Money, Money, Money: Stories of Human Behavior

By

Teemu Lampovaara

DEDICATION

This book is dedicated to all the people around the world who inspired these stories – you know who you are.

STORIES

ACKNOWLEDGMENTS

A big thank you to Veera for ideas and suggestions offered. Still loving you.

PREFACE

"Money is the root of all evil."

"Money is a terrible master but an excellent servant."

"Time is money."

"Money doesn't buy happiness."

Where have such sayings come from, and do they have any truth to them? The older I get, the more fascinated I become with money, finance, and people. I am especially intrigued by the different approaches people have towards handling their personal money matters and how they pose it to the outside. You might think that an individual's financial situation is of no one else's business but theirs, but oh, are you so wrong.

Whereas it is true that in theory everyone should only mind their own business when it comes to money, it does not work like that in real life. The way you appear to the outside will always send constant signals to other people about who you are and what you are like – whether you like it or not. Judging by your looks only, people will draw conclusions about you as well as your financial situation. Funnily, they will do so even without any factual evidence. Most of their ways of making assumptions have been taught to them by our society constantly ever since the moment they were born.

Everyone on some level knows that they are constantly being observed and evaluated by others and will thus modify their exterior to please their surroundings. The ones more caring of what others may think of them will do so more than the rest. In fact, some may not even care about what other people think of them at all.

Upon growing up, money was not discussed in my family. From what I have gathered, that is also not an exception, but closer to a rule in most of the families. I even remember one time asking from my mother how much her monthly salary was, and she refused to answer. She straight up told me she did not want to let me know. Pretty much the only discussions we had of money involved how much my monthly allowance I got from my parents should be.

Even right now, I cannot think of one good reason why I would not let my own kids know how much I make in my current job. That is one hell of a great way to break the ice and start teaching your offspring about money, which you most definitely should do. Please do note that this does not mean that I would broadcast my salary and possessions publicly – that would be simply foolish. Not only would it pose a security risk, but it would also cause plenty of negative feelings in people, such as envy, greed, or shame. Some would take it as me bragging, and others would mock me for not making enough money.

Even though people do not speak publicly about money, they do let public opinions guide the way they spend their money. Some will feel pressured to attend a night out at a restaurant simply because they do not want to appear as poor to their friends, even if they really could not afford a night out at that time. Because of the same reason, others will not want to buy items at a discount price. The third group of people would not want to buy anything costly even if they could, just simply for being afraid that others might construe them as snobby or arrogant.

Is the answer to breaking this code simply not to care about what others think? Perhaps, but once taken to an extreme, it will probably backfire as well. You would become the miserly lunatic who is too frugal to ever spend money on anything or go bankrupt in an instant.

All the short stories in this book depict fictional events, companies, organizations, and people. Still, they are all inspired by actions of people in real life all across the world. Many of the plots and actions are inspired by what I have personally witnessed in life, and some others are inspired by real life events that I have heard and read about. There are very few sets of events in the book that have been given birth to by imagination only, and even those are events which more than likely have taken place somewhere in the history of humanity.

Besides hoping that you find the stories entertaining, I wish that upon reading them you will take the time to identify certain patterns of behavior that people tend to exhibit when wealth and money step into play – or on the contrary, are taken off the table. What better way to learn than from other people's successes and mistakes?

Finally, as a sincere wish I hope that you, the reader, find the time to leave a review about the book on Amazon.

For questions, comments, or discussions, contact: teemu.lampovaara@gmail.com.

THE ARC OF RICHES

"Bullshit," Ethan sighed, almost crying. His spontaneous self felt like shouting and considering that he had always found it important to appear strong on the exterior, he wished he had the inner strength required to shout the word out loud. Alas, he had none left. Despite all the mahogany-framed shelves full of books, the great library of his family manor now seemed big and empty. Despite all the books and all the prestigious ornaments and a spacious room full of earthly matter, it all felt eerily hollow now.

Since he did not even know what he had been reading anymore, Ethan slammed shut the book in his hands, and began walking around in circles. At first, he simply circled the spacious room, but soon he found himself wandering almost aimlessly around the manor. Considering that the Baxter family manor had three floors with nearly 30 rooms total – excluding the smallest closets – he had plenty of area to cover.

He had no idea what he was doing or would do. Sadness, desperation, loneliness, anxiety, fear, and anger all gnawed at him at the same time. On the bright side, the greatest anger had begun to subside, since he lacked the strength to be angry any longer. For that, he felt thankful. The initial shockwave of all those negative emotions had made him feel like his head was about to explode, or that he came close to losing his grip of sanity. Now, despite the deathlike depression, managing those emotions turned out to be easier than before.

All those negative feelings stepped aside for a while when he stumbled into another room. Not just any room, in fact, for it was here where Ethan had spent countless hours and even days completely and absolutely happy, oblivious to the outside world. The reason he had managed to escape the tightening grasp of all those negative emotions was hardly nostalgia, however, but the line he had spotted lying on the desk. The rush of adrenaline and dopamine he now experienced reminded him still of the same kinds of feelings as nearly 15 years ago, back when Ethan first saw that same kind of a line. Back then his spontaneity and impulsiveness aroused those good feelings in him, but now, mostly just the knowledge of what to expect made his mind burst into flames of ecstasy and relief.

Ethan walked hastily towards the desk, grabbing a straw sitting right next to the white line, and snorted the cocaine deep inside his nostrils. It was not even the intoxicating effect of the drug that soothed him so much as the comfort of knowing it lay there, and that he could return to it and all those parties any time he wanted to. Although the recent events threatened his entire lifestyle, drugs made the awareness of it all go away – even if only for a little while that constantly grew ever shorter.

The next day Ethan woke up feeling sharp and well-rested. It was early; 5:15 AM according to the alarm clock on his nightstand. Ever since he had attempted to stop using stimulants, he had noticed that even the slightest pause gave his body some much-needed time to reduce some of its tolerance to substances. Waking up early after only a short night's sleep without feelings of drowsiness was one of the nicer side effects. He knew there would be no point in attempting to lie in bed any longer, so he grabbed his slippers and his bathrobe and headed downstairs to fix some breakfast.

The moment he reached luxurious kitchen of which even Michelin star chefs would be envious, the mobile phone he had left on the kitchen table began to ring. Normally he might not have bothered answering, especially at such a weird time, but since he felt awake and clear headed, he made an exception and picked the phone up. The number on the screen was unknown. He slid on the green phone icon.

"Ethan," he answered.

"Hi, this is Peter. I am sorry to disturb you at this hour, but I was wondering if the Bentley…"

The caller went on, but Ethan just heard a high humming in his ears. For a moment he had lost grip of the fact he had to sell his car to be able to cover other expenses. Now, yet again, the reality of it hit him right in the face. Once he recovered from the sensation, he realized a complete silence stood on the phone conversation which had but begun a few moments ago.

"Yes, that is right," Ethan answered, despite having no idea what the caller had said after the magic word of Bentley.

"So would tomorrow afternoon work for you?"

"It will. Let's meet at four. The address is 13000 High Valley Road. Just drive towards the big gate and push the buzzer next to it and I'll let you in."

"Wait… you're not Ethan Baxter, are you? Wow, that is quite a coincidence and…"

"Shit," Ethan thought to himself. He was hardly a celebrity, but having enough high-ticket possessions was enough to gain some popularity in a city small enough, such as Garden City.

"Yes, that is right," Ethan cut Peter off. "Come meet me tomorrow at four if you're interested and we'll continue this then. Have a good day," Ethan hung up without letting Peter finish his thought.

He immediately began to regret ever answering the phone. Not because of Peter or the fact that he knew he had to sell his luxury car, but because the call had thrown him right back into all the misery of what his life had become. For days he had been looking for answers to get out of this financial mess. Alas, he had none.

At first, he had been thinking back to all the success and glory that his life used to be, and how he owed it all to his mother and his grandfather. Obviously, he knew that while growing up he had never listened to his mother or his grandfather. That is why he had thought of combing through books and literature – as if there was a magical secret hidden somewhere in between those pages. They did indeed contain lots of information, but Ethan could not distinguish what he should do differently, and how. More importantly, he felt like he could not read more than three sentences without having his mind start to wander off. He just could not focus on written words.

That is when it struck him. Staring at the kitchen sink, he understood that he could not be saved by his family's book collection. He saw that to achieve the same kind of success his parents and grandparents had seen, he needed to start acting like them. Still staring at the onyx marbled kitchen sink, he began to reminisce.

Ethan was running on the streets of Garden City. Alongside him ran his childhood friends Matt, and George. It was a summer day, and the sun shone scorching hot. Ethan felt sweat running down his forehead and his throat was completely dry. Not from the running, but because of the excitement of the chase. Tossing some rotten eggs on the frontage of a local farmer's house had been the grand idea of day for the boys. Well, it was Ethan's idea, to be fair. Matt and George had just gone along with it. Even at the early age of eight Ethan had always wanted to lead people, and to do even reckless things to get people to follow him felt completely natural. He simply enjoyed the excitement too much. Now, standing in the kitchen of his manor, he chuckled at the memory, and kept on thinking back to the days of the past.

After having escaped from the angry farmer, Ethan shortly parted ways with his friends and headed home. It was way past the time he should have been back at home, and Ethan knew that. The first few times he had run late his mother, had verbally disciplined him, and threatened to ground Ethan. At first, Ethan had taken it seriously, but quickly noticed that he simply did not care enough. He knew he was supposed to be home earlier, and he knew he should not to have been raising all kinds of hell around the town, yet he did not care. Arriving home, to an average house not nearly as fancy as the manor he would move into later in life, he opened the door, stepped inside, and shut the door – not even bothering to attempt to hide the fact that he had been out for too long.

"And what's your excuse this time, young man?" Ethan heard his mother calling out to him from the living room.

"I went out with Matt and George," Ethan replied nonchalantly, and started heading towards his room.

Before Ethan could reach his room, Amelia, a woman in her early thirties, as well-groomed and beautiful as ever, stepped in front of him, with a faint and sad smile on her face.

"That's not what I asked."

"…no?" Ethan replied, not as much baffled by his mother's response but by her facial expression, which seemed oddly calm, even though he had accepted that she might be mad.

"No. Come on, your dinner is getting cold."

Ethan felt a sudden urge to rebel against his mother and not go to dinner, but some sound deep inside him told him that for now it would be wiser to obey. So, he followed his mother to the kitchen.

The Baxter family had no separate dining room back then. Amelia had set the small wooden dining table for her and her son. There was nothing particularly special about anything there. The kitchen and the table were both quite small and extremely basic. The meal consisted of potatoes, beans, and some chicken. Ethan sat down and began to eat.

"Big things are happening, Ethan," Amelia said, while sitting down on the other side of the table.

"And from now on I need you to focus more than ever before."

"What?" Ethan replied, while chewing on a mouth full of cooked potatoes.

"When I was your age, your grandfather sat me down, every Friday evening, just like this. Our day might have been long and filled with arduous work, but in the end, he insisted on talking to me. He would talk about the world, our livelihood, our town, or about managing ordinary everyday life," Amelia started.

"He told me I had to start growing up, to be able to take responsibility. And ever since, every Friday, he sat me down like that."

"Now, Ethan, I need you to start growing up. Times are changing, and good things are about to happen to us."

At this point Ethan was hardly listening anymore. His mind drifted and wandered towards the coming summer holiday weeks. Amelia noticed that she was speaking to deaf ears. Her mood darkened, she raised her voice and said:

"Go to your room. Now."

Ethan quickly ate what little food that remained on his plate, stood up, and started heading out of the kitchen.

"And the next time you're late for dinner, you're grounded for two weeks!" Amelia shouted after him.

It was the summer of 1998. But a month had passed since the mysterious lecture Amelia had tried giving to Ethan. The only thing he at that time had acknowledged were the threats of being grounded. The rest of it quickly came back to him when, during an otherwise normal day, Amelia announced to Ethan that they were moving. Ethan's eyes grew wide with surprise as she revealed that her parents, Ethan's grandparents, could no longer manage to keep their business up and running. His grandfather, Henry, had been struggling with his health for a while now, and it was time to let go of the family business now and pass it on to Amelia, his only child. Ethan's grandmother Clarice had never taken much part in farming equipment industry, and now her focus shifted solely towards taking care of Henry.

"Grandpa and grandma are moving. They are leaving the manor and the workshop to me, and because of his health, I will need your help here, sweetie."

Amelia grabbed Ethan by both shoulders, looked deep into his eyes and said:

"Now I need you more than ever."

Ethan, as probably any eight-year-old boy in a situation like that would have been, was mystified. His grandparents had always been rather distant to him, yet he knew they were extraordinarily rich and successful because of Henry's work. Because of the distance – both physical and emotional – between them he could not feel particularly sad about the imminent death of his grandfather. More than that, the reality of it started to sink in now: they were about to become rich! At that point, in spite of still not knowing it back then, Ethan's mindset and life had changed forever.

In the coming months, despite paying more attention to hanging out with friends and the luxurious new home they had, Ethan did eventually learn something about business, entrepreneurship, and his family history as well. Henry Baxter had built the family business from the scratch all by himself. At that point in time, in the 1960's, farming and agriculture were one of the leading fields in the state of Kansas. The need for equipment, staff, and materials was constant. Henry, a self-learned car mechanic, despite having no degrees or certifications, spotted a need for ever more efficient systems and machinery.

All the while taking care of the livelihood of his small family in his workshop situated a couple of miles from the city center, he had been forming an innovation of his own: a new kind of an automated irrigation system for sprinkling on crops. His secret lay in sensor technology, which allowed the sprinklers to act automatically, and thus reducing the need for manual labor. On top of that, the design he used turned out to be extremely cost-effective to build. During daytime, Henry worked on cars the locals needed to get fixed and maintained. After that, he worked on his invention like a madman.

Long story short, all the hard work ended up being worth it – and even more. Ethan could never find the interest in learning to become an engineer like his grandfather had been, be it a self-learned one or not. What he did find interest in, however, was the wealth and possessions the Baxter family had amassed. His grandfather never needed to build a factory, production lines, or to hire staff, since he could outsource all of this. Nevertheless, he was able to profit from his patented solutions and inventions. When the business flourished at its peak, Henry had the luxurious manor built right next to his workshop. Besides that, he invested a great deal of the profits into land and his stock portfolio. Apart from being literally loaded with money, Henry, Clarice, and their daughter Amelia led a rather normal life, with Henry managing his business, Clarice taking care of the house, and Amelia going to school and attending college later – all the while taking short lessons about life from Henry every Friday evening.

The years passed by, and Henry's business grew. Now that Ethan thought about it, what Henry did was rather brilliant. He managed to scale the business up without hiring employees, but instead innovated repeatedly. This was nothing Ethan had ever considered himself to be capable of.

What Ethan had not even realized before was at that point Amelia did not lack skills in business either. Gradually, as she grew older and attended more lessons with her father, she started to partake in supporting what had now become a family business. The company called Baxter Irrigation brought in more wealth to them than ever before, and since many of the production processes had now been outsourced and automated, effort-wise it was now also easier than in the early days of the invention Henry had made. Before she even knew it, Amelia had learned everything there was to learn about the upkeep of the business.

Henry had taught her daughter more than just that, however. Some of the most life-changing lessons given to Amelia involved money and how to value it.

"You need money to live. To earn money, you need to work. Work takes time," Henry told her, again and again.

"And time is something you will never get back once it's lost," he went on.

Had Ethan been there and had Henry said something like that to Ethan back then, he would have probably called it brainwashing. However, Henry never had the chance to even try.

Right around the time that Amelia turned 20, she bought a house of her own. A rather simple yet beautiful 750 square feet home right next to the city center, but not too far from her parents either. Despite the wealth of her parents, she insisted on mortgaging it herself. Just like her father, she by that point had learned the value of self-sufficiency and responsibility. A couple of years later, a passionate albeit short-lived romance with a local farmer called David Roberts resulted in Ethan. Amelia's and David's love towards each other alongside his life came to a tragic end with David succumbing to a heart condition which led to cardiac arrest in 1990. He never got to see Ethan, nor Ethan his father. All that remained of him for Ethan were his mother's descriptions of David as a decent, hard-working man.

Much thanks to the lessons given to her by his father, Amelia faced being a young single parent rather admirably. Each and every day she devoted herself to working for Baxter Irrigation with tasks supporting the main line of business, such as invoicing and managing subcontractors needed to keep the business running. Working remotely from home at that time was very rare, especially in rural areas, but Amelia and Henry succeeded in this together. The rest of her waking hours were spent taking care of her beloved son, Ethan. Already that early in her life Amelia had learned what persistence, durability, and diligence truly meant. It was as if her father had intentionally been preparing her for all this.

Alongside such strength and business skills, Henry had taught Amelia the value of money. Just like her parents, she lived a rather ordinary life, and was very frugal. Avoiding excess spending got integrated and programmed into her way of life. This helped her to invest and to pay off significant amounts of her mortgage even before Ethan had reached school age.

Amelia's frugality and unwillingness to show off their wealth to other people made Ethan despise that way of life. He never could understand why they had to live as if they were just another normal family, when in fact they were not. Growing up, Ethan never had a lack of anything. There was always warm food on the table, the fridge always had more contents in it than just a light, there were toys for him as a kid, and some spending money too as he grew older. But they lived in a regular house, just like everyone else. When Ethan's friends got bicycles, so did Ethan. When they went to the movies, so did Ethan most of the times as well. But there never was anything more. Nothing to make anyone jealous of him, even though Amelia very well could have afforded that and much more. And that lack of wealthy lifestyle is what Ethan for the life of it could never fathom.

Ethan felt like they were living in poverty, even though deep inside he knew they were not. But the thought of having all those riches so close to him, yet so far away created the illusion of poverty. On top of that, Ethan was never one to chicken out of trying new things. When the other kids got something, he had to have it too. Where they went, Ethan went. And whenever possible, Ethan came up with droll ideas of what to do. He still could remember a particular instance in his youth where he got dared to leave a piece of gum on his teacher's chair. As always, craving for attention and validation from his peers, he went one step further and place a sharp pin on it. And every single time he caused an incident like this he got caught and had to pay the price as well. Needless to say, he spent quite some time of his youth in detention, doing some extra homework, or being grounded at home by her mother.

Ethan did not mind the punishments, for what he got in return in the form of social acceptance, validation, and countless friends made it worth it. Everyone in his age bracket in Garden City knew Ethan. Even if some thought of him as the class clown, Ethan would not care since he enjoyed the constant popularity. It was like a drug to him.

Unfortunately, what rebellious nature in Ethan resulted in childhood pranks and mischiefs only escalated in his teen years. At that point he and Amelia had moved to the Baxter family manor and enjoyed a more luxurious lifestyle. Amelia had managed to sell their smaller house and they lived there full-time now. As incredible as it was, this living in a house built exclusively for very rich people did not quench Ethan's appetite for prestige. Three floors of seemingly countless rooms, a fountain, a swimming pool, and a great garden in the back were not enough for him. Apart from the manor, Amelia still led a frugal lifestyle, and would not "Resort to excess spending," as she so bluntly put it.

So, Ethan found a way to excitement and luxury in his life in other ways. By the time he turned 13, it was safe to say anyone who lived in Garden City knew who Ethan was. Not only because of his reputation but also due to the mysterious life he had in the eyes of the other people, living in the great Baxter manor only with her mother. Whereas Amelia Baxter was a well-known and respected businesswoman, Ethan stood alongside her as the mysterious and wild wayward son of hers.

One autumn afternoon after school hours when Ethan and his friends were spending time together in the downtown, "just chilling", as they would have called it, something that would later turn out to be life changing for Ethan happened. As they were sitting on a railing built right next to the road, they were approached by two older boys. Ethan recognized both of them immediately, since they attended the same school in the ninth grade, whereas Ethan and his friends were in the seventh. One of the older boys was called Jake, Ethan remembered. The other one he did not know by name. They both wore black leather jackets and blue jeans which made them seem that much cooler as well.

"Hey," Jake opened, and before anyone could answer, he went on.

"I know you. You're the jackass son of that snobby bitch."

Being popular and known was nothing new to Ethan. Being insulted without any provocation, especially when his mother also got targeted, however, was whole another deal. His face turned red from all the surprise and anger, and he could hear blood rushing up to his face. It produced this strange flowing sound in his ears, so he could quite literally hear it. Ethan instinctively clenched his hands in a fist and stood up. Jake's friend noticed this, stepped in front of Jake, and went on:

"Relax, man," he told Ethan, turning then to Jake, and said: "This guy look like a snob to you? Shut up."

Now it was Jake whose face turned red.

"Hi, I'm Jesse, and this mofo here is Jake," Jesse introduced them, shortly glancing at Jake with a slight contempt on his face.

Ethan hesitated. For a while, he had been mentally preparing himself for a physical fight, which he at this point was no stranger to either. After a short silence, Ethan said:

"So, what's his deal?" nodding his head towards Jake, who still remained silent.

"Look, I'm sorry for his attitude problem. He's just been having a rough time, that's all."

By this point Ethan had calmed down a little bit, and thus gained a lot of his confidence back. He knew that three of his closest friends were right beside him, observing his every move and word, and had to perform in front of them, and not to act embarrassingly.

"…Well? What do you want?" Ethan asked with as stern a look on his face as he could muster.

"We were actually looking to do business with you. But just with you, not with the rest of them," Jesse clarified, with a friendly smile on his face, eyes locked on Ethan while doing a gentle swinging motion with his hand as if trying to send his friends away.

Ethan had mixed feelings. Just like he had seen back home and as his nature had guided him, he wanted to become a popular leader and a businessman as well. Besides that, his constant curiosity immediately guided him towards trying out new things. On the other hand, he knew the guys would probably be up to no good. Just like everyone else, he had heard warnings and lectures about the dangers of smoking, alcohol, and drugs, and figured this 'business' would probably have something to do with those – or even worse. Plus, he was still trembling a bit from the fact that he had almost gotten into a fight because of what Jake blurted out earlier. Ethan's instincts told him to decline, but he did not want to show it openly to his friends, so he said:

"Get back to me later and I'll think about it. I'm busy now." Ethan actually surprised himself with how confident he managed to sound. What then surprised him even more was Jesse's reply.

"Sure thing. Be seeing you around!"

Jesse and Jake then turned around, heading back down the street to where they had come from, and then disappeared around the corner. They were as quickly gone as they had arrived.

Ethan let out a sigh of relief – just small enough so that his friends would not hear – and then turned back to them, simply saying: "Let's get lost."

The four of them headed down to the local mall, and to Ethan's recollection, if we do not count Ethan arriving home on time, nothing else extraordinary happened that day.

It would be an understatement to say that Ethan could not stop thinking about this weird business proposal offered by Jesse and Jake. In fact, he was tormented by it. The fear of missing out on something big, some incredible opportunity was eating away at Ethan. That very evening he decided he wanted to hear more about the idea. In his head he had already built up several images of what it might have been.

The next day at school classes felt like they were longer than ever. Ethan tried to look for Jesse and Jake in between classes so that they could approach him once more. Alas, during the day, he never saw them. In the evening, he stayed out with his friends for much longer than usual with the hopes of running into them. But they were nowhere to be seen. Ethan came home frustrated and sad, convinced that this one unique and great chance had been blown. When he opened the front door to their manor, Amelia was standing there.

"What's going on, Ethan?" she asked, with sorrow on her face.

"Nothing. All is good," he replied, with a blank expression on his face, at once knowing that his mother would not buy it.

Amelia stepped closer to Ethan.

"What's going on, for real?"

"Nothing."

Ethan then started heading towards the second floor on which his room lay. With the sound of his steps echoing in the large hallway of their big home, he could hear her mother saying – almost crying out:

"I'm worried about you, Ethan."

That conversation had haunted Ethan ever since. His mother did not usually act that way.

The next day Ethan woke up to the same feelings of disappointment and missing out on something big. He was certain that his unique business opportunity had passed, and there was nothing that he could do about it. Still, he remained slightly hopeful that he might run into Jesse and Jake that day. After a rushed breakfast, he headed straight to school and the first class. Even though he felt calmer, he was still consumed by the images of success he had conjured up in his own head.

The school day started with mathematics. Not that Ethan could concentrate on any of it, though. After the fuzzy lesson, Ethan strolled around the school yard, and his eyes widened with excitement once he noticed Jesse and Jake in the group of several other ninth graders. He thought about approaching them directly, but it would have been too unordinary; in the Garden City elementary, kids from different classes rarely mixed, and it was even rarer for younger and older kids to spend time with each other. Instead of heading to them, Ethan decided to stay still, leaning on the wall next to the front door. That way, even if he would not manage to get their attention, they most likely would have to pass by Ethan to enter the school building. That is, if they were intent on heading back inside.

He did not have to wait for long. Soon, he saw Jake noticing him, and then saying something to Jesse, while nodding at Ethan. Ethan felt his heart racing, as this could only mean that the deal might still be on. Not even knowing yet what it was all about, he felt certain that this would change his life. To his slight disappointment, Jesse and Jake, along with the rest of their group, did not head back to the school, but entirely off the school yard, towards downtown. Nevertheless, Ethan felt much more confident now. He knew something would happen soon.

School was out for the day, and Ethan began packing his things up. By instinct, he knew that the older guys would be waiting for him. It turns out his instincts did not fail him either. He stepped out of the school building, letting the heavy fire door slam shut behind him, and began walking home. After passing the school yard and a field nearby, he made it just around the corner of the first building – an abandoned warehouse of some kind – and there they were: Jesse, Jake, and a third person with them. He was now glad he had decided to walk home alone.

Ethan did not recognize the third guy from anywhere. The boy seemed older than them, perhaps even a grown-up young man. Not only did his face look older, but he was also sporting a beard and slim fit black jeans that were not typical to teenagers in Kansas back then. Ethan could not help noticing that despite warm weather, he was wearing some kind of thin, black gloves. Ethan's confidence shriveled, and he felt as if a big lump had just got shoved in his throat.

"Hey," Jesse began.

"Hey," replied Ethan with a weak, excited voice, cursing in his mind how wound-up he had suddenly become, hoping that it would not show.

"Ethan, we want you to perform a slight task for us. Take care of it and there'll be a small prize for you."

Ethan had a hundred questions popping up in his mind, especially how did Jesse even know his name. Because of the fear of possibly getting left out, he did not dare to ask anything, and simply stated:

"Ok."

"Malcolm here wants a small package delivered to the Sunmill mall tomorrow. Hold on to it until tomorrow afternoon and deliver it to his friend at three. Can you do that, Ethan?"

Malcolm, upon hearing his name threw a quick glance at Jesse. Ethan wondered if it was because he did not want his name mentioned in front of him, or whether Malcolm was even his real name.

"Sure thing," Ethan said, so quickly and without hesitation he surprised even himself.

Malcolm put his gloved hand into his ridiculously tight jeans' front pocket, and pulled a small bag out, handing it out to Ethan.

"Mind the bag so it won't rupture," Malcolm said, in a way more high-pitched voice than Ethan would have imagined for him to have. Ethan extended his hand, took the bag from Malcolm, and without even daring to look at it, put it into his front pocket, just like Malcolm had.

"I will. So, three o' clock tomorrow at Sunmill's?"

"Right," said Jesse, smiling, and went on: "You take care of this for us, and there'll be more you can do for us. The bigger the job, the bigger the prize."

Ethan could not figure out what to say to sound clever, so yet again, he simply said: "Ok."

Since he realized now knew of the thing that they wanted him to take care of and had no will to stay chatting with them any longer, he started to walk away.

Not before too many steps, Jake raised his voice at Ethan: "Don't screw this up or it's you who'll end up paying us!"

Ethan looked at them over his shoulder. Not knowing what to say, Ethan kept on walking, grasping the small, precious baggage that had just been handed to him a minute ago tightly in his hand.

Amelia held a rainbow-colored duster, quickly attempting to cleanse surfaces in their huge home. It was just like the hand-held dusters everyone had grown accustomed to seeing in vintage commercials, which was probably why she liked it so much. She felt certain that it did not actually help her clean the house but would just send dust particles flying off wildly in all directions. But she did like the colors of it, and she was extremely nervous and needed some menial physical labor to help her to gather her thoughts.

With her wildly performing the rather short ranged but very rapid swings and thrusts with the duster, she could not shake the feeling of concern she had for her son. Ever since Ethan could walk, he had been wild, and this came to Amelia as no surprise. She had always been able to rely on the fact that she knew her son, even if he was wild and spontaneous. But that was just it – for the first time ever, she had the feeling that she did not know everything about him. It was not that Ethan had done anything particularly suspicious, but it was just the feeling – a gut instinct that only a mother can have – which made Amelia feel even more confused and frustrated.

She of course knew that she had not raised Ethan the same way her father Henry had raised her. Ever since her childhood years, in contrast to her son, Amelia had always been calmer, less temperamental, and in many ways, more reasonable. On the other hand, she knew she did not have as big ambitions as Ethan had. For the last two years, she had been waiting for

Ethan's nature to stabilize. Since that had not happened, she had put off giving any significant responsibilities to him.

"Well, no more," she thought to herself. Since Ethan would not become more stable by himself, she would have to take a more active stance in raising her son. Realizing that, she suddenly felt very lonely. With her parents away and her closest acquaintances staying in touch with her only because of the family business, she did not have anyone else to rely on but herself. This made her even more nervous. Even though she had been raising Ethan and providing for him for the last 13 years, this was the first time that raising a son did not feel natural to her.

Before she had time to recover from all those feelings of uncertainty and nervousness, she heard keys jingling and the front door of the manor opening. Ethan was home.

Amelia swept ever faster with the duster as she thought about what to say to him.

Ethan slammed shut the great door behind him. Usually, at this point he announced his mother of his homecoming with a loud greeting. Just as the door closed, however, Ethan realized he had not thought this through. He knew that he had crossed some kind of a line and would not want her mother to know about it, so just a casual greeting felt completely wrong. On the other hand, acting different than usual would appear suspicious as well. Just as he had made his mind up and was about to shout out loud that he was home, Amelia appeared on the balcony upstairs.

"Ethan!"

"Mom, I'm home!" Ethan shouted so loud it made the situation awkward, with his mother being in his line of sight right above him.

"I can see that, dear," Amelia went on.

"Assuming you have the time, young man, I would like to have a word with you before dinner. Join me in the living room, please."

Now Ethan got even more nervous. The mysterious package handed to him by Malcolm felt like it simultaneously weighed him down and burnt a hole in his pocket, and to top it all off, his mother was acting in an extremely weird way.

"I-... I need to go to bathroom," Ethan said, passing Amelia by, and started to almost run up the stairs. He could not believe he had just stuttered out of fear.

Amelia yelled after him: "I'll be waiting!"

Ethan did not need to go to the bathroom, but he soon reached his room and closed the door behind him. He was gasping for air out of sheer excitement. Even though he was afraid of getting caught, he felt this incredible rush of adrenaline he had been missing for a long time. The way his mother had told Ethan she would be waiting for him implied she was not angry, but rather demanding, and would be serious about wanting to talk. Since Ethan had no intention of confronting his mother with something in his pocket that might very well be illegal, he quickly grabbed the small plastic bag Malcolm had given him. He dared to take a proper look at it for the first time now.

The bag was an ordinary, small Ziploc bag used in refrigeration or freezing food. The contents did not surprise Ethan, for it looked like some kind of white powder. There was not very much of it, maybe two ounces at most. The bag was tightly shut, with both a Ziploc seal and a clip. Even without opening it Ethan immediately noticed the pungent smell coming out of it. Now that he knew he was dealing with drugs, he had to quickly hide the bag somewhere his mother would never look. The place of choice ended up being his bed, right under his pillow. Now that Ethan had disposed of the evidence making him a drug mule, he opened the door to his room, stepped outside, went to quickly flush the toilet, and started heading downstairs.

What Amelia called living room was something most commoners would describe as a ballroom. Henry Baxter had not been minimalistic when designing the almost 700 square foot room, nor had Clarice when decorating it. Housing a great fireplace, a grand piano, and a pool table, and with 10-foot-high windows reaching almost all the way up to the ceiling, the room indeed was a sight to be seen. The room at once signaled to everyone that the owners of the house were wealthy.

Obviously, the sight of the room appeared as nothing new to Ethan. He stepped inside and sat on leather sofa, right across from the couch where Amelia sat. A brief silence ensued, and then she began:

"Ethan, I know that you and I are different, and there's nothing wrong with that. I cannot completely change your nature just like you cannot mine."

"I also know that I may perhaps have not been the best at teaching you about life, and I am sorry about that. And I don't mean the things they teach you about in school, but about the things a mother should teach her son. Now, that is about to change."

"When I was your age, your grandfather would sit me down every Friday, and teach me about economy, money, and life in general. From now on, I intend to do the same with you."

Ethan could not believe his ears. At the same time, he was both intrigued and mystified. All these years, he had craved for a chance to be involved in something bigger than himself, and now, in just one day he had already been presented with a chance and was now about to receive another one. He was also a little uncertain because this was not something he had been expecting. Despite all the love his mother had for Ethan, he had gotten used to his mother being a side character in his life, even a bit distant. He could feel his confidence growing due to all the acceptance he had received, and looked his mother boldly in the eyes and stated:

"Well, what are we waiting for?"

Amelia replied with a warm smile. Words could not describe how relieved by Ethan's reaction she became.

"I thought we might warm up by talking about your future plans and aspirations, Ethan. What do you want in life?"

An hour and a half later, Ethan stepped back into his room, and closed the door. He immediately checked to see if the bag was still where he had left it. He grabbed it, stashing it inside the wooden drawer right next to his bed, on which he lay down right after. He felt he had a decision to make which he already knew the answer to. For almost one hour, they had talked about Ethan's life and what he would like to become once he had grown up. At times Ethan had trouble concentrating. Especially her mother's suggestions of Ethan enrolling into college involved ideas of long term work he had never seen himself doing. He wanted to live in the moment, and profit quickly. At that moment Ethan had gotten sidetracked in his thoughts and started thinking about his side gig with Jesse and Jake. Nevertheless, Ethan and Amelia had discussed his future, after which they had sat down for dinner.

Now, lying on his bed, Ethan saw himself at a crossroads. He had a choice of working with Jesse and Jake, or the choice of attempting to live up to the expectations of his mother. Ethan chuckled at the thought, and grinned. Right there, at that moment, he chose both.

The next day Ethan stood on the corner of Sunmill mall, which back then was the only shopping center in Garden City. To make it there on time, he had skipped the last class of the day. Now, with the scorching afternoon sun shining bright on his face, he was waiting for whoever would appear to pick up the Malcolm's bag from him. Earlier at school, Jesse had told Ethan that he would not need to worry about recognizing the recipient. He would recognize Ethan, instead. Jesse had instructed Ethan to arrive at that very corner, located right next to what used to be a video rental shop of some kind.

Ethan did not have to wait for long. The clock was almost three, when a guy from one of the doors leading inside the mall appeared and started walking towards him. A slim young man, dressed in a hoodie and jeans. He was shorter than the 13-year-old Ethan. Even from up close, Ethan did not feel intimidated in the slightest. The guy was clearly older than him – in his early twenties perhaps – and looked odd and sickly. Simultaneously, Ethan felt pity towards him and yet was disgusted by him.

"You got something for me?" the stranger asked with a raspy voice.

Ethan said nothing, but just reached inside his pocket, and handed Malcolm's bag to the stranger.

"Thanks, bro," the thin stranger thanked Ethan, with a joy on his face that seemed authentic. Then, he passed by Ethan and went on towards downtown on foot.

At this point Ethan felt uncertain about what to do next. Since he had no further instructions, he stood there for a while, simply because he was about to head towards the same direction as the man he had been dealing with and did not want to run into him again. Then, he left the mall and headed home.

The next day at school it did not take long for Jesse and Jake to track Ethan down. They came to him out in the yard, and for the first time ever, even Jake seemed genuinely pleased with Ethan.

"Cheers for a job well done," he said, handing Ethan a 50-dollar bill.

"Thank you," Ethan replied, and could not disguise his feelings of happiness for taking this step and performing successfully.

"You wanna do more of these gigs?"

"Does a bear shit in the woods?" Ethan spat out the sarcastic question he had learned of just the other day.

It seemed as if it took a while for Jesse and Jake to get it, since they just stood there for a while, in silence, after which they burst out laughing.

"That's my man! I knew I could count on you," claimed Jesse, patting Ethan on the shoulder.

"What's the next job?" Ethan asked excitedly.

"Patience! All in due time. But I promise you this: the next ones will be bigger, as will the payments. This first gig was sort of a test of reliability. And believe me, we're just getting started here!"

It looked like at this point even Jesse was not able to sustain his cool approach, but it seemed obvious he had gotten pretty excited as well. With that, they left Ethan in the school yard, holding the bill in his hand. Understandably, considering his wealthy background, it was not as much the money that Ethan was after, rather than the feelings of success. The idea that he had started and finished this endeavor by himself and had managed to earn money while doing it felt incredible. More than that, he had made new friends and connections. This remained one of the best possible feelings out there for Ethan. He could not wait for more jobs and projects like this.

Ever since, Ethan did these 'side gigs' – as he used to call them – for Jesse and Jake. Almost all of them involved storing or moving drugs from one place to another. At times, Ethan had a stash of multiple boxes and bags hidden away in his room. Despite his raucous lifestyle, he could execute all of them without making mistakes. He had deemed his partnership with Jesse and Jake to be of so high value he would not dare to risk endangering this business they had going on.

Weeks turned into months and months turned into years. Jesse and Jake no longer went to school, but Ethan still kept in close touch with them. At first, just for the sake of business, but later on they also began spending time together. People rarely got into the business of handling illegal substances just for the sake of profit, and Ethan was no exception. Shortly after starting the courier jobs, he got offered the chance to try some of the stuff he handled. So, aside from doing business, that was just what the three of them also did together: partying. Already at the young age of 15 Ethan had learned to love the rush stuff like amphetamine gave him.

All the while Ethan was living what he imagined would be his dream life, he had her mother giving lessons to him at least once a week. Amelia tried to offer him as much of the same knowledge as Henry had offered her in her childhood years. At first, Ethan was as much excited about this as he had been about illegal drug trafficking – at least almost as much. But as time passed, Ethan noticed his interest in his mother's teachings fading. He had been introduced to the world of dopamine and quick profits, so attempting to learn about the family business and especially about frugality sounded incredible tedious and long-winded to him. By the time Ethan was sixteen, he barely acknowledged a thing she told him in those weekly gatherings.

In his defense, Ethan never had a problem with substance abuse that grew big enough to prevent him from taking care of other daily tasks. He attended school just like before, receiving average or slightly below average grades. He stayed in touch with all his other friends as well, not just with Jesse and Jake. Most importantly, he never let drugs interfere with his business. Besides social acceptance and the thrill his new-found life gave him, Ethan valued his business and success in the field. He even felt a bit disgusted by all the junkies he continuously met and thought of them as a reminder to himself never to let himself sink to that level. This business had made him what he now was, and he would never let go of it.

Miraculously, during all that time he never got caught, not by his mother or by law enforcement. His mother he could easily trick, for she was so stuck in her ways he could predict practically all her moves every single day. Ethan could not recall a time when his mother catching him under the influence of anything or storing anything in his room would have even been a close call. Still, the lack of police attention he, Jesse and Jake drew to themselves always amazed Ethan, and he figured it was just because they were too small of a target for the Garden City police, who at that time were infamous for struggling with low funding and overall inefficiency incompetence.

Five years had passed, and Ethan would soon graduate from high school. He was about to enroll into college, just as his mother had hoped he would. He did not have any interest in it but figured it would be the best way for him to hold up the appearances of living a rather normal life – at least as normal as it could be for a rich young man moving and dealing drugs. In any case, he could not wait for the graduation day. That way, even if attending college studies, he felt his real life could now begin. He had some savings tucked away with which he could afford a housing of his own. Amelia had also promised to support him living independently on his own. All in all, especially because of the rather lucrative side job he had been practicing, Ethan was rather well off financially.

Alas, now that Ethan stood in the kitchen of the Baxter family mansion reminiscing, he still thought this was the time in his life when things started to go awry.

It all began to collapse the very same week Ethan finally graduated from high school. In the biggest drug bust of the decade in Garden City, the local police had finally caught up with Jesse and Jake. It even made the headlines in local papers. As soon as Ethan heard of it, his first thought was how lucky he was he did not happen to be dealing with them that particular moment they got caught. For a second, he felt invincible. But soon that all passed, since he came to understand that he would not have much time left before law enforcement would come after him as well. It would only make sense to try and stay calm and to act as rationally as possible.

First, Ethan got rid of everything that might be incriminating, even though that included flushing a few thousand dollars' worth of amphetamine and cocaine down the toilet. The second thing was temporarily shutting down all his current operations involving drugs. This proved to be the hardest step for him since that business had by then become his life blood. Finally, he had to make the choice of whether he would tell of the ensuing trouble to his mother in advance or not. Since he knew his family wealth would come in handy when dealing with the justice system, he decided to tell her — after a fashion.

The following morning it was a beautiful summer day. School was off, and Ethan should have been enjoying the holidays, but instead, he sat at the kitchen table, having breakfast with his mother, wondering what to say. He knew she would soon be heading to work, probably to do invoicing or some other tasks which Ethan found completely menial and boring. In other words, Ethan knew he did not have much time to tell, since every wasted minute meant that the risk of her finding out because of the police coming to arrest him would grow. He quickly went over the plan he had come up with the previous evening and began.

"Mother, did you read the news?"

"Yesterday, yes. Today, no. Why is that?" Amelia wondered.

"I am talking about the police catching guys dealing drugs here in Garden City. I knew the two of them, they used to go to the same school as me."

"Really? Well, it's no surprise really, we don't have that many elementaries," she figured.

"Or high schools. In any case, I used to hang out with those two as well. I never knew of the kinds of business they were apparently involved in. But now… now I am worried I could be accused of something as well."

After hearing this, Amelia placed her cup of coffee down carefully and slowly. She then crossed her hands, looked straight downwards at them for a short while, and remained completely silent. After a couple of seconds, she asked Ethan:

"Are you using drugs?"

Even though Ethan had guessed beforehand his mother might react fiercely, the question still shocked him. He was obviously fully aware that he had been using drugs, but hearing his own mother ask him this so directly still felt chilling.

"No! I was just about to say, I never had anything like that to do with them. But that doesn't help me with my concerns in the slightest. You know what this can end up like for me!"

Amelia quickly raised her head, and looked Ethan in the eye:

"Ethan…"

Before she could go on, he stopped her:

"Mother, you must believe me!"

Amelia looked at her son with a blank expression on her face. Deep down, she had known something was wrong. All that time – on some level – she knew. Yet, as she looked at her son, knowing that besides wealth and her own, nowadays rather distant parents he remained all she had left. Therefore, she decided to believe him. More than that, she wanted to believe him. She could feel a tear running down her face.

"I believe you, dear."

They both just sat there, in silence. Ethan, trying to function as rationally as possible, and Amelia, still in emotional turmoil from what she had just heard. But even though Ethan and Amelia had their differences, they both shared the ability of being able to act rationally and calmly even under stressful situations. It was something Ethan had been relying on, too. He decided to break the silence:

"So... the police might want to ask some questions from me too."

"So, they'll ask, and you'll answer. Truthfully," said Amelia now that she had been able to gather her thoughts.

"You say you are innocent, and I believe you. And since you are innocent, we will have nothing to worry about. Isn't that right?"

Ethan felt relieved.

"Absolutely."

To his mother's shock and as a no surprise to himself, the police arrived at the Baxter mansion later that day and took Ethan in for questioning. It all went down undramatically and quickly. In the evening, the police allowed for Ethan to call his mother to inform her that he was being arrested and would be spending the night in jail. With Amelia horrified by this, she began arranging for a lawyer for Ethan, for it was not like they could not afford one.

The very next day things started to collapse. While Ethan remained at the police station, being questioned, Amelia, while waiting for a call back from one of the lawyers she had contacted, picked the phone up only to receive another very disturbing call. It came from a doctor in Nebraska. By instinct, she immediately knew what it was going to be about. Almost ten years ago, when she and Ethan had been able to move to the mansion, her parents Henry and Clarice had moved to the neighboring state to enjoy their days of retirement.

But now, Amelia's guess turned out to be correct. Her parents had been driven to the local county hospital in an ambulance, with Henry having suffered a major heart attack. It was at this point that Amelia's focus started to crack; the bad news had gotten simply too much to bear, even for her. Even though she did not remain convinced of her son's innocence, it was something she now just had to believe in, and to fight for, so she would not lose everything precious to her.

Quickly, she called every possible attorney in Garden City and the nearby locations and told the first available one to get to the police station to assist Ethan. She felt so stressed that by the time she looked for her car keys she could no longer even remember the name of the attorney she had just hired. Amelia quickly packed the essentials she needed and jumped in her sedan. She would call Ethan about the attorney on the way over once her nerves had calmed down.

Ethan was fed up. After a night of very little rest, he was again in the same small box of a room at the police station. The detective whose questions he had been answering to had stepped out on a break, and Ethan sat alone in the room in which there stood but a simple table, four plastic chairs, and very little room to move around. Even though he maybe should have been, Ethan was not particularly afraid. He knew there would be little to no evidence against him, and some legal help would soon be on its way. Even if Jesse and Jake had told the police everything about his involvement, he felt certain that without concrete evidence, it would not be enough to get him convicted of anything. Mostly he was simply annoyed. Annoyed by how he had been thrown in a jail cell and annoyed by how arrogantly he had been handled by the cops. Because of that treatment, he did not even feel remorse for the things he had done but gladly denied them all.

Just as he began wondering what took the detective so long, the only door out of the room right in front of him opened, and a man came in. Ethan did not know him, and before he had a chance to say anything, the stranger opened the conversation:

"Mr. Ethan Baxter? My name is Michael Williams, I'm an attorney at law, and I'm here to assist you in this investigation you're under," he said, taking a brief pause, after which he went on: "Your mother Amelia did tell you I was coming, did she?"

It was just now that Ethan got a good look at his newly appointed attorney. Without that introduction and the environment he was in, he never would have imagined Mr. Michael Williams to be practicing law. He could swear the guy was almost seven feet tall, and extremely muscular as well. He had a sharp look in his eyes, a blue suit which fit him well, and unlike many other men in their forties, no distinctive beer belly. The initial impression he gave off told everyone that this was a man not to be messed with. Michael proceeded to place the bag which assumably contained his laptop on the table, and sat down right next to Ethan.

"She did," Ethan replied.

"Good! For a second there I got scared I might have gotten into the wrong interrogation room," Michael grinned.

"Here's to show you I am who I say I am," Michael said, proceeding to hand Ethan his business card.

"So! We'll take care of this step by step. I did get a brief explanation of the events over the phone. Can you confirm that you are absolutely certain there is no chance the police can have any other evidence against you besides testimonials of others?"

"Yes," Ethan said, without hesitation.

"Good. That'll make the first step of our journey a lot easier. I'll make sure you get released from here as soon as possible. Based on my experience, I'd say you most likely will get to go home tonight at the latest. That is, if everything goes smoothly," explained Michael, winking at Ethan.

"We'll talk about the rest of the steps once we're out of here."

Ethan could not figure out what to say, so he went on by simply saying:

"Ok. Thank you."

After the brief meeting with Ethan, Michael stepped out of the room, leaving Ethan there. Ethan was getting anxious about being released and kept staring at the clock on the wall of the room. According to it, roughly one hour had passed since Michael had left. Then, the door opened. The detective that had been questioning Ethan stood there.

"We'll continue with the questions later. You're free to go."

Without saying a word, Ethan stood up, shortly looking at the detective, and then walked out. He got escorted out of the section of the police station that was reserved only for staff and their 'customers'. In the lobby, Michael awaited him.

"Now, the first obstacle is cleared. As you suspected, they have no hard evidence against you at this point. Therefore, they cannot hold you."

"I see," Ethan could not help smiling a bit.

"But by no means are they going to be dropping the case against you. So, I would recommend we do some planning together. Even though we can play this the way the police will not find any reason to hold you for any longer than necessary, they will still be detaining you for more questioning in the future," Michal explained.

"Before that, I assume you will want to rest and clean up a little. I suggest we meet later this week to discuss the process, preferably already tomorrow if that will do for you?"

"Sure, tomorrow any time will do. It's the Baxter mansion, you probably know the place."

"I do. I'll come there tomorrow around four in the afternoon. And remember: do not talk to the police without discussing it with me first. Now, do you need me to drive you back home?"

"It's ok, I'll walk."

Ethan had the feeling that Michael had already done more for him than required so he did not want to ask him for any more favors.

As Ethan stepped out of the police station and started walking home, he felt incredible. He remained confident that he would not get caught, and having a top-notch lawyer by his side made him feel like he was someone important. For better or for worse, the whole ordeal turned out to be a huge boost to his ego.

As Ethan arrived home, he was greeted by silence. This was not something he had grown accustomed to. Especially under the conditions, he could not understand where his mother might have gone at a time like this without letting him know. At that moment, he did not worry about it too much, though, for she would surely call him or come home soon. After grabbing a bite to eat of what was left in the fridge, Ethan took a long shower, after which he just collapsed on his bed. The mental energy boost he had gotten had passed, and the night spent at the police station was about to take its toll.

The next day Ethan opened his eyes to see the time was six in the morning, and he could not get any more sleep. This came as no big wonder, since after he quickly did the math in his head, he realized he had been asleep for 12 hours. For a while, the events of the last few days seemed like a distant dream, but then he remembered it had all actually happened. He reached for his phone to see if Amelia, Michael, or the police had been trying to reach him. To his disappointment, there were no calls or messages he had missed. He felt a shiver run down his spine.

Later that day, Michael showed up at the mansion at precisely four, just as they had discussed. They went over some of the details involving mostly the answers Ethan should be giving to the police. In short, he should hardly be answering their questions at all. This was the main takeaway Ethan got from that meeting. Just as Michael was about to leave, he reminded Ethan not to talk to the police without him present. Ethan then asked:

"Have you heard from my mother?"

Michael seemed a bit surprised by the question. Most likely he had been expecting Ethan to ask him questions concerning the case against him.

"No, I haven't. Why? Haven't you?" he replied.

"No."

Michal and Ethan were both silent for a moment, after which Michael simply said:

"Well, I'm sure you have nothing to worry about. She'll hopefully call you back soon."

"Yeah, most likely."

Even though he would not admit it to Michael, it just hit Ethan; he had not tried to call Amelia even once. He had just waited for her to call or to come home.

As soon as Michael had left, Ethan grabbed his phone and called his mother on her cellphone. The phone kept ringing for maybe ten seconds, after which Ethan heard a beeping sound. Someone else tried to reach him on his phone. He decided to prioritize the call to her mother, and then call that someone back. Even if her phone had gotten stolen and she was trying to reach him on that other line, surely, she would respond as soon as he called her back.

The phone kept ringing, and soon the beeping sounds stopped, indicating that whoever was calling him had given up. He held the phone, and it rang for a long time. There was no answer. Finally, he got disconnected, most likely because of the long delay in the recipient's end. Ethan stood there, holding his phone, wondering what to do next. Just as he would check his phone log to see who had been trying to reach him, the doorbell rang. By instinct, he quickly checked to see who the caller was, wondering if the call and the sudden visitor would be connected. Of course, it could just be Michael who had forgotten something. Much to Ethan's disappointment, the caller had hidden his number.

Ethan rushed to the front door. His earlier feelings of confidence and might were gone, and now for the first time ever during these recent events, he was afraid. As he opened the door, the first thing he saw was the police vehicle parked in front of the mansion front door. Only after that did he at once recognize the same detective who had been questioning him earlier. He was not wearing a uniform but a regular black jacket with blue jeans, with badge and what looked like identification hanging from his neck. He stood on the front steps of the mansions with some other man who did not wear a badge and was in civilian clothing as well. Before they could say anything, Ethan reacted just like Michael had advised him to:

"I'm not saying anything without my lawyer."

Neither of the men seemed surprised by what Ethan had just said. In fact, what he had said produced no reaction in them whatsoever.

"We are not here to talk about that case, Ethan. Or drugs or anything related to those," detective whose family name Ethan now remembered to be Sullivan said.

With Ethan just standing there in silence, holding the door in one hand, detective Sullivan took a brief look at the man he had arrived with, then looked at the doorstep in front of Ethan, and stated:

"It is about Amelia, Ethan. I am sorry to have to tell you that she is dead."

The detective then slowly raised his head so that his eyes could meet Ethan's, and began talking for what felt like eternity:

"The Nebraskan coroner's office asked us to deliver this information to you. Apparently, on the highway just north of the state line, her car drifted into the oncoming lane, and a truck collided with her. According to the local rescue service, it was all over very quickly."

Detective Sullivan paused for a moment, nodding in the direction of the other man who was with him:

"We are very sorry for your loss. Aaron here is a social worker of our PD. If you wish for any kind of support in this time of crisis, we're here to help."

Ethan could not believe his ears. Astounded, he asked:

"Is this some kind of a trick?"

Detective Sullivan again looked Ethan in the eyes and slowly shook his head.

Ethan sat on sofa in the living room. It was the very same sofa which he used to sit on whenever Amelia had been teaching him about money or life in general, which by now had been countless times over the course of all these years. The police were gone, and Ethan remained all by himself. Since he had a hard time believing this was really happening, he had asked them for contact information of the officials in Nebraska. Over the phone, they had confirmed Amelia's death to Ethan and extended their condolences. Aaron the social worker had given him some phone numbers and websites of victim advocacy and grief counseling, since Ethan had refused to talk with them any longer and sent them away.

Even though the facts were clear, the reality sank in slowly. First, the fact that he would never see his mother again. Second, that he was practically alone. With her gone, no father in his life, and his only known grandparents living a very distant life, there were no relatives left. His so-called friends, which Ethan hardly thought of as friends, but more like business partners, were either caught by the police, gone underground because of the police, or complete drug addicts. Third, Ethan figured that on some level this would be exactly what he on some level had been anticipating for quite some time. He had now become now the boss of the family and of himself. Behind all these thoughts his ever-rational thought processes were wondering what all the practical arrangements would be that he had to take care of now that his mother had passed. On some level, he was still wondering whether this might be an attempt to trick him into confessing his crimes.

At that time, the only person Ethan could think of calling and wanted to call was Michael. Even that call ended up being rather short; Ethan informed him of the latest developments, and Michael told Ethan to think of the police case as little as possible to allow himself some time to grieve. Together, they decided that at this point it would be wise to just lay low and wait for the police to make the first move. Finally, Michael told Ethan he would be emailing him to confirm that his assignment to Ethan's case would still be ongoing with him as the principal instead of Amelia. Michael from Ethan's point of view then ended the call quite abruptly.

Ethan stared at the vast living room around him, thinking that this was all his now. For a minute, he in his mind stepped into this world of fantasy where he was the great drug baron, respected by many and feared by the most, running his operations from this great manor. In that fantasy he lived a very carefree life.

Alas, his life was not carefree, and he came to understand that as soon as he snapped out of that fantasy. The fact is, he would soon be a college student, just like everyone else, and that he was a suspect in a criminal case. For the first time – even if only for a brief moment – he felt shame for what he had been doing with Jesse and Jake. More importantly, he was completely alone, and no amount of wealth he would inherit could ever change that.

Over the next weeks, Ethan got questioned by the police two more times, with Michael present at both. All in all, from the day police had come to detain Ethan for the first time, it took less than half a year for the district attorney to come to the decision not to prosecute him because of lack of evidence. Before ending their collaboration on Ethan's case, Michael reminded Ethan that the case could be reopened, should the police be able to come up with any new evidence. Ethan took Michael's hint seriously and decided to hold off on doing that business for now.

During that summer, Ethan learned he now remained the only living relative well enough to take care of his mother's funeral arrangements. His grandfather Henry had died as well, due to this rapidly deteriorated health, and his grandmother Clarice was in ill health, not able to travel. After all these years, Ethan would not be interested in contacting his distant grandmother. He took care that a good spot would be reserved for his mother at the local cemetery and asked the funeral home to send out invitations for a simple ceremony. Besides Ethan, only three people attended. All of them were Amelia's former partners in the family business. Another thing about the funeral that Ethan knew he would never forget was that even though he wanted to, he could not cry.

During that autumn, Ethan was supposed to begin his college studies. In reality, he did not only do any studying, but his life became very fuzzy. Even though he had been accustomed to being wealthy, with the access to the family business and funds, he had in fact become a millionaire overnight. He knew there would be no need for him to ever study or work again, and that he could have everything he ever wanted just with what he already had.

In the end, Ethan got classified as a no-show student, and his admission into college was cancelled. He did not care. He felt certain that as soon as the criminal case had been dealt with, he would in all sense and purpose be a free man. In the meantime, he bought the best computer for gaming purposes that money could buy and spent his days mostly online.

Then came the day he had been anxiously waiting for: he had been acquitted and he and Michael parted ways. For that one evening, Ethan felt sincerely happy. He spent it playing World of Warcraft with his online friends and getting drunk. He knew that now he could do anything he ever wanted to.

Alas, Ethan ended up spending his days at the computer, drinking. He loved the feeling of success that he achieved in the simulated worlds of games alongside his friends. The high alcohol and occasional spikes of dopamine that developing characters in the games gave him boosted that feeling even further. It was as if apart from a few days he spent hungover he had entered the life of a party.

However, as weeks and months passed, this way of life started to numb him. Each day, it felt as if the feelings of high were a little lower than they were yesterday. Many of Ethan's online friends disappeared since they had to work and study —

some even had a family of their own. New games were not as exhilarating as the old ones used to be, and the old ones had become too boring to grind. Even getting drunk was not like it used to be, Ethan felt that alcohol just made him slow and passive instead of the good feelings it used to bring up in him.

Had anyone known Ethan well enough back then, they would not have been shocked by what Ethan did to try to resolve this. Even though he was not in the business anymore, because of his past experience he knew exactly where to find the top dealers of other substances in Garden City. To regain his feelings of greatness, Ethan turned to the world of stimulants. Cocaine especially became his drug of choice since he had no problems affording it. On some level he was also still fascinated by how all the rich and influential people did just the same. He wanted to fit in with them, despite not being in the same social groups – not even close.

Since life in the games had become boring, Ethan found some new contacts while buying drugs. Besides wasting time online, he frequented bars and nightclubs with his new friends. Of them, Ethan was the only one financially well off, so naturally he ended up paying for his friends as well. In his life, days quickly turned into weeks and months of partying, and months turned into years. Aside from more serious crimes than substance abuse, Ethan and his friends did pretty much anything one could in Garden City, with the sole purpose of having fun.

Now, Ethan stood still in the kitchen. He had been walking in circles, both literally and figuratively. The year was 2023, and here he was, reminiscing about something that could only be described as wasted years. He had no idea what he had done with the last 15 years of his life. Nothing accomplished, nothing gained. Now, all those years of fuzzy carelessness had finally resulted in what seemed to be his immeasurable wealth running out. Him selling his luxury car was not because of his own will, but because it would be a necessary action for him to survive financially. The family mansion would probably be next on the list of things he had to get rid of. In just 15 years, Ethan had squandered that which took one lifetime and more for Henry Baxter to build and for Amelia Baxter to grow and to preserve.

Suddenly, Ethan found it hard to breathe. All the anxiousness that previously made him feel as if his head would explode had now transformed into him having to sit down or to lose consciousness trying to stand still. The anguish he went through was indescribable. With his last strength, he wandered into the hallway leading towards the living room, and quickly sat down on a wooden chair in the hallway, placing his face against the palms of his hands.

The next day, at five o'clock in the afternoon, he saw what used to be his Bentley cruise off the mansion property for what was probably the last time. The buyer, after taking a relatively quick test drive had immediately fallen in love with Ethan's car and wanted to buy it. Since Ethan desperately needed the money, he sold the car to a young man who judging by the looks had probably gotten his first well-paying job in some fancy field such as law or medicine.

One might have figured the 60 000 $ deal helped Ethan overcome his financial troubles, but he knew this would only be the beginning. The mansion upkeep costs combined with frivolous spending, debt, and family business that was now worthless meant that Ethan could no longer afford to go without working. Ever since Amelia's death, Ethan had found no will to keep on developing the Baxter irrigation business. He had simply paid off all the little business debt they had, and let the business stay completely passive. Competitors had invaded that product sector, and there were no customers left. Since Ethan had no clue how to run the business, and the existing revenue was minimal, there were no chances left for him to be able to revive the company, either. The only option left seemed to be declaring bankruptcy.

Ethan headed back inside. As he stepped on the porch, he had tears running down his face. He could not remember the last time he had cried, and for those who knew him, it would have been unheard of to see the infamous Ethan Baxter crying. But there he was, crying in front of his huge mansion. It was what some would describe as manly crying, lasting only for a moment, and done in silence.

He dried his face off on the sleeve of his shirt and turned on his heels. He needed something to help ease the pain. He had run out of drugs, but obviously knew who to approach in times of need. With no car, Ethan began walking towards the suburbs of Garden City.

"Hey bro…" a thin, almost skeleton-like figure in a black hoodie and baggy jeans greeted Ethan as he walked towards an old house he has previously visited only a couple of times. The house and the neighborhood around were in terrible shape. Some windows had been smashed, the paint on the facades had worn off, with graffiti here and there. The neighboring house even looked like something had crashed through its roof. It is as if something had fallen out of the sky and directly towards that rooftop. Even though Garden City did not have too many places that could be considered as slums or ghettos, if one place had to be chosen for the role, it would be these parts just north of downtown.

Ethan did not stay there wondering about the roof for too long, but went directly to the point: "You got anything for me today?"

He got no reply, but was greeted by the figure gasping for air, with his face wildly twisting first from a surprised expression to the one of maniacal laughter. After that, he just sat there on the front steps of that old rotten house, staring at Ethan in the eyes.

"Dude…" he gasped, so faintly and unclearly Ethan could barely understand. At that point it truly dawned on Ethan: this was indeed just some figure, a shell of what used to be a man. There were many names for what Ethan might have called him, such as junkie, drug addict, criminal, lowlife, or simply just a thing. In that shell, however, Ethan saw no humanity left. The feelings of disgust Ethan felt at that moment were almost overwhelming.

"Are you high?" Ethan finally asked, only to be given the same exact greeting as before: "Dude... bro..."

The man who used to be one of the dealers Ethan rarely had associated himself with had his eyes roll in his head one last time before he finally passed out on the front steps. He did it in a surprisingly clean way. His head simply collapsed in front of him while the rest of his body managed to stay firmly in sitting position he had been in. Had it been in any other neighborhood, for some it might even have looked like just a traveler resting his eyes for a little bit.

Ethan took a few steps towards the passed-out addict. Once he saw there was no initial reaction, he checked to see if the guy might have any cocaine or methamphetamine on him. He could not even remember the guy's name, and he did not care. As he got up close to him, he could smell the stench of old vomit and dirt from those baggy clothes and saw there were abscesses, some of which were emitting pus all over his hands. Now, Ethan felt as if he himself might throw up any second.

"Yeah, I'm most definitely not your bro," Ethan quietly said, all the while going through the pockets of those baggy jeans.

Three weeks later, Ethan sat in the living room of the Baxter mansion. He still had a small amount of methamphetamine he had bought from the passed-out junkie. He did not consider it to be stealing, since after taking the drugs, he had replaced them with a hefty amount of cash. Definitely more than what he could have gotten when selling the stuff on street, in any case.

All these days, Ethan had been craving to use it, but had been reluctant to do so. Over the course of those three weeks, Ethan had lost the business as he had anticipated, and it had also dawned on him that he would have to get rid of the mansion as well. Nothing in his life was about to take a turn for better, and this remained the only thing imaginable to him that he could find some joy in.

The one thing that had prevented Ethan from using drugs was the sight of that addict. Even though he craved the stuff, he was too horrified by what he had seen to actually enjoy it. He could not believe that for all those years he had been living in the fantasy of thinking that line of business would be the road to fame and wealth. The illusion had been unbreakable for such a long time for him it was like the whole world had now been turned upside down for Ethan. As if the last 20 years of his life – everything apart from the early childhood – had been a lie and completely and utterly for nothing. The thought of that made Ethan shudder.

But it was true. There was nothing left in his life, and the values and ideas he had lived by had turned out to be false. And even though he so deeply yearned for that feeling and those thoughts to go away even for just a little while, the drugs he held were a part of that same illusion, that same lie. Hence, he had not been able to use them, even at this point when his whole life the way it used to be was finally going to disintegrate. In a way, it was probably even for the better. All this waiting for the inevitable had been a terrible time for Ethan, and now a new chapter could finally begin.

He could hear faint steps echoing from across the hall. They were getting closer, as if the sound of those steps would symbolize all of his problems finally managing to creep up to him after all these years. Then, Ethan could hear the steps right outside the living room, after which the source of those steps entered the room.

"Thanks for letting me use the bathroom. I'm finished with the contract now as well, so I suppose all that's left are the keys," the man announced.

He was a real estate agent. Ethan looked at him. As a man in his forties, with a mid-sized body, glasses, shaved face with a short and clean haircut combined with semi-formal clothing, he resembled everything Ethan had always pictured an average American worker to be, and something that Ethan had dreaded of becoming like himself. Yet, if given the choice, he would now switch places with him in the blink of an eye with no hesitation.

Ethan reached for the keys in his pocket, grabbed them in his fist, and extended his arm. For a short moment, there was an awkward silence as they both looked at each other. Then, the agent took two steps towards Ethan, placing his hand right under the fist which Ethan held the keys with, and looked at him from under his eyebrows.

Ethan opened his fist, releasing the keys from his grip. As they landed on the agent's hand, they made a soft jingling sound, which to Ethan sounded like a loud explosion had gone off in his ears.

"Thank you."

Again, a short and an awkward silence befell them, as Ethan just stared at him. After a while, the man broke the silence by saying:

"I think we should go now," as if he was asking Ethan a question. In reality, he indicated that Ethan no longer had any right to stay in the mansion which used to belong to Baxter family.

"Yes," Ethan replied.

"Let's go."

As they went outside and the door closed behind them, the agent turned towards Ethan and said:

"Well, I need to get going now. Have a nice day."

Ethan said nothing.

Once the real estate agent's car had vanished around the bushes circling the property, Ethan began walking around the mansion. He stopped at the gardens at the back of the house and looked around. Besides the overgrown gardens and crumbling walls there was no one to be seen. It was as if the building was a physical manifestation of the ruins his life had become.

Having no more strength to stand up, Ethan fell on his knees, where he for the second time felt he wanted to cry within a relatively short period in his life. Only this time, it was not just for a teardrop or two, but he now could and did turn on the whole waterworks.

As the sun was starting to set, tears streaming down his face, he knew he could blame no one but himself. Even though his physical life was far from over, his spirit was crushed, and whatever family legacy had been handed over to him was gone as well, banished by his own actions. Now, he would have to start all over again.

A TALE OF WEALTH AND WOE

Just south of downtown Minneapolis, there is a neighborhood called Powderhorn. For the locals, it is especially known for several diverse restaurants and shops. At the heart of Powderhorn, there is a park, surrounded by what many would describe as a typical American residential neighborhood. Albeit nothing too fancy, it is exactly what one would expect from the typical American Dream. You would not be able to find huge mansions, garages, or swimming pools there, but mostly just middle-income families living in relative peace and quiet.

Right across the park, on the eastern side to be precise, stood a blue house at the corner of an intersection. It was much bigger than most of the properties found in the area. Even from the outside it was clear that the house had been taken care of well, and despite it being old, it gave off that particular feeling of a new house, for it had obviously been thoroughly renovated all the way from top to bottom.

In that house, lived Kurt Henderson, a 68-year-old widower by himself. After the death of his wife, he had not remarried, nor had he had any other spouses for that matter either. Ten years ago, when Kurt and his wife Hannah had moved there, they had decided that they wanted to be able to live in a house that was in good condition. With both of them being almost able to retire, it seemed like a wise choice back then.

For Kurt, it still was a wise choice. In fact, he thanked whatever divine powers might exist that at least he had a good home to reside in. Kurt and Hannah had been married for almost forty years. With his wife falling ill with pancreatic cancer three years ago and her imminent death which ensued quickly afterwards, trying to handle caretaking of his home at the same time would have been too much for him to manage.

However, would Kurt have received any visitors, they might have noticed the lack of furniture and décor in the house. Besides the master bedroom, kitchen, and the living room there were very few things in Kurt's home. He had gotten rid of much of the stuff which had been precious mostly to Hannah. He himself did not care much for home decorations. The home of Kurt Henderson was minimalistic. In the bedroom there stood the same king-sized bed which Kurt and Hannah had owned for the last twenty years. In the kitchen stood a simple table with two chairs, and the only visible appliances appeared to be fridge, stove, oven, dish washer, and microwave oven. Everything was very cleanly organized and in nearly pristine condition.

The living room was much like the kitchen and the bedroom were: very simple and modest. On the wall right around the middle section of the house stood a fireplace which looked like it had not seen much use for a while. Almost in front of it there was an armchair made of brown leather, with a footrest in front of the armchair made of similar brown leather. In the corner, there lay a basket made of straws. It had old newspapers and magazines in it. Right next to the only window in that room there was a drawer with some framed photographs on top of it. Just like in the other rooms, all the surfaces were in excellent shape.

In that living room, in what some might describe as dark or dim lighting, sat Kurt Henderson in the brown leather armchair, browsing a newspaper. Even in the year 2022, Kurt had not gotten used to reading the news on the Internet, but preferred a newspaper he could physically hold in his own hands, just as he had for all his life. He kept the lights in the room in a dim setting for two reasons. Firstly, since he wanted to save electricity, and secondly, because he thought that too much brightness made his eyes feel worn out. He was sitting in a relaxed and comfortable position, resting his feet high up on the footrest, and just like many elderly people used to, read the news with his head tilted upwards so he could see from under his glasses. His vision up close was not what it used to be, and he had not bothered purchasing separate glasses for reading. As he was reading opinion columns written in part by regular columnists of the paper, and in part by the readers, while gazing upon a certain headline, his eyebrows jumped upwards.

The text had been titled "You only live once". A man in his thirties described how he was having a very hard time surviving with the rising costs of living. He described his accurate calculations of how inflation and the rate hikes had caused havoc in his life, and how his family of three could now no longer perhaps afford to live in their large home, or they might have to sell their third car. The writer did admit to having made choices which did not reflect the average household spending, but his choices had been more prestigious and luxurious ones. In his defense, he claimed that nobody will get to keep their wealth once they are gone, and that one should be allowed to nevertheless enjoy their life.

This struck Mr. Kurt Henderson hard. All his life he had been valuing the concepts of frugality, minimalism, and saving money. Long ago, his father had taught him that each man has only one life, and the time they get on Earth is a limited gift. That is why nobody should sell their most precious asset of time too easily, and if one did end up doing so, the money earned by exchanging time for it should be treated with the respect it deserved and was never to be spent frivolously. Kurt had seen his father lead a life of doing long hours to provide for his family, and in the end witnessed him dying at the relatively young age of 55. He had decided to heed the advice of his father and was intent on not working himself to death.

Kurt, who had succeeded in being able to provide by working only part-time for the last eight years of his career up until his retirement at the age of 58, read the young man's story with contempt. Kurt had worked a long career at Xerox. At the moment of his retirement his title was sales manager. He knew what doing hard work for a good paycheck meant. The writer who signed off as "Mike, 33", according to himself, fell in the bracket of high-income earners as well. Unlike Kurt, however, he seemed to be clueless about the value of his own work.

Kurt had half a mind to go fire up his laptop to write a column of his own in reply to Mike. He closed the wide, rustling newspaper in his hands and wrapped it in a tight roll.

"Oh, who cares!" said Kurt to himself with frustration in his voice. He tied the newspaper roll with a small rubber band and threw it in the basket that was sitting in the corner. The basket was now halfway full of old newspapers. Kurt sat there, staring at the fireplace, with an annoyed and cranky look on his face. Then, he stood up and with his old, brown, and almost worn-out trousers producing a swishing sound as he took steps towards the coat rack, he grabbed his leather jacket and left the house.

Each day for the last three years, apart from the few days he had been ill with flu, Kurt Henderson had visited Minneapolis city center. He considered movement and exercise to be very important and would nowadays never go without his daily walk. Up until that point he had done a lot of biking, but ever since he had started coming down with slight tremor in his hands, due to risk of injury, he would not dare to ride a bicycle anymore. So instead, he walked.

Now, it was almost noon, and the swishing of his pants was combined with the occasional crunching sound his jacket made as Kurt strolled along the familiar streets of Powderhorn. Autumn was almost at an end, and the famously cold winter of Minnesota would soon be on its way. It was Wednesday, so the streets were mostly packed with leaves that had fallen from trees, with most of the people working or at school. This was one of the reasons why Kurt usually began his walk before noon. Even though he enjoyed the company of people, he disliked big crowds and intentionally wanted to avoid them.

After having walked for a while, he soon reached what might be described as the southern border of downtown. There, after passing a street which seemingly came to a dead end, he entered a local kiosk. The sign above the door said "Burgham Place Kiosk". Kurt had never understood how it would be possible for that little business to survive in such an isolated corner of this residential area, nor what the name meant. Nevertheless, ever since discovering that place nearly one year ago, he had in his own way been a loyal customer. He very rarely bought anything, but mostly just enjoyed shooting the breeze with Mike, the owner of the place.

Kurt did not actually even know Mike's full name, but ever since he visited the place for the first time, they had immediately hit it off. Mike was a huge, tall, black guy in his forties who had been a restaurant chef before starting the kiosk. Even though Mike and Kurt were nothing alike when it came to their looks or the lives they had led, they enjoyed each other's company. Mike worked long hours at the kiosk which saw relatively few customers every day, and Kurt was a retired old man living alone, so they both naturally had some time to kill every day that Mike was working – which also was almost every day.

As Kurt stepped inside, he was instantly greeted by the familiar scent of hot dogs and candy. If you had to name three main sources of income the kiosk produced, those would definitely be hot dogs, candy, and gambling in the form of lottery tickets and other kinds of betting. Needless to say, customers were mostly comprised of children and elderly people. Besides the scent that was so usual here that it had probably crawled its way permanently into the walls, the place was in spotless condition. There stood a small wooden coffee table and three chairs sitting right next to the window.

While the little bell placed above the door made its usual jingling as the door to the kiosk closed behind Kurt, he was already pulling back one of the chairs next to that old table. Behind the counter stood Mike. Crouched over cardboard boxes, he kept opening and unloading boxes of what looked like milk cartons. Just as the bell began to jingle, he raised his head, and a smile appeared on his face as he noticed Kurt sitting down.

"Hey there! How's it hanging?" began Mike.

Kurt, while looking at Mike with a blank expression, slowly shook his head: "Same old, same old. As a retired man, every day is very much alike for me."

Then, there was a moment of silence, which was broken by Kurt continuing: "How's business?"

Mike laughed a little, and then proclaimed: "Same old here too! But that's all good and all right by me."

Kurt twitched in his chair and wrinkled his forehead – it was as if he suddenly got very uncomfortable – and then asked: "How are you still managing here? Everything is so expensive nowadays, and judging by how screwed up even regular people are… aren't you in trouble?"

Mike laughed again, then said: "Nuh-uh, I don't need that much. Business is good enough and there is no trouble in sight. I've got it all just where I want it."

"I do get where you're coming from, though. These are crazy times," he went on.

Kurt looked at Mike for a while and the wrinkles on his forehead would not disappear. Then, he sighed, looked around, and looked more restful again.

"I'm sorry for being so nosy all the time. You know I don't mean anything by it, it's just who I am," Kurt shrugged his shoulders.

Mike, who had just finished unboxing the milk cartons leaned over the counter. With his arms completely straightened and his palms towards the glass surface of the window that covered some lottery coupons, one might have thought that he was about to say something dramatic.

"Mr. Henderson, like I have said, you are obsessed by thoughts that are way too depressing. When's the last time you truly loosened up and had fun without worrying about something?" Mike asked, with a look on his face that seemed sincerely curious.

Kurt just sat there with a baffled look on his face. He had always been bad at answering surprising questions, and he had gotten ever slower with age. After a while, he realized he probably had to come up with something to say, but just as he opened his mouth, he understood he still did not know how to answer, so all he could produce turned out to be a whisper-like:

"Uuuhmm…"

"Oh, for crying out loud," Mike went on. "Even though I don't know about your financial situation, I know from our previous conversations that you're loaded. Why not just take a vacation? Go somewhere? Have you ever even been outside the states?"

As he heard Mike's suggestion, Kurts eyes widened:

"Nonsense! I'm a pensioner with very little to use, and the only reason I've managed to live this far without working every day of my life is because I refuse to waste money." Kurt then stood up, placing the chair carefully right next to the table where it had been.

"And refusing to refuse to…" Kurt stopped for a while, evidently tripping up in the words he was going to say.

"I mean, live like that and you'll never retire! Just watch and see!"

Mike sighed, shrugging his shoulders: "Very well then, see you tomorrow."

As Kurt headed outside, it was high noon. Clouds had dissolved and sun was shining against the leaves that were covering most of the sidewalks. Even a bird could be heard singing somewhere in the distance. All in all, it was a much more beautiful day than an average autumn day in Minneapolis usually looked like.

But Kurt Henderson did not see the beauty around him, for he remained too flabbergasted by the conversation he had just had with Mike. Muttering to himself, he decided to head home via a slightly longer route than he had walked on his way over to Burgham Place Kiosk.

As usual, Kurt came back home empty handed. It was very rare for him to buy anything during his daily walks, despite his frequent visits to Mike's kiosk or nearby stores. Upon his arrival back home, squeaking of the door hinges and jingling of his keys created a very rustic ambience as he entered the house. Over the years, he had become a creature of habit, and now he immediately placed his keys in a small bowl right next to the door and hung his coat on the rack as he had grown accustomed to.

All the way from the hallway, he could immediately tell that something was off. He noticed the living room seemed somewhat different from how he had left it. Crouching his back and squinting his eyes, he decided to head right over there to see what was going on. As Kurt came closer, he soon understood what was different from before. It was nothing inside his home, but rather on the outside of it. The backyard of his house had always directly faced the backyard of the neighboring house, providing a clear line of sight towards it. The house next door had been empty for two years now, and Kurt had gotten used to silence in that apartment.

But now, Kurt clearly saw a woman moving in the neighboring backyard, arranging garden furniture. He estimated that she was in her late twenties or early thirties and judging by her actions of carrying chairs and flowerpots openly in daylight, she most likely would not be there to loot an empty apartment. After the previous neighbors who seemed like a typical nuclear family had moved out, the place had been for sale for quite some time. Apparently, someone had finally bought it, Kurt figured. For a while now, Kurt had gotten used to the neighboring house being empty, and had grown to like it, so he could not help feeling a little disappointed.

In any case, Kurt's initial reaction was to step outside to take a closer look at his new neighbor, and that he did. The even older hinges than what were attached to the door on the other side of his home sounded off an even louder creak than before at the front door as he stepped into the backyard. Calling Kurt Henderson's backyard a garden would have been a gross exaggeration, for there was hardly anything there. The grass he had always kept in neat condition, but just like inside, he did not care for décor. His yard had just some clean-cut green grass there, and a path built of stones to walk on across the yard to a small gate leading to the sidewalk. Besides the pair of flip-flops next to the back door of the house, there were no other items there.

Kurt slipped on his flip-flops and headed towards the fence situated at the border of the two houses. The lady next door had not even noticed him. Apparently, she had a pair of earphones on. Kurt stopped right next to the old fence that the passing of years had covered partly in rust.

"Hi there," Kurt began.

She had his back turned towards Kurt and gave Kurt no response. Apparently, whatever she was listening to on her headphones prevented her from hearing him speak. As Kurt waited for a reaction for a while, he for the first time paid closer attention to his new potential neighbor. In Kurt's standards, she was young, just as he had gauged from the distance. Despite the chilly weather, she wore a red dress and a denim jacket. In her feet, she had no shoes, but just thick socks made of wool.

Kurt tried clearing his throat loudly but got no reaction. It looked like she focused on planting flowers in a pot. Alas, he was too curious to find out what was going on, so he just stood there, waiting for her to notice him. After a while, she tried reaching for something behind her without turning around at first. Then, since she could not find whatever she was looking for by just feeling it out, she looked to her right, and then onto the ground behind her. As she found the gardening spade she had been reaching for, it dawned on Kurt that she also noticed him standing there, since she quickly jumped up, screaming:

"Oh my gosh!"

Startled by her reaction, Kurt tried to calm the situation down:

"Hey, sorry, didn't mean to scare you."

He then kept a brief pause and went on:

"I live here and was intrigued when I saw you. This neighboring house here has been empty for quite a while now."

Judging by her hyperventilating, she still had not regained her composure. With her right hand still holding the gardening spade she had apparently grabbed in panic, she used her left hand to pull the earphones out of her ears, after which she placed both of her hands on her chest. In between her breaths she managed to puff out:

"It's ok. You caught me off-guard there."

She let out a couple more deep breaths, and asked:

"I'm sorry, what were you saying before?"

Relieved that he had not managed to cause a bigger scene upon making the first impression on her, Kurt repeated himself:

"I was just wondering whether we'll be neighbors. The backyard you're standing in has been isolated for years now."

"Ah, yes," she smiled now.

"I noticed the place was for sale and price-wise it was a bargain, really. Since the place had not been properly looked after for a long time now, I managed to drive the cost even further down, nearly 20 % off what the original price was," she explained.

"Quite a change for me, considering I used to live in a multi-story apartment house of not much more than 300 square feet!" she laughed.

Kurt, stunned by how quickly she had calmed down and was now telling her life story to him, would not know exactly what to say, so nodding his head slowly, he just said:

"Ah. Well, it's a nice and calm neighborhood we have here."

"Tell me about it! It's quite a change from NYC where I used to live."

"So how did you…" before Kurt had a chance to finish his sentence, she continued:

"…decide to move here?" She laughed again, and Kurt just stood there with a baffled look on his face.

"Because of the house! Like, you know, New York City has its problems, and I wanted some more room for myself with a less crowded and safer area. Nowadays, it's so easy to do anything over the internet. Can you imagine I just arrived in Minnesota two days ago for the first time in my life, and now I'm already settled in here? Just a few weeks ago I was still in another state and looking for another place to live in."

"Well, where are my manners? Hi, I'm Mia," she introduced herself, extending her hand, and laughing again.

Kurt shook his hand and said: "Kurt Henderson. Nice to meet you."

At that point Kurt came to realization that he would probably be stuck there talking to his new neighbor for the rest of the afternoon unless he made a move to exit the situation.

"Well, it's been nice talking to you, Mia. Welcome to the neighborhood."

Mia then smiled cheerfully and replied: "Thank you! Can you imagine that I…"

At that point it was Kurt's turn to interrupt her: "I'm sorry Mia, but we'll have to continue this conversation at another time. You see, I have something to take care of and you obviously need time to get settled in as well. Be seeing you around here."

Mia had a surprised look on her face for a while, but said: "Oh of course, I hope I haven't been talking for too long. See you and have a lovely day!"

She blew a kiss at Kurt, which obviously sent him into even more confusion. Since he did not know how to respond to that, he simply turned around with an uncomfortable smile on his face and walked across the yard back inside.

As he reached the living room and closed the door behind him, Kurt was completely blown away. He could not remember a time in his life where he had met such a person that had given so much information about themselves to someone who at the time was still a complete stranger. Clearly, Mia was very extrovert and rather peculiar by nature. The extreme reactions of getting that easily scared, calming down quickly and finally blowing Kurt a kiss which obviously had nothing sexual to it, but was something she probably did with all people made that very clear. For a second Kurt considered the possibility that she might be mentally unstable, but even despite his suspicious nature he quickly discarded that thought, wanting to believe that was not the case.

But most of all Kurt could not believe his ears when Mia had told him she had just spontaneously moved across the country on what seemed to be a whim – and without even seeing her new home first. She had even very openly told him of the costs involved, which amazed Kurt, who had always been very reserved when it came to speaking of money. He had always planned out his life very carefully in advance. In his twenties, he had already been making plans for his early retirement and had been living and spending money accordingly. The thought of buying a new home like that and just going sounded frivolous and irresponsible to him.

For the rest of the day, Kurt avoided going outside, since he did not want to get caught off guard by Mia and be stuck in another lengthy conversation. Earlier, he had lied to Mia. In reality, he did not actually have anything particularly important to do. He spent the rest of the day cooking, cleaning the house and reading before finally turning in that night.

Weeks passed and the infamous Minnesotan winter was about to arrive. Kurt lived his life like always, sticking to his routines just as he had before. But besides his daily walks and chatting with local shopkeepers like Mike, he had gotten to know his new neighbor better now as well. Mia had her stuff in place in her new home in no time, and within a few weeks she had managed to land a simple job as a cashier at a supermarket Kurt had never heard of. Besides the cleaning she had done, her house still remained in the same condition she had bought it in. Kurt had never been inside but had seen pictures of it in the sales ad. Especially the bathroom wall tiles, and floor were in almost original, really rough shape, considering that the house had been built in the 1950s. But that did not seem to bother Mia, and it is not like she would have had money with which to renovate it either.

What amazed Kurt about Mia the most was her trusting, spontaneous, and open nature. In this regard, she had proven to be the complete opposite to him. Barely a week had passed after her moving in, and he already knew almost everything about her life, history, and even finances. He himself had always been very reserved about sharing such information about himself to even those close to him. He found such topics to be extremely private in nature. Kurt had been wondering if that was the reason why she seemed to have no problem with finding new friends and getting acquainted with people; a field in which Kurt had been struggling his entire life.

Most of all, he found it impossible to fathom how Mia could just decide to do something, and then do it. For Kurt, even trying out a new brand of coffee could take days of planning and preparing for. Mia could just decide to relocate completely, with no fear of uncertainty about a source of income or being unable to stay in touch with friends and family. Even though Kurt did not know her situation that precisely money-wise, he bet she was just as spontaneous when it came to spending as well. To Kurt, Mia was like Mike the kiosk owner on steroids. Their values and ideas were nothing like Kurt's, yet he had managed to form a kind of a friendship with both of them.

Even if Kurt regarded himself frugal, he never thought of him as being miserly. In fact, he had always enjoyed giving small, purely altruistic gifts to people near him. This year, as the Thanksgiving was close by, he had already made plans to prepare a traditional, albeit simple traditional dinner the way he and Hannah together used to. As a part of that, this year he would bake two additional pumpkin pies to give out as gifts, one for Mike and another for Mia. After all, he had never exactly given a proper housewarming gift to her, which would be the neighborly thing to do.

On November 23rd, the eve of Thanksgiving, Kurt was standing at the front door of his neighbor. He had delivered the other pie to Mike along with his greetings earlier that day. As was to be expected, he got invited to join Mike's family for dinner the coming day, just like he had been the years before. And just like before, he kindly declined the offer, for he did not want to feel like he would be imposing on them. After exchanging some wide smiles and pleasantries, he left to deliver the other pie to Mia.

Now, as he rang the doorbell, he could not help feeling a bit troubled by how worn Mia's home seemed. No matter how frugal and minimalistic life Kurt himself had always led, excluding the two years he served in the military as a young man, he had always been very strict on some standards of living. He considered a clean and whole home to be one of the most important things in life. Judging by how Mia had settled to live in the neighboring house, which was in dire need of renovating, she did not share the same set of values.

As Mia answered the door, she seemed genuinely surprised and happy at the same time.

"Kurt! What a nice surprise!"

Before Kurt had a chance to say anything, she went on: "I was just making some coffee, come on in!"

Even though Kurt had come to know his neighbor up to the point that she was a spontaneous and open person, he had still not gotten completely used to Mia's sheer openness. Ergo, Kurt declined by instinct.

"No, thank you. I really need to be going soon. I…"

Kurt never had a chance to finish the sentence when Mia interrupted him.

"Nonsense. Come on in," Mia stated, not even bothering to wait for Kurt's response before she already turned on her way back to what Kurt deciphered to be kitchen. As Mia made her way back, Kurt was both baffled and annoyed by her attitude, which to him felt even arrogant and intruding. Besides that, she was wearing a pair of slippers on her feet which made the most aggravating squeaking sound as she walked.

"…really just came to drop this thing off," Kurt finished his sentence in an annoyed and frustrated tone. But Mia was already gone and could not hear a word. Kurt sighed, kicked off his old pair of brown leather shoes, and went in.

With the pan of pumpkin pie in his hands, he slowly walked in Mia's footsteps. As he was approaching the room in which he heard Mia humming by herself, he got too intrigued not to look around the house. The living room right next to the hallway had old vintage wallpapers, just like one might expect to see in the home of their grandparents. As he took a few more steps, he noticed the door to his right had been left open, revealing the bathroom which seemed to be in the exact shape it probably had been designed and built roughly 70 years ago. Kurt shivered as he saw the bathtub which at some point probably used to be white. Now, the years had colored it yellow.

After the seemingly endless self-hosted house tour, Kurt finally reached the kitchen, where Mia had already ground some coffee beans and was now preparing coffee maker. The kitchen, which seemed to serve its purpose also as a dining room was not in as bad condition as Kurt had expected it to be. Naturally, it was not in a pristine condition either, but at least it had been taken care of somewhat at some point in the lifetime of that house Mia called home now. At the other end of the room there was a small dining table. Kurt pulled a chair and sat down at the table.

"So, what you got there with you under the foil?" Mia leered at Kurt.

"It's a small housewarming and Thanksgiving gift for you. A pumpkin pie," Kurt replied.

"Oh, how lovely!" Mia quickly moved in to grab the pan and took a quick look at it. "I need to place this in the fridge. Thank you!" she smiled.

"I'm not much of a baker. I hope it's good," Kurt said, feeling his irritation of Mia fade away.

"Nonsense, I'm sure it'll be fantastic," Mia said, switching on the coffee maker. "There, that's all set now."

Mia opened her fridge to place the pie there, and Kurt could not help noticing how empty her fridge seemed. At the quick glance he got from the other end of the room, it seemed that there was a partial stick of butter, a few weird jars which probably included mustard and pickles, and some bread. Besides the emptiness of it, Kurt wondered who on earth would store bread inside their fridge. Kurt did not have much time to bury that thought as Mia sat down across the table.

"So, any plans for tomorrow?" Mia began to inquire.

Kurt could sense where this was going and wondered whether to answer truthfully or not. After some quick thinking, he decided to go with the truth:

"I plan on just preparing a small dinner for myself. It's kind of a tradition for me now."

"Oh, that's nice," Mia responded smiling, but with a face that clearly signaled she felt bad for him having to spend Thanksgiving all by himself.

"It is. I mean, I've had a long life with plenty of people around I love and enjoy spending time with. It's about time I get some time to spend in peace as well," he gave a short laugh.

Mia went on: "You know, I'm heading for drinks with a couple of friends from work. Even though they kinda invited me, I'm sure if you wanted to, I could ask them if it'd be ok to…"

"Stop right there," Kurt interrupted. "In all honesty, I want to spend the evening alone. For goodness sake, I am seeing people every day! I don't need someone to be with me around the clock."

Mia raised her hands up to signal that she was not going to argue with him about it, rolled her eyes a bit, and then smiled.

There was a short, slightly uncomfortable silence, which was broken by Mia: "I'll check on the coffee!" she seemed relieved she had found something to say. Kurt just nodded.

As Mia stood up to fetch the cups for them, she switched topics: "You know, I could not help noticing in how great shape the home of yours is in. I mean, I've obviously just seen the exterior, but kudos on keeping the house in such a great shape."

"Can't say the previous owner of this place did the same here," Mia chuckled.

"Thank you," Kurt responded. "You know, I can recommend this one small company to you, if you would be interested in having some work done here as well. They did marvels with my bathroom for a reasonably good price as well."

Mia looked at him slily. "Do I look like I could afford that?"

She went on: "That was rhetoric, sorry. I could never get a hold of such money. I can barely take care of my mortgage as is."

Kurt was not surprised. In fact, judging by Mia's life, he had kind of anticipated this. In any case, he could not help asking: "Aren't you worried about your home losing its value?"

Mia poured coffee for the two of them.

"You know, I'm more like someone who likes to live in the moment, you know? Milk or sugar?"

"I'll have it black, please."

"So, you don't mind the risk of losing your home or your money?" Kurt went on.

"What's the point?" Mia wondered. "They money will be gone either way, no matter if I invest it into the house or spend it for fun." Carrying the two cups of coffee simultaneously to the table, she said: "Why would I want to save for later when I can live my life today? You never know when your life is going to end. Just that every day it will be somewhat closer by."

Kurt had always been fascinated by conversations about money. Not just about investing and saving, but about ideas and philosophy people have towards money. Even now, even though he could not understand her point of view, he was intrigued to find out more about Mia's way of thinking when it came to spending money.

"But what'll you do if you do end up living a long life? With that way, you will never be able to retire and stop working. Doesn't that scare you?" he asked.

"How boring is that! I could never travel, go to restaurants, have fun… well, not the way I do now, anyway," she took a long sip of her coffee. "On the other hand, if I only saved up small amounts, it would never amount to anything great enough to make a difference, anyway."

Kurt waved a finger at her: "That's where you're wrong! Even small amounts can matter."

"I know, but that's just not me, I guess. Let's turn this the other way around, now. When was the last time you had a night out? Ate out? Or even better, travelled? Do you spend any money on your hobbies?"

Kurt answered with a serious look on his face: "I was a happily married man for decades, Mia. I don't really go out the way young people do. Even before, I never really enjoyed that kind of partying. As for eating out or travelling, I don't do a lot of them either, since I simply can't afford them! The last time I travelled was to Las Vegas, I think, back when there was a work-related conference there."

There was a short silence, and just as Mia was about to speak up, Kurt added: "I enjoy simple things. Reading and writing… I also have my own record collection at home I've had since the eighties now, and still find great joy in listening to them. I have my daily routines I enjoy, and especially my freedom of not having to work for money. Instead, I save money. I don't work to earn it. Well, anymore, that is."

"Well, I for sure could not live like that," Mia declared.

"I get that we are in completely different age brackets, but still, living like that would be exhaustingly boring to me," she continued.

Kurt could feel blood rising up to his cheeks and his feelings of frustration and anger returning. Did Mia just insult him in his face and call him boring?

"My life is not boring," Kurt said in a very serious tone. "It's responsible and frugal. I don't find pleasure in consumerism the way that you young people especially nowadays do."

Much to Kurt's dislike, Mia rolled her eyes in the way one might do to signal contempt, while simply replying: "Whatever."

Kurt frantically thought whether to answer to that immediately, even at the cost of risking their good relations as neighbors, to storm out of the place, or to just stay silent. He decided to go with the latter option and said nothing. Both of them just sat there, slowly sipping their coffee, when Mia finally broke the silence. With a voice that sounded genuinely curious, she asked:

"Don't you ever miss it, though? Yearning for things or experiences?"

"Miss what?" Kurt snidely asked.

"Literally anything you could do with the money you have. Getting a nice car, new clothes, new records. Or if not that stuff, you could see the world, get excited by gambling, eat out, or try new hobbies. I know if I stood on a big pile of cash, I would not waste a second before starting to think about the things I could do."

"I know I'm a little bit of an odd bird the way I don't like routines or days similar to each other. But even if I did, I definitely know I would want to experience and see some of those things every now and then, at least."

Kurt emptied the last of what remained in his cup of coffee. Then, he simply stated: "I'm quite content with my life, thank you. Anyway, thank you for the coffee. I need to be running now. I wish you a nice thanksgiving."

Mia stood up at the same time as Kurt did. Smiling, she said:

"Thanks, and you too. I'm sorry, I didn't mean to offend. I just meant is as some food for thought... for me, that is. I just like thinking about these things and have a bad habit of blurting my thoughts out loud without thinking about them first."

With that, Kurt nodded at her, smiled a little, and left Mia's home.

A week later, Minneapolis received its first layer of snow for that winter. With the temperatures being chilly instead of outright cold, it was obvious that the snow would not last for long. For some reason unbeknownst to Kurt Henderson, the city and its population somehow also changed a lot alongside seasons of the year. Especially winters made Powderhorn a lot quieter than it was in autumn or during summer months. The people came and went as they did all around the year, but the area and ambience were a lot quieter. Still, Kurt would not change his ways, and just as he used to do his daily walk in the autumn, he did so in the beginning of December.

When returning back home, and upon inspecting the mailbox he found a letter sent to him. Since he received very little mail overall, and even fewer hand-written letters, he could not wait to get back inside, and just opened it up in the yard. Much to his surprise, it turned out to be an invitation. An old colleague of his, Sterling Winslow, was retiring. Sterling used to be in the same sales team back at Xerox as Kurt, and they were rather close back then. The moment Kurt retired early, however, the connection between them got severed, and there was very little that bound them together outside anything work-related.

Kurt and Sterling were both the same age and the only major difference in their careers was that Kurt had managed to retire almost 11 years before him. Now, his old colleague was about to leave working life for good as well and was inviting Kurt to festivities that would be held at the local Xerox office where Kurt used to work, too. The moment he read the invitation it was obvious to Kurt that he would attend. Overall, he did not have too many friends, and it would be nice to meet old acquaintances, too, Kurt figured. The event would take place right before Christmas, after which Sterling would retire.

Kurt Henderson very rarely got excited about anything. He hardly tried new things but valued his routines and old habits. In his younger days there used to be times when he found exciting opportunities in his work, but even those got rather bland to him after a while. Overall, many had found him difficult to persuade into attending things or to even please at all.

Now, as Kurt slipped his accepting response to the invitation inside an envelope, he felt truly excited.

On December 23rd, Kurt was getting ready for the retirement party. It was one o'clock, and the party was scheduled to begin in one hour. Since the Xerox office was located at the very heart of the city, not too far away, Kurt had decided to walk there, as per his usual habits. He thought of a two to three mile walk as a good chance to get some exercise, as well as to save gas by not using car.

As Kurt stepped outside, he noticed Mia rushing to her car parked on the street. After getting inside, she immediately started the car and stepped on the gas. She must have been running late for work, Kurt thought to himself. They had not talked ever since their heated-up conversation prior to Thanksgiving. He had thought about what Mia said back then, however. Especially the thoughts of his allegedly boring life and of living day to day without fear of tomorrow were new to Kurt. Up until now, he had not done much critical introspection of his life choices and philosophy. Sure, there had been times when someone had questioned his frugal and minimalistic lifestyle, but those were remarks Kurt found easy to bypass. He knew he was far better off and happier than any of those people were in their lives.

Now, as Kurt began striding towards the city center along the snow-covered streets of Minneapolis, those thoughts returned to him. He saw something different in Mia that he did not in those naysayers he had met before. Unlike those people, albeit broke, she seemed actually content and happy. Despite him finding Mia's attitude towards life irresponsible for not thinking about the future, he saw in her the same kind of happiness and excitement Kurt used to have at an even younger age than what she was now.

Throughout the decades of his life, Kurt had been enthusiastic about many things. Work and family life as in what many considered the classic American dream used to inspire him to work hard with the goal of one day achieving all of that. Unfortunately, as human beings usually do, he got tired of the concept after a couple of years. Days became a repetitive grind, and to reach for new titles, more responsibility, and higher salaries while climbing the corporate ladder took years of working in a position which quickly got old even after a short while.

Convinced that work was ruining his life, he created one major goal for himself: to live as frugally as possible to be able to quit paid work. Now, for the first time ever, as Kurt was stomping through piles of snow which at times had not been properly plowed off the sidewalks, he wondered if somewhere along that long journey of saving money he had lost his true self. Could he have wasted a large portion of his life on a goal which had changed him for the worse?

Consumed by that question in his mind, he arrived at Xerox Minneapolis branch office. He had no recollection of his journey there, just of the mental debate he had been going through. Now, pushing those thoughts aside, he opened the door of the old and gray office building and headed to the lobby.

Kurt stood in the corner of a mid-sized auditorium with a glass of budget champagne in his hand. He had not seen exactly what it was the waiter of the catering service of the business park had poured into his glass, but he knew enough of quality drinks to tell the cheap from the good. The lack of fizzing and oddly sweet scent were enough to paint the picture to him. Nevertheless, Sterling's employer was considerate enough to arrange something like that in his honor, which was commendable.

Upon entering the lobby, he had been guided inside the office building common auditorium to wait for the other guests. He seemed to be the only one to arrive on time, and outstrider in contrast to the current staff of Xerox, perhaps even the only one in that regard, too. Even though Kurt had been excited to come here, waiting for others in there with a glass of bubbly in hand five minutes to two o'clock made him feel awkward, to say the least.

A couple of minutes after two, the rest of the attendants started pouring inside. At that moment, Kurt's suspicions came true. He was the only one to attend not currently employed by Xerox. Most of the people he did not know; they were probably front office staff working at the Minneapolis branch headquarters. In fact, the only one besides Sterling he recognized was his former superior Phil, a sales manager. Doubts about arriving started creeping up to Kurt. Not because he was uncomfortable talking to strangers, but because it was obvious he stood as the odd man out, the strange fellow who had appeared out of nowhere and that no one knew. His doubts only grew stronger as Sterling passed him by in the stairs heading down to the stage in front of the auditorium, and all he had to say to Kurt right there was: "Hey there!" to which Kurt replied with a simple hello.

The so-called ceremony did not alleviate his thoughts. It felt so endless it was like watching paint dry. First, Sterling was awarded with a retirement present by his soon to be former employer. Probably the same kind of gold watch he himself had received ten years ago, Kurt thought to himself. Then, the almost mandatory short speeches which to his taste contained way too many cheesy reminders of how great people Sterling had the chance to work with, even though it would now be the time to move on. Finally, after a few toasts with the cheap champagne and perhaps twenty minutes later, it was finally over.

The event continued in a smaller conference room right next to the auditorium where there was a coffee and cake serving alongside the chance for some more casual mingling with people. The ones who apparently were the least enthusiastic about Sterling retiring, vanished back upstairs to finish their work before the weekend right after the official part of the festivities in the auditorium was over. Kurt was now yearning for a good reason for his showing up and wanted to catch up with Sterling and thus refused to leave just yet. Right after the now-smaller crowd had moved into the conference room, he saw his chance had come as Sterling had been left standing in the corner with nothing but a cup of coffee and that stupid retirement gift in his hand.

As he approached him, Sterling's face lighted up so brightly it looked like cheap overacting. Sterling opened up with: "Henderson, psst! Henderson, over here!" while waving the hand with which he held the gift box up in the air.

In Kurt, that initial reaction awakened a sudden need to flee, but instead, he just smiled, waving his right hand calmly back, while walking to Sterling.

"It's been a while, huh?" Kurt asked.

"And look at you! Looks like you haven't aged a day. How long has it been, anyway?"

"Almost ten years," Kurt said calmly.

"How time flies! Looks like I finally caught up to you now." Sterling paused for a second, and then asked:

"How has your retirement been? I mean, you must be a pro at it already at this point."

Smiling, Kurt answered truthfully: "Full of freedom. I haven't had a use for an alarm clock in all this time. I've structured my days so that they involve exercise and calmness in just the correct balance. Unlike I could when working here. What's best is I get to do whatever I want."

"Do you ever miss it? Working here?"

"No," Kurt said without hesitation. "I liked the people, but that's it. I wouldn't come back here for any price, that's for sure."

Sterling seemed a little troubled for a while. Then, he took a quick look around as if to see if anyone else was listening in on the conversation, leaned towards Kurt and lowered his voice:

"But how do you manage your time? Do you have anything to do with all that time?"

Since Kurt did not know how to respond and looked baffled, Sterling went on:

"Because I'm terrified. Most of my days have been filled with this work, and I'm a divorced man with no kids or close relatives. Hell, even all of my friends are colleagues here at work." At the end of that sentence, his voice had taken on an anxious, hissing tone.

Yet again, Kurt did not immediately know how to respond. Sterling stared at him with that anxious look on his face. Then, Kurt said:

"Well, I… I just have things to do. I've dedicated my whole life to getting to know people outside of work and enjoying peace and quiet. Don't you have any hobbies?"

Before Sterling was given a chance to answer that question, they were approached by a young guy holding another glass of champagne. Kurt had picked him out from the crowd earlier, too, since he rocked a Hawaiian shirt so yellow and bright it almost hurt his eyes this up close.

"Hey Ster', just came by to congratulate you and wish you luck in your future endeavors, whatever they might be." They shook hands. Then, he turned to Kurt, extending his hand: "We must not have met before. I'm Bran from sales."

Kurt shook hands with him.

"Kurt Henderson. I used to be in sales. Now, I've been retired for ten years."

"Isn't that nice!" Bran shouted, as if choosing pleasant words would have masked his fake cheeriness.

"Well, I must be running now to my final closing before the weekend. Have a good one… both of you!" Bran rushed off as quickly as he had appeared.

Before Kurt had a chance to say anything, Sterling hissed at him: "See what I mean?!"

Kurt had not had nearly enough time to digest the conversation. He cleared his throat loudly, as if to say something, but before he could, Sterling went on. At this point, he seemed almost aggravated:

"At least you have a wife! Me, I have no one! And from now on, there will be no one to respect me either since I've already served my purpose!"

His words hit Kurt hard. Not only because of what he said, but because of how he said it. He had never seen Sterling like this, even though they had been working alongside each other for years. In fact, he could barely contain himself enough not to raise his voice so high that everyone in the room would hear it.

"Without this position, besides not having anyone, I, too, will become no one. Hell, I don't even know what I will do to spend all the time I have from now on," Sterling finished.

At that point, all Kurt could respond with was: "Wow," which came out in such an exhaustive and sincere manner it had to sound sincere. He could not go on before one of the few people he had initially recognized joined them. It was Kurt's former superior who still apparently was the acting manager of the office branch, Augustus. A man now in his forties, he had joined the Minnesota branch almost ten years ago. All three of them had always gotten along well despite their obvious differences in age as well as in their career goals.

"Who do we have here?" Augustus patted Kurt on the back while grabbing his hand to shake it. He was smiling gently. "Why did you ever even leave us in the first place?" he asked, followed by a raucous laughter.

"Gus. How have you been?" Kurt replied, smiling back at him.

"Missing you," he now had a more serious look on his face.

"In all honesty, I believe that the team us three were still the best line-up we've had in our sales in all the time I've been in here."

Augustus leaned back, raising his hands to his sides, and shrugged.

"Alas, what do you do? Things change and that's just the way it is. Speaking of which, we have someone else leaving after today," he now turned to Sterling and extended his hand to him:

"Once again, thank you. It's been an honor."

Sterling shook hands with Augustus, replying: "Likewise."

Before turning on his heels, Augustus looked at both of them, saying: "For the old times' sake, we really need to catch up over a beer someday," winking at them. Then, he disappeared into the crowd of other employees.

"Well, wasn't he in a jolly mood!" Kurt said.

"All just an act. I've seen him say the same things to everyone here. Some of the words and phrases were even precisely the same as what I've heard him saying in some previous retirement parties… including yours, Kurt."

"Probably. Which brings me back to what we were discussing about the importance of working. Why do you care? I mean, why do you care so much about what others may think of your position? Their shallowness shouldn't bring you down."

Sterling nodded slowly, looking down at his cup, and said:

"That may work for you, but I'm not like you, Kurt. These things bother me, especially when I know there will be no one back home waiting for me, and without too many friends it feels like my life will become shallow."

Not bothering to let Sterling know of Hannah's death, Kurt just said: "Maybe that's something you should try to work on." At that point he also knew he had seen enough and was looking forward to going back home.

"Look, I need to get going, but I wish you all the best in your coming retirement. Enjoy the freedom. I mean it," then, after exchanging short smiles, Kurt walked away.

Kurt went to drop off his empty glass of champagne before leaving. As he left the glass on a tray at the serving table and was heading out, he overheard his name being spoken. The voice belonged to Augustus. He was talking to a colleague of his:

"…yes, and you can't believe it, it was Kurt Henderson, my former subordinate. The old guy retired like, what, ten years ago, and still comes back here for this? Just between us, he was always rather simple and demented, even at a younger age. This one time…"

Augustus' voice faded out as he and the other guy began walking the other way. Apparently, he had not seen Kurt so close by.

With that, Kurt headed outside where it was snowing heavily and began his walk back home.

That night, Kurt could not sleep. At eleven o'clock, he lay awake in his bed, thinking of Sterling's retirement. He thought of his words and the meeting of the two other acquaintances, Bran, and Augustus. Obviously, he had met rude and distastefully acting people before, so seeing Bran behave that way did not shock Kurt all that much. Augustus was whole another thing, though. Kurt had always regarded him as a decent boss and even a friend. Judging by his words Kurt had overheard, Augustus did not think the same of him. Two-faced deceitfulness of people had always managed to take him by surprise.

On the other hand, he could not shake the thoughts of Sterling's fears, either. He had never regarded work, titles, and positions to be of high value in life. People's characteristics and persona were much more meaningful to Kurt in relation to how he thought of them. Despite seeing many others thinking differently, his patterns of thinking had not altered too much. But today was different. Seeing Sterling absolutely terrified of retirement, and thus thinking of losing all his purpose and value in life was something Kurt had not witnessed firsthand before. He had never been much of a worrier of other people's problems, and instead, he now thought if he had been missing out on something by retiring early.

Lastly, he was thinking of what he had said to Sterling. More precisely, he had encouraged him not to care too much about what others might think of him. Apart from perhaps his teen years, Kurt had always found it easy not to care about what others thought of him. Sure, being thought of as a good person in general was important to him, but never before had he found himself worrying or feeling bad about what someone might have thought of him – even if in a negative light. Clearly, Sterling was very different from him in that way.

But now, he was not too certain anymore. Now he found out that he actually cared about what the others he had met today thought of him.

On the 2nd of May, spring had arrived in Minneapolis. The winter had been colder than in many years, but now, snow and ice were gone, sun was shining, and birds were singing to signal the start of a new nesting season. Nothing particularly eventful had happened in the state of Minnesota, in Minneapolis, or more locally in Powderhorn.

In spite of that, should one look at it from the street, the view towards Kurt Henderson's home was quite different. The most distinctive change lay in the color of the house. The old, calm blue paint had been painted over, and the house now glistened with bright yellow color. As was apparent from the clean and new look of the façade, the paint had not yet been dry for too many weeks. Another noteworthy addition to point out was a brand-new Audi standing right next to the driveway right where a garage could have stood.

Inside sat Kurt. He was wearing clothes that differed greatly from how he had used to dress for years now. Dress pants and collared shirt which had been tailored for him made him feel as if he worked in an office again. The insides of the house had changed a lot, too. All of the living room had been built anew, and the only old thing left was Kurt's brown armchair made of leather. A new television sat on top of a TV mount. The old drawers were gone, and in their place were a couple of new ones, and a large part of the living room had been taken over by a home theater system.

The reason for Kurt wearing his new clothes was not coincidental. Even though it was true that he had just gotten the clothes and wanted to try them out, more importantly, he was about to head outside. He stood up, put on his shining pair of Santoni leather shoes, grabbed keys to his Audi, and stepped out.

As Kurt backed up from the driveway onto the street, navigating system was already giving him directions on how to reach his destination, a casino located a reasonable drive from Minneapolis downtown. Apart from an odd go at a slot game as a kid, Kurt had never gambled. This was one of the reasons why he wanted to try it now. Even more than that, he wanted to see if he was able to get a thrill out of getting a chance to win or lose money.

Kurt had just turned 69 one month ago. The initial thought of trying to gamble at that age had made him feel stupid. Seeing as it was one of the things he had not tried yet, he decided to go for it. The engine of his new Audi thundered as he entered freeway and stepped on the gas. He could barely hear a thing due to the well soundproofed interior of the vehicle.

A great deal had happened in Kurt's way of thinking ever since Christmas. Seeing Mia's carefree way of life topped with Mike's ideas and seeing Sterling as a nervous wreck that he had become because of his colleagues' values and behavior had triggered a moment of introspection in Kurt. Because of his minimalistic and frugal life, he was rather wealthy. He had refused to spend money on things he had considered unworthy, and he deemed anything which did not increase his happiness not worth spending on. In the end, relentless saving and investing had allowed him to retire early, as well as to have a substantial amount of wealth which he never used for anything.

But now, in his late years, he had suddenly begun to wonder whether he kept missing out on something others had been able to experience. He had no children and no close relatives he had stayed in touch with. In other words, he had no important heirs to assume his possessions once he was gone, so he might as well spend some of it on himself. He had pondered about having a will made, but postponed it, since he could not think of an ideal person, organization, or charity to donate his possessions after his death. In any case, potential heirs were not a concern for him during this experiment. Mostly he worried about crossing his own values of several decades and how it would affect him.

So far, he had bought the Audi, had some work done on the house, and bought electronics for entertainment. His newest purchase were the clothes he was wearing on his way to casino. In February, he had also taken a trip to Paris. Aside from his home, buying the car, plane tickets, and paying for the hotel were one of the most expensive purchases Kurt had ever made. Paying for them had been mentally painful to him, as he had expected. He thought of it as a challenge for the mind as well.

As for the challenge, he had succeeded. He had bought everything he had intended, and he had visited Paris, which was also the first time ever he had left the United States. Besides the cost, it bothered him that he had felt no satisfaction from getting all those new things. The car and the new color of the house had looked fancy for the first two weeks, after which Kurt had gotten used to them. All the miscellaneous entertainment such as his new TV had grown old even faster — basically right after the first time he had used them.

Visiting France was something he had been looking forward to. On the day of arrival, he had felt some excitement, but once he glanced outside from the window of his hotel room, he understood he had no idea what to do. Apart from seeing the Eiffel tower, what was there? How would he spend his days? In the end, he had wandered around the streets of Paris, visited a few cafés, and spent time in his hotel room for the seven days he was there. Needless to say, after the first day, he was already longing to return home.

When he arrived at the casino it was early evening. The sun had not yet begun to set and radiated beautifully across the parking lot as Kurt parked his car. The prestigious place was a combination of hotel, holiday resort, restaurants, a night club, and of course the casino. Never before had he been in a setting like this. From his general knowledge of which most was based on movies he had seen he knew that he would have to change some cash for tokens. Upon entering the building, he managed to do this without too much trouble at the reception desk located at the back of a grand lobby with bright, colorful lights and gold colored floor. He decided to start with 1000 dollars' worth of gambling tokens.

Again, judging purely from the movies he had seen, Kurt thought that a game of dice might be a good place for a beginner to start. In the main lounge where most of the games were located, it did not take too long for him to find a table. Besides the casino employees, there were four people standing around the table, who seemed like two couples of a man and a wife. With wide smiles on their faces amidst the loud chatter, they seemed to be having good time. All of them were dressed even more formally than Kurt was. The game itself appeared extremely confusing to him, and he could only hear everyone frequently mentioning the words of "passing" and "seven" while dice were rapidly slamming against the side of the mahogany table.

Kurt sighed, took a step forward, and placed his tokens on the table in a slot that apparently had been reserved for them.

"Hi, I haven't played before."

"Come-out round, place your bets pass or no pass, please," an employee said to Kurt, while handing dice over to a woman next to him. She picked up two dice, leaned over to Kurt and whispered:

"If you bet for me to pass, you will win if I shoot a 7 or 11. If I shoot 2,3, or 12, you will lose. If there's some other number, you might still win. Those are the rules."

Covering his frustration of not understanding all of the game, Kurt noted that there was a minimum bet of 5 $, so he placed that amount on her making the pass line. Then, after bets had been placed, she threw the dice. The results were a three and a four, and Kurt won ten dollars. He figured we would learn more as the game went on.

After a little more than a half an hour and multiple rounds of craps, Kurt decided to call it quits. He had gotten a grasp of the basic rules of the game, although he did not know what a winning strategy might be. He had placed small bets only, some of which he won and some of which he lost. In the end, he had made a loss of roughly 100 dollars. He did not feel particularly excited or annoyed, and wondered if it was because he did not care about the game, or that he simply did not bet enough money to make it exciting.

Then, he noticed the classic symbol of any casino: a roulette wheel. This was a simple game that he also knew. He marched over to the table with only two players there and observed for two rounds. Since betting on a single number had terrible odds of winning, he decided to go all in and placed the remainder of his tokens on red. The croupier made a quick count and announced that it was 910 dollars. He got a couple of funny looks from the two fellows who were there before him. They were playing with much smaller amounts.

"Feeling lucky, are we?" one of them asked Kurt. Kurt did not bother looking back at him, but just replied with a grunt:

"Mm-hmm". The bets were in place and the croupier span the wheel.

Two hours later, Kurt was back home. If emotions could be described with colors, he now felt gray. That is, he felt absolutely nothing. He had won in roulette, almost doubling what money he had when entering the casino. Back there at the game table, because of the cheerful reaction of the bystanders, he had acted as if it meant something to him, even though it did not. After all, it was nothing more than just money to be invested in something which would make him more money. Or alternatively, he could just put it in a savings account. The only thing that he was certain of was that he would not consume it the way he had been consuming for the last several months. Clearly, it brought him no joy.

Kurt sat down in his armchair. The money still weighed heavily in his pockets, but not just in the form of material weight. It weighed him emotionally down to know that he could not gain joy from it, even though he tried to. He lacked something that other people had. He could not help but wonder about everything he might have gotten and experienced had it not been for his extreme frugality and minimalism. He might have had children, more friends, and more connections with his relatives. Besides people, he could have led a life of exciting experiences, travelling, and trying new things. He might be able to enjoy such a simple thing as a new television.

Now, buried in the solitude of his own home, what had once felt like freedom seemed more like a prison now. His eyes were fixed on the ceiling. A tear ran down his cheek.

Mia had just finished packing her groceries in a brown paper bag. It was weird coming to her workplace on her day off, but she had a craving for something sweet. So, she had decided to drive to the supermarket she worked at to pick up some ice cream and candy. On the other hand, this gave her an opportunity to chat with some of her friends she had made there. As she left the store, she shouted a hello to the store manager who was also her boss.

On her way back home, she began to think of the upcoming summer, which was almost here. She had a short leave coming up, and as a relatively new employee, she would be expected to be among the first ones to spend their holidays in the coming summer season. She lived mostly from one paycheck to another, so the only option for travelling would be trying to catch some last-minute cancellation tickets. It was not as if she had not gotten used to doing so. In fact, she had plenty of experience of travelling on a strict budget. It just meant that there would be very little planning for vacation in advance.

She had just reached her home street and was slowly driving towards home. Just as she received the first glimpse of her beloved albeit old house, she saw her neighbor Kurt driving towards her in his new car. By instinct, Mia waved at her, and Kurt responded by waving back with his hand out from the open window of his car. Then, she noticed Kurt stopped there with an open car window, clearly waiting for Mia. As the street was as quiet and empty as always, she slowed down and stopped right next to Kurt's car, so they faced each other and rolled open her car window.

"Hi! Long time no see. I gotta warn you, I have some ice cream in a car that has AC broken, so I cannot talk for long," Mia cheerfully greeted Kurt.

"Oh, it's ok. Just wanted to see how you were doing," a faint smile appeared on Kurt's face as he went on:

"I was just heading out to do some shopping myself as well. Lately, I've been trying to learn to appreciate the little things one can find in life."

"I can see that. Nice Audi!" Mia made an exaggerated whistle while looking at his car. Kurt chuckled a little.

"Yeah. Heh. Truth be told, it's not going so well. I'm having trouble enjoying the things I buy."

Mia shook her head, smiling. At this point she knew that Kurt led a very unconventional life, so it did not surprise her. Kindly, yet sarcastically, she replied:

"Yea, must be a drag," she then burst into laugh.

Kurt held lightly onto the Audi's steering wheel with both hands and smiled again.

"It must be that I…"

Kurt's phrase got cut short by an expression of grin on his face. As he grabbed onto the steering wheel more tightly and a vein on his forehead began bulging, it was clear that this was not a grin of happiness, but of aching. At this point, only a sharp, gasping sound came out of his mouth. Mia noticed that something was terribly wrong.

"Kurt? Are you ok?"

Kurt violently shook his head from one side to another, as if to signal that everything was not ok, and that he could not speak. His face turned red, and he was obviously in pain.

"Kurt?"

He turned his head towards Mia, and his expression was one of physical agony. The grin was the ugliest she had ever seen on someone's face. Then, before either of them could say anything, Kurt's eyes rolled over in his head, and he slammed unconsciously towards the steering wheel, causing the signal horn to go off in a continuous loud noise.

"Shit, what a terrible lunch. I keep reminding my wife not to take all the Tupperware we have to her own work without returning it, but she does it anyway. I wish I was able to pack my own lunch as usual. That was absolutely disgusting," a voice echoed from behind a closed door.

"I hear you," another voice responded, now closer by.

"You go on ahead, I'll be there in a second," the voice was now right behind the door.

The door slammed wide open. A man dressed in all green hospital clothes, a surgical mask and a head cover entered the room, leaving the door behind him open. The room was standard of what one might expect to find in a hospital ward used to receive or examine patients. The ceiling, the walls, and the floor were all white. Right next to the door leading out to the hallway there stood a desk with a computer and a saddle chair. Some medical instruments and equipment lay on portable metallic trays. There was also a big portable computer cart on the other side of the room. The man walked to the portable computer, inserted a card of his inside a slot in the computer, and began typing on the keyboard. In the center of the room there was a hospital bed with a patient lying on his back. Tucked in nice and tightly, only his head could be seen from under the blankets.

Over the typing sound the man made on keyboard, there was the sound of a toilet being flushed. Then, another, older man entered. He was dressed otherwise similarly, but he was also wearing a lab coat.

"That's it for the break then, I guess. Let's get this over with," he said, while taking off his coat and hanging it on a peg at the wall.

He sat down on the computer next to the door, inserted a card of his own in a slot, logged in, and started reading.

Meanwhile, the other man was leaning against the computer cart he stood at, waiting. For a while, there lay complete silence. Then, it got broken by the older man pressing the button of a recorder.

"Dictating, dictating… the patient is a 69-year-old man, deceased from what appears to be myocardial infarction. Found today on a public street, a bystander called an ambulance to spot. Prehospital care started at approximately two o'clock in the afternoon. Resuscitated on spot, defibrillation back to sinus rhythm successful, transported to Abbott Northwestern. Suffered another cardiac arrest in the emergency ward, resuscitated for 35 minutes, after which pronounced dead by colleague Jackson. Now here for a postmortem examination to confirm the cause of death."

He pressed the recording button again to stop recording and turned around on his chair to gaze blankly at Kurt Henderson's motionless face.

"Have his next of kin been informed?"

The other man who was still leaning against the computer said: "He had none we could contact."

"None? I see," the older man paused for a while. He seemed sincerely depressed by the setting.

"Very well, then. Judging from the medical records, we can move on to external and internal examination. Prepare to open him up."

"Next!"

Sally stood up, walked slowly towards a shelf, carefully picked a place to put the blue folder in her hands in, put it there and then took the folder sitting right next to it, walked slowly back to her desk, and opened the folder.

"Kurt Henderson, 265-77-0032," she said, almost robotically.

Caitlin, her boss, and administrator of the unclaimed property unit typed the name on her keyboard and pressed enter.

"Kurt Henderson. E 33rd Street real estate and property, alongside a vehicle and stocks, funds, cash money, and physical gold under his name."

"That is correct," Sally confirmed.

Caitlin performed a quick database search on her computer.

"No next of kin or a will?"

"None I can find."

Caitlin read out loud as she typed on her computer:

"No next of kin nor will by the individual. No children, no other relatives. Possessions subject to escheat by the state of Minnesota."

Sally routinely closed the blue folder in front of her.

"Next!"

MEAT DISCOUNT

"Ben, breakfast!" Sarah shouted.

A quick, thumping sound could be heard as Ben made his way down the stairs of the small house. The eight-year-old second-grader threw his backpack next to the door and came into the kitchen where Sarah had just poured some cereal for him.

"Hurry, or you'll be late."

"I will, I will," Ben stated as he sat down, poured milk onto the cereal, and started to quickly shovel the breakfast into his mouth.

Sarah just sat and watched with a cup of tea in her hand from the other side of the table. She had never been a morning person. But sleeping in was not a luxury she could afford, for she had to look after Ben getting to school on time and then heading to work herself, too. It was Tuesday, and to her it felt like she had been working for a whole week in a row already, despite it being just the second day of the week.

"Done!" Ben stated cheerfully, dropping his spoon loudly against the bowl. He stood up and headed towards his backpack at a brisk pace. Sarah had gotten lost in her thoughts and lost the track of time. She instinctively looked at the clock on the wall and was thankful to notice that but a few minutes had passed and neither of them was going to be late.

"See you in the evening, sweetie!"

"Bye, mom!"

Ben stepped out of the house and closed the door behind him. Sarah heard him ringing his bicycle bell as he began biking towards school not too far away from their home. Even though Sarah enjoyed sleeping a little longer in the mornings, she disliked how her new hours at work did not allow her to be back at home before her son. Before, even after grocery shopping and household work, she used to have an hour or two to herself before Ben got back home. Now, all she had were these 15 minutes after he had left before she had to leave for work.

After finishing her cup of tea, she went to bathroom to take a look at herself in the mirror, and decided she would be ready to leave the house. Grabbing her purse and keys to her car – an old silver Ford Fiesta – she stepped outside. It was a beautiful autumn day. The school year had just begun, the sun was shining and there were still some hints of summer in the air. Sarah pushed the remote control on her car key, only to be reminded of the fact the battery had run out last week. So instead, she manually opened the lock using the key, stepped inside, and started the car.

The journey was not going to be a long one. From their home village of Bibury, England, she drove across the local streets surrounded by green mounds of grass until she reached the road heading down south, with farming fields on both sides. After no more than five minutes of driving, she reached the first buildings of the village of Fairford. Having finally arrived at her destination, she parked her car in a place reserved for the staff of the local elementary school and headed inside the building. She worked as a teaching assistant at the first elementary school of Fairford.

Her workday would start at nine o'clock, and it was now fifteen minutes to nine. Typically, her days consisted of attending various classes where teachers would need assistance. Most of them were in the fields of physical education, arts and crafts, or activities which required escorting pupils outside the school grounds. The last two hours of her working time she attended after-school activities the school had for pupils, such as homework clubs. The after-school clubs made her employer mandate her to work different hours than she previously used to.

Occasionally, Sarah had considered the possibility of working closer to her home, in the village school of Bibury. That was the same school her son Ben attended, which would have its pros and cons. That way, she would be able to look after her son more closely, but on the other hand, that could not affect the way she did her work at the school. An obvious plus would be the shorter commute, too.

But right now, she was still working in Fairford. As she entered the staffroom, Tim and Jane, two class teachers greeted her. It was typical to see some of the teachers in the staffroom at this hour, either taking a break or preparing for the next class. As she gazed at the bulletin board on the wall which included timetables for all the grades as well as for the education staff members, she noticed no changes had been made to her day. With Sarah being the only assistant in the school, there was always plenty of demand for her. Usually, her day from nine to three consisted of hopping from one class to another.

This day did not prove to be an exception. From nine until noon, she would be assisting in physical education as well as with the supervision of lunch, and in the afternoon there would be a class on textile work, followed by after-school clubs. Sarah grabbed a quick cup of coffee before heading out into the yard where pupils would be waiting to play football.

The day had been uneventful. Now, it was almost five in the afternoon and Sarah was heading back to her car. Ben was most likely at home already and she still had shopping to do before heading home. The roads of Fairford began to see some slight traffic with people heading from work to their homes as Sarah drove to the nearby supermarket.

Considering the small size of the town, the two grocery stores were surprisingly packed at that time of day. A lone and single cashier at the only checkout probably had something to do with that. As a single mother living with her son, the weekly shopping Sarah did consisted mostly of simple and budget friendly pickings. She had always taken great pride in being able to support herself and her son financially despite having a job that did not pay very well. She refused to live like they were struggling, even though the truth was that after the monthly expenses, she was never able to save even a penny.

Regular foodstuffs found their way into her shopping cart: vegetables, fruit, cereal, milk, butter, and tea. At that point, the only thing she was still missing was meat. Mostly, she preferred minced meat or chicken since they were quite affordable, easy to prepare, and she and Ben both liked them. She was taken aback upon gazing at the deli counter. There was nothing there but a written sign indicating that the local producers had been experiencing trouble in delivering the products, so there would be significant delays in re-stocking the shelves.

Sarah felt a wave of annoyance washing over her. This meant two things. First, she had to spend time going to the local butcher's shop next door. Second, she would have to pay more for the same amount of meat that she would have gotten at the store. She had a quick passing thought of driving to another supermarket but dumped the idea because she had to get home earlier than that. Also, if this store was experiencing delays in delivery, then most likely the other place would be as well. So, she decided to pay for her groceries and head to the butcher's shop for meat products.

Upon entering, Sarah immediately noticed the scent of red meat stored in cold. Despite the place being very hands-on rural workshop, it had kind of a cozy ambience to it. It was a small shop, consisting of but a few square meters worth of room for the customers to move around before the counter in which the products for sale were kept for the customers to choose from. Behind the desk, stood the town butcher himself, a thin and seemingly happy old man, who looked nothing like clichés of typical butchers in the old horror movies. Some meat products were also hanging on hooks placed at the back wall. In the corner behind the counter, right next to the butcher, there was also a tiny table with a laptop on it. Besides that, there was nothing else to the place. Sarah was the only customer at the moment. The butcher greeted Sarah.

"Good day, how may I help you?"

"Hi. They had no meat at the market next door. I'm looking for some affordable chicken and minced beef."

"The minced beef I can do, but I'm all out of poultry for today, sorry."

"That'll do fine. How much for the beef?"

"For a kilogram, seven pounds for the 15 % fat. But I would definitely recommend the 5 % organic meat from the local producers here in Fairford, it's far better. That'd be 12 pounds for a kilogram."

Sarah could not help but get a slightly sad look on her face. She had no doubt in her mind that the meat would be of great quality, but the cost was also more than what she could afford.

"You know, I would love to try the better one, but I'm looking more for the budget options right now. Perhaps I'll go with the 15 % one, if you could do 700 grams for me, please?"

"Sure thing," the butcher began working on the meat. As he weighed the correct amount and began wrapping it in paper, he said:

"If it's budget solutions you're looking for, you should know that I try to avoid excess food waste by selling meat that would soon expire for half the price in the last opening hour every day. That's from six until seven."

Sarah had always avoided such products in regular supermarkets. In part because she had not bothered thinking about the prices more than she absolutely had to, but mostly because she did not trust those products. From early on, she had been taught they were for the poor and desperate people.

She also found herself worrying about possible health risks involved, since it was meat that would soon expire.

On the other hand, she now thought to herself that if there was still time left until the expiration date, it should be safe to cook and to eat. Plus, with the rising costs of living, she would really have use for more affordable meat.

Seeing that Sarah hesitated, the butcher went on: "I have some diced beef here, for example. Seeing as there's just half an hour to go until six o'clock, I can sell it to you now if you are interested. Five pounds for one kilogram."

The price was really good. Sarah could use it to prepare a stew for them that would last days. Without further doubts, she accepted.

"I'll have one kilogram of that as well, then."

"Absolutely, I'll pack it up for you. That'll be 9.90."

"Thank you. I just might end up visiting here more often, I should have done so years ago already," Sarah laughed.

"Have a good day," the butcher waved at her as she left the shop.

On the drive back home, Sarah gazed at the endless fields all around her. She had lived in Bibury all her life and got used to the life here. The contrast to a big city such as London was incredible. In here, everything just sort of slowed down, and was typically far more beautiful. The people cared of each other, and everyone basically knew one another. Fairford as a tad bigger town could still be considered to belong to the same community as Bibury.

Unlike many, Sarah had never taken part in the farming lifestyle or catered to tourists who often frequented Bibury. In that way, she belonged to a minority amongst local residents. She knew very well that there were some groups in the village she had been excluded from because of that, but she did not mind. To her it even seemed natural that the local farmers wanted to have an inner circle of their own.

At home, after greeting Ben who was in his room taking care of his homework, Sarah went immediately to kitchen to prepare the stew. Ben had always had the peculiar habit of preferring to take care of his homework as soon as he got home, instead of doing it at the last minute like most kids did. That was one thing in him that Sarah was particularly proud of. As soon as she had the food in the oven, Sarah got some time for herself to relax and just sat down with phone in her hand. Before starting up any social media applications, she began thinking about her visit to the butcher's shop, and especially the meat the butcher had for sale every evening. Taking full advantage of that could in the long run save her a big penny and be good for the environment too.

She did a quick search on the internet if it would be safe for her to buy the discounted meat in bulk and then freeze it for later use; something which sounded so simple, yet she had never thought of. As it turns out, it is possible. She did not have to check the freezer to see if there was room in there for any excess meat, she knew by heart they never had much food stored up for later use. But that would change soon.

"Ben! Dinner!" Sarah shouted as she lifted a big pot of beef stew out of the oven. Almost immediately, Ben came rushing into the kitchen.

"Finally, I'm starving!"

"Sorry it took so long, but now we have food for many days in a row. Why didn't you grab a snack?"

"Wanted to take care of the school project first," Ben said as he scooped stew to his plate.

"What project is that?"

"History. About Julius Caesar."

"Really? Sounds demanding, considering you're in the second grade."

"Nah, it's easy. Remember tomorrow I have football after school."

Ben played football three times in a week. This was yet another thing Sarah could barely afford but had always found it important for her child to have a hobby that included both physical exercise as well as members of his own age and peer group. Thankfully, it was relatively easy to arrange since the practices were always in Bibury and Ben could take himself there and back by bike.

"How could I forget. You'll be home around seven, right? I'll have food ready by then."

"We finish sometime around half past six."

"I hope the food is good, we'll have that for a couple of days now."

"It's good. Thank you, mom."

"You're welcome, sweetie."

The next morning was as regular as any weekday for Sarah and Ben. Ben had headed to school and Sarah was on her way to work. As he knew Ben would be playing football, she could stop by the butcher's shop again for some more discounted meat to fill up the freezer with. This would mean she had to exceed her weekly – and perhaps even monthly – budget she had for food, but the exercise would pay back for itself in the long run.

This time there sat only Jane in the staffroom as Sarah entered. After greeting each other with a smile, Sarah went to check out her schedule for the day. That time the whole day would consist of her assisting in the arts and crafts classroom for students of different grades. Then, at three o'clock, there would be the after-school activities to assist with, as usual. This reminded Sarah of the one thing that she did not like in her job was how many days quickly began to resemble one another. On the other hand, she loved working with the children so that made it worth it to her.

Yet again, another day of work was over, and Sarah headed directly to the butcher's shop, as she had planned. It was half past five in the afternoon. Sarah opened the door and heard a bell on it jingling to signal that a customer had entered the shop. The same butcher stood up to greet Sarah, this time from the table he had been sitting on at the laptop. She opened up the conversation, this time far more confidently:

"Hi again!"

"Good day to you, how can I help this time?"

"I came here solely for the purpose of seeing if you have any meat that's about to expire for sale."

"Almost every day but only starting six o'clock."

"Damn. I come here from Bibury, and I'm usually finished with my work at five. Guess I'll have to start to figure out something to do for one hour if I'm to make this my habit in the future," Sarah laughed.

The butcher looked at her, stayed silent for a moment, and then said:

"You know what, I'll make one more exception for you. But the next time, starting at six o'clock only. I have other customers who'll be disappointed if I'll let someone grab everything in advance."

"That would be so great, thank you!"

"Don't mention it," the butcher said, with a strange smirk on his face.

A while later, Sarah walked out of the shop with two large bags in her hands. She had enough pork, beef, and poultry to fill up her freezer until it was halfway full. She aimed to try to get it almost as full as possible, with these prices anything else would feel foolish to her. She would only leave a small spot open for the occasional vegetables, fruit, or ice cream that required their freezer.

As she unlocked her car and started to pack the bags inside the trunk of her Mondeo, she heard a woman calling her name.

"Sarah, isn't this a delightful surprise!"

Sarah turned around to see Agnes, who was one of the locals from Bibury she had become good friends with. Agnes and her husband lived but a few houses away from hers, and as the style of life in places like Bibury basically demanded, they had run into each other quite often and chatted a lot. Agnes was more than ten years older than Sarah, and her children had already moved out of their parents' house. As Sarah recalled, they were both students. One of them lived in Cambridge and another in London.

"Agnes, what a coincidence running into you here," Sarah said, trying to clumsily wave her hand despite holding two big paper bags that read 'Butchers Ltd'.

"Timothy and I were just here shopping. There's this marvelous Nepalese restaurant just around the corner we were planning to try out. You are welcome to join us if you have the time."

"Oh, no, thank you. I need to head home before Ben gets back from football practice."

"And I can see you have already bought something to eat as well!" Agnes laughed.

Sarah grinned uncomfortably.

"Yes, gotta stock up when there's an opportunity, you know."

"Of course. Well, I won't be keeping you for any longer now. See you in a few weeks at the harvest festival. You will be there, won't you?"

"We certainly will. Catch you later."

Sarah packed the big bags of meat inside the trunk and stepped in the car. As she drove home, she understood she had completely forgotten about the upcoming festival. In Bibury, it was customary for the locals to have small gatherings in the form of festivities a couple of times in a year, and the harvest festival was to celebrate the end of summer. Typically, these were warm events with lots of drink and food, and everyone was expected to bring something there for the serving. These events were one of the things Sarah had always liked about living in Bibury.

Upon arrival, Sarah stashed all the meat she had accumulated in the freezer, which now got significantly fuller than before. There was still some room left which she planned to fill up in the coming week. She checked the fridge to make sure there would still be enough stew left for the two of them to warm up in the microwave for tonight, which there was. Grateful for that, she sighed, and fell down on the living room sofa. She checked her bank account statement on her mobile phone and saw that she had spent many times more money on food than she usually used to each week, just as she expected. But because of this, the coming weeks would be significantly easier for her budget-wise.

"Mom, I'm home!"

Sarah jumped up from the sofa she had just sat down on. Without realizing it, she had fallen asleep with the phone in her hand, and it was almost seven in the evening. As she felt her heart still racing from the surprise her son had given her, she thought that she must have been more tired than she understood.

"Hi, dear!" She shouted in as normal tone as possible. She did not want Ben to know she had been sleeping.

"You go wash up and I'll fix the dinner for us meanwhile, ok?"

Ben appeared from behind the corner, looking at her in a funny way. Sarah wondered if he had seen her sleeping on the couch.

"Ok, Mom," he said, after which he hurried to his room.

As soon as Sarah saw he had disappeared, she rubbed her eyes, stood up, and walked to kitchen to begin setting the table. This night and the coming day she would dedicate to as good sleep and rest as possible.

Sarah's plan of having a good night's sleep did not work out as she had planned. After saying good night to Ben, she headed straight to bed herself, but could not sleep. The combination of the lessening hours of daylight that came with the season and the nap she had probably played havoc with her circadian rhythm. The sleep she got was of good quality, but having to get up early in the morning meant that she did not get enough of it. Now, she was about to start a new day of work in Fairford. Thankfully, tomorrow would be Friday.

At work, as she was checking her daily schedule right before nine o'clock lessons, the school headmaster who was also her supervisor popped in the staffroom. Tim and Jane were there as well, sipping their coffees as usual. The tension in the room immediately altered. It was as if the air had become thicker than before. The headmaster Margareth was an elderly woman who had worked at the Fairford primary school all her career. Generally, she was considered a fair boss, albeit very strict, traditional, and conservative person. She appeared the same way both to the rest of the school staff as well as the pupils.

When she was not working with local education authorities or teaching, she typically stayed in her own office, and rarely mingled with the rest of the staff. This is why it was strange seeing her appear in the staffroom on an otherwise normal Thursday morning. Apart from the casual good mornings, no one said anything, yet Sarah swore she noticed Tim and Jane glancing at each other, after which they quickly jumped their chairs and rushed to prepare for their next classes.

"Hello, Sarah."

"Margareth, hi. Long time no see," Sarah said as nonchalantly as possible, even though she felt anxious because of the unusual setting.

"How have you been doing?"

"Oh, everything's great. At work, nothing special, and long hours at home, looking after Ben," Sarah smiled, then understood Margareth may not remember who Ben was, so she went on to explain: "My son."

"Oh. Good, good."

Margareth cleared her throat, and said:

"I would actually like to talk to you about your input at work when there's time.

Sarah felt blood rushing up to her face.

"Sure thing. But what exactly…"

"I need to get going now, and you probably have a class starting up as well. But let's get together soon, ok? Have a good day."

Margareth left the room and Sarah froze up. She cursed to herself in her mind that she did not have the guts to stop Margareth and ask her what she was talking about. Now, this would most likely bother her for the rest of the day or even longer. But anything she did now would cause an even more uncomfortable scenario, so instead of running after her, she just decided to take a deep breath and head to the first class of the day.

After assisting with physical education and after-school activities, Sarah was done for the day. She was exhausted. Not because of the physical education, which was rather easy for the staff, but because of the bad sleep and being mentally tired. She had always found weird comments such as what Margareth had said to her hard to shake off, and now they continued to bother her.

Now, she felt grateful that she did not have an even longer commute back home. As she turned to her home street, she saw Agnes in her and Tim's front yard, doing what seemed to be gardening. Sarah slowed down and waved at her through the window. When Agnes noticed Sarah, she had a concerned look on her face at first. Then, as if checking to see if there was anyone there to see them, she quickly looked around, and then gave Sarah a mild smile which seemed almost forced. Instead of waving back at her Sarah witnessed a wave of a hand which could be interpreted as Agnes telling her to go away. Her smile faded, and she drove to their home where she parked the car.

Sarah felt lousy. The interactions both at work as well as with Agnes just now had left a bitter taste in her mouth, especially since she had no idea of the reasons for their weird behavior. Like many people, she had always found it difficult to get over the feeling of being cast out. Of course, now she did not know whether this was even the case, or if it was all just in her head. She had after all been sleeping badly and was very tired.

To top it all off, after dinner with Ben that night she noted that she would have to cook for them again tomorrow. And in the coming week, she would stock their freezer so that she would not have to do any meat shopping for at least two months.

The next week, Sarah was once again heading to work, as usual. The Friday and the weekend had been uneventful; Ben had spent a lot of time at football practice and then with his friends, while Sarah had gotten some household work done. On Monday, right after work, Sarah had headed to the butcher shop in Fairfield and taken care of filling their freezer up with discounted meat. It was now Tuesday, and Sarah had planned to see some of her friends in Bibury after work. Ben would once again head to play football right after school, so she would be in no rush to get back home.

As Sarah turned to park her car in the familiar spot at the gravel paved yard of the Fairford elementary, she was feeling good. After she was done with her work today, there would be no distractions left for her in the evening. For the rest of the week, there would be no mandatory tasks to occupy her days – as much as that could ever be the case for a single parent, anyway. The only thing for her to take care of would probably be the planning of the servings she would be bringing to the village gathering but two weeks from now.

At school, before Sarah could reach the staffroom, she saw Margareth standing in the hallway of the school. It was the same, exceptionally great hallway for a school of that size which Sarah passed by every day on her way to the staffroom. As Sarah greeted Margareth just as she would anyone else in the mornings, the memory of the brief but strange conversation they had had the previous week came back to her mind. Instead of simply greeting her back, Margareth asked Sarah to join her in her office. Sarah's face flushed and her heart was racing as she followed Margareth into her office.

The headmaster's office was very traditional for a school building of such an old age. Whereas the classrooms and other areas of the school had been built and kept in a very primitive state, entering the headmaster's office immediately gave off the sign that you were in the presence of someone high in the hierarchy. The desk seemed absurdly wide for the room, leaving barely enough room for one to pass by it and walk to the other side to sit down. The armchair behind the desk was equally impressive and comfortable looking, whereas someone entering the room to talk to the headmaster would have to settle for the simple wooden chairs next to the wall. In the corner, there stood a plain wooden table with two more of those chairs around it.

As Sarah entered the room, she was about to head to grab one of the chairs lined up next to the wall, expecting Margareth to sit behind her desk. Instead, Margareth pulled a chair from under the round table, urging Sarah to sit there instead. Then, she pulled the other chair for herself and sat down, facing Sarah.

"So how have you been?"

"I'm o….k," Sarah extended the phrase and forced a fake smile on her face to try to cover up her nervousness.

"And how is your son?"

"He's good. With all due respect, I really don't understand what it is we are…"

"There have been concerns about you, dear. People have been questioning your judgement and capabilities of working safely and responsibly with children and adolescents," Margareth interrupted.

"What?" Sarah could not believe her ears.

Margareth crossed her hands on the table and leaned towards Sarah.

"These are very serious allegations, and we as an educational community do obviously have to take these claims equally seriously."

"To avoid any petitions filed against the school, we will have to remove you from any assignments where you would be involved in teaching or helping to assist in teaching of children."

Margareth looked at Sarah in the eye with a serious stare. Sarah was left speechless for a while, after which she said, barely holding back tears:

"What is happening? Why? I don't understand this."

"For reasons of privacy protection, I cannot tell you where these complaints have come from, but we have received many of them. I assume child protection or perhaps the police will be in touch with you, they might be able to tell you more."

At this point, Sarah burst out crying.

"The main reason I am telling you this, is that since we have no tasks for you to perform after three o'clock in the afternoon that would involve no contact with pupils, your position will be altered to a part-time one."

Margareth went silent for a while. Then, she went on:

"It is possible that our school facility cleaner might be taking a longer leave in a while, and at that point we can offer you to substitute for her, that way you could be employed full-time with full pay again. Assuming that this case won't be over by then. It could take some time."

Sarah sobbed uncontrollably. Obviously, she had known that something was wrong, but now, she had no idea where all this was coming from, and not of the reasons for the actions of Margareth. Margareth was still in the same posture she had taken before, leaning against the table with her hands crossed. She glanced at the clock on the wall. Turning her eyes down to the table in front of her, she said:

"Why don't you take the rest of the day off. We have no tasks to assign to you now in any case. Try to get some rest and we'll talk again later."

At that moment, Sarah was just happy to get out of the room and the situation she was in, so she quickly nodded her head, still sobbing. Then, she stood up and left Margareth's office. In her mind she knew that what was being done to her was unfair and perhaps even illegal, but she simply had no strength at that moment to confront her boss about those matters. With quick steps, she rushed out of the office and school building, went to her car, and just sat in the driver's seat for a long while, attempting to gather the remnants of her willpower to be able to drive back home without accidentally swirling into a ditch on the way.

Sarah had always been quick-tempered and emotional. Fortunately for her, this also meant that she was quick to calm down. On her way home, she already felt slightly better. She made up her mind that she would not settle for this without a proper inquiry. On the other hand, she knew that she would be terrified of approaching Margareth again, but she was also convinced that she could not rest easy being wronged like that.

In the coming evening, she also had a meeting with her old friends to look forward to. Even though she now did not feel like heading out at all, she was also aware that she would feel better after seeing them. Before that, she would have to make up her mind on whether she should tell them what had just happened or not. Friendly support and advice would be exactly what she needed right now. Then again, for no rational reason, she felt ashamed of the whole incident.

Sarah parked the car in front of their house. Thankfully, Ben was still at school, so she would not have to explain her early return back home just yet to him. After Sarah had engaged the hand brake, her cell phone vibrated. It was a WhatsApp message from Alice, a close friend of hers who lived in Bibury. Alice was a teacher in the same school Ben went to and she would be joining Sarah for drinks in the evening. Except that as Sarah opened the message, she saw this was not the case any longer. It said:

"Really sorry but can't come tonight after all. Something has come up. Maybe some other time?"

Sarah decided to chalk it up to bad luck and sent Alice a simple "OK" back. At least she would still see Emily and Charlotte tonight. Emily was a childhood friend of hers who now lived in Oxford and would be joining them since it was not that long a drive away. Charlotte was yet another local from Bibury who Sarah had gotten to know from all the different village gatherings she had attended over the course of all those years they had lived there.

Sarah felt she had to drag her feet to get inside. Once she had made it, she fell sitting on the living room couch, focusing on just how tired she was. But as she knew herself well enough, she deemed it would be impossible for her to sleep right now, being still too shaken up by what had happened at work. Perhaps she would take a nap in the afternoon before heading out with Emily and Charlotte.

A few hours later, just as Sarah was thinking of trying to get some sleep, her phone rang. The caller was Charlotte.

"Hey! What's up?" Sarah answered.

"Hi Sarah. I'm really sorry, but Jonah's come up with flu. I need to take a rain check tonight. Joe is working evening shift, so he is not here to help me either."

Jonah was Charlotte's youngest son, and several years younger than Ben, so it was understandable the she would want to stay in and take care of him. Her husband worked at a factory, so it was plausible that he would not be home every evening. Still, Sarah could not help feeling that this was an excuse or even a lie on Charlotte's part.

"Aww, that's too bad."

"I hate the timing but can't help it. We must try this some other time. Please give my regards to Alice and Emily."

"I will, hope Jonah gets better soon. Talk to you later, bye."

"Bye-bye."

Sarah's plans for the evening were rapidly collapsing. She had half a mind to just call Emily and cancel altogether. Then she thought that she would not want to be the one to call the whole thing off. Besides, if Emily did not feel like coming, she would have to inform her more than Sarah because of the drive from Oxford. With that in mind, Sarah closed her eyes and lay down on the sofa, uncertain whether she would be able to sleep.

That afternoon, five minutes to five o'clock, Sarah entered The Thirsty Falconer. The place was an old, cozy, traditional English pub, and an obvious choice for all kinds of meet-ups and gatherings for anyone in Bibury. Because she did not have to work that day, she arrived at the pub well ahead of her schedule. The rest of them had originally intended to meet at five, whereas Sarah was the one who was supposed to be running late.

Unlike she had expected, she had been able to sleep before heading out. Maybe that was the reason for having enough energy to come and meet her friends for drinks. For a long while, she had hesitated whether to show up at all. But as Emily had not cancelled, and the local pub being but a short trip from her home, she had decided to go as planned, even if it was going to be just Emily and her.

As she closed the wooden door behind her, she noted that the place was practically empty. It was easy to see that the holiday season was over and that it was a regular weekday. While the emptiness of the place did not surprise Sarah, she was disappointed to not to see Emily there already. In her experience, usually the ones who had the longest travel were the ones also showing up the earliest as well.

Sarah headed to a table next to the window, hung her coat on a rack which was basically just a nail on the wall, and sat down. Just as she did that, the door opened, and a red-headed woman in her thirties, dressed in a long wool coat entered the restaurant. A while had passed since Sarah had seen Emily before, and now, she looked like a proper professional attorney. By the looks of her, she could have passed as a businesswoman too.

The last time they had met was just as Emily was about to begin in her first job in the field of law, after graduating from university. When they were young, she had chosen a different route than Sarah and left Bibury as soon as she managed to enroll into Oxford. Sarah felt that ever since Emily had left, they had been drifting apart from one another, which was a shame, since they had known each other since their early childhood.

Sarah noticed Emily greeting the waiter of the pub very formally, after which she headed towards the table where Sarah was sitting. She smiled as she walked. Once she got to the table, Sarah stood up and they hugged each other.

"So great you could make it."

"You're looking so lovely, dear. I can't wait to see the others, too."

As Emily began hanging her coat next to Sarah's, still standing, Sarah said:

"Yeah… that might be a problem. Charlotte and Alice both cancelled."

"Really? They didn't bother mentioning that to me. That's too bad."

Sarah felt relief as Emily sat down and acted so casually upon hearing the news of the others not coming. On some level, she had been worried that Emily would not have been interested in seeing her alone. She pulled a chair and sat down as well.

"I don't know. Somehow, I got the impression that they were both just making an excuse. But it all could be in my head as well. This day has been such a mess for me so far."

"How so?"

With the waiter approaching their table, Sarah did not have the time to answer her. As soon as they had ordered two glasses of wine, she went on to explain what had happened to her at work. Emily did not seem shocked to hear about it, which did not surprise her. Emily had always kept up an exterior which did not reveal her emotions – to some, she might even have seemed like a cold person. Sarah knew this, of course, but was still disappointed on some level by this seemingly uncompassionate approach towards her situation.

"Wow," Emily said.

"If I did not know any better, I'd have a hard time believing such events. It does not sound like it's legal, let alone ethical. Do you have any idea where this is all coming from?" she asked.

"That's just it, I don't know! Everything at work has been as usual, there's a new semester that just started, and it's just like the many others before. I just don't get it," Sarah once more had a hard time holding back tears.

"That's quite a pickle."

After that, there lay silence. Now Sarah felt her anger growing.

"That's it? That's all you can say to help me?"

"I really don't know what else to say. The whole situation sounds so unbelievable. It is something that I have never encountered before."

"If you are asking me for legal advice, I'm afraid I will fall short there, too. You know I specialize in corporate level contracts and public procurements and purchases. Labor legislation is something I am not familiar with. I think the correct approach would be to ask your boss for more information, and preferably to have a union representative to back you up there as well."

"I'm not sure I can. I am not a member of any union and confronting her alone is a very intimidating thought."

After a short silence, Emily said:

"Well then I guess you are just fucked."

Both of them burst out laughing. They had always had a common preference towards this kind of black humor.

"In all seriousness, the whole thing sounds so absurd and insane it's hard to say anything. Try to get someone to support you on spot and then confront them, that's all I can say."

"I will. You know another thing that is bothering me in all of this? The rumors. These towns are so small everyone is bound to find out that I will not be doing the same tasks at work as I used to."

"Mm-hmm. That is one of the things I did not end up longing for when I moved out."

"And I cannot help thinking that Alice and Charlotte might have found out already. Or worse, that tonight they cancelled for the same reason that I am having trouble at work now. That maybe there is already a rumor circulating somewhere."

"You told me you got canned to a part-time position. Will you survive financially?"

"I don't know yet. Margareth said there will be a chance of full-time work again soon, but if it doesn't work out, I might have to get a second job. Our costs of living are not that bad, but there is no chance of doing anything fun every once in a while with only part-time wage."

At seven, Sarah was walking home. In the end, she was glad she had summoned up the grit to come see Emily and she felt much better than before. The conversations with her coupled together with two glasses of strong organic wine strengthened her resolve in that she would fight to see this whole thing through, and not give up easily on the wrongdoings she was now facing.

The next morning was yet another regular school morning in the household of Sarah and Ben. It was Wednesday, and the first day that Sarah was supposed to be working part-time. As Ben sat at the other end of the kitchen table, eating his bowl of cereal, Sarah held her cup of tea and wondered how to phrase the situation to him. Before she had a chance, however, Ben opened up the conversation.

"Is everything ok?"

The question startled Sarah. She began wondering if she had unintentionally been acting in a strange way and if this would be a good moment to tell Ben.

"Sure thing, honey. Why?"

"Two guys at school. Aaron and some other boy. They asked me if I needed help dealing with you."

"What?"

"It sounded like they were worried you were doing something wrong. I don't know what."

Now Sarah knew for sure that there were some rumors floating around about her situation at work. People in these small communities loved to gossip, and word travels fast.

"It probably has to do with some changes to my work routine in Fairford," Sarah said, as calmly and convincingly as she could.

"I will be working different hours and doing tasks that are a bit different than before. But it's all of my own free will just so I get some more time to us, plus it's all temporary."

"Oh. Ok."

Ben seemed as calm as ever. Sarah was not sure whether he believed her, but it was all she would tell him for now. After all, what kind of a mother would she be if she unloaded all the burden she was carrying on her own son?

"I will be going to work every day the same as before, at nine. I will just occasionally finish up and be home earlier than before. That's all."

"Ok," said Ben, then proceeding to eat the last of what remained of his cereal.

"Now go on and finish your breakfast or you're going to be running late."

After Ben had left for school, Sarah headed to her car. She wanted to be at her workplace earlier than usual because she wanted to have another talk with Margareth. She had not been able to find anyone for support but had been going through the lines she was going to be using in her head. At least she knew now that she would be able to retain her calm better than she could yesterday. Her old Mondeo made a thundering sound as she backed onto the street. Driving onto the Bibury main street, she saw Agnes on the porch of her house. They made eye contact. Sarah waved at her, just as always whenever they ran into each other. Agnes quickly turned away and rushed back inside, not responding to Sarah.

"She must have heard something, too…" Sarah quietly said to herself in the car.

Sarah arrived at the school half an hour before the start of her shift. First, she wanted to ensure that even in the event of being given new kinds of assignments, all her rights as an employee would be respected. Second, she wanted more information about what it would be that she was going to be taking care of, since she in the meantime would not be allowed to work with pupils. Instead of heading to the staffroom, she walked right through the echoing hallway towards the headmaster's office. She knocked firmly on the door.

Slightly to her surprise, she was greeted quickly with a "Come in!" from inside the office. She half expected Margareth not to be in her office. Sarah grabbed the doorknob and pulled the creaky and old wooden door open and stepped inside.

Margareth sat behind her desk, with both hands on the desk in a wide stance. Her palms were open and facing downwards, right towards the desk which seemed to be solid wood and must have weighed a ton. The setting reminded Sarah of a pupil heading inside the headmaster's office for a talking-to in a conservative, religious school. All that was missing was Margareth wearing the uniform of a nun.

"Ah, Sarah. Step inside, please."

Sarah did as told and stepped inside, closing the door behind her. Then she headed to the small wooden chair placed right in front of the huge desk and sat down on it.

"Good morning," Margareth said with such a delay and emphasis that it sounded weird.

"Morning. I wanted to talk more about what you told me yesterday."

"I see. Was I unclear somehow?"

Sarah was not certain whether Margareth sounded so inapt on purpose, or if this was simply the nature of what she was like. In any case, it was intimidating.

"Yes. Since you will be demoting me to a position in which I will be paid less than before, I think I am allowed to hear the reasons for this. Also, I would like to know the exact time this measure will last, and what will my assignments be like during this period."

Sarah was proud of herself for being able to speak so directly and firmly. She had been practicing her lines beforehand and had now managed to open up with her main points almost up to a word of how she had perfectly imagined it.

"You have me confused now. I thought that we went through this already. Accusations towards you have been made, and they involve your ability to take care of yourself, as well as the welfare of your child. I have been advised by the authorities not to say any more, they will be in contact with you."

Sarah opened her mouth to try to say something, but Margareth went on, with a heavier tone:

"In the meantime, I will be required to find you some other kind of work to perform instead of working with children."

Margareth took a deep breath, closed her eyes for a while, opened them, and then extended her hand towards Sarah to let her know it was her turn to talk.

"That doesn't sound legal. And what right do you have to reduce my pay unilaterally?"

"Of course, you will not be paid in full since we have no full-time work to offer you. It's as simple as that."

"And what will I be doing now?"

"I thought that today you could start in the kitchen."

"What?"

"Yes. Not preparing food, of course. But there is always a need for support staff taking care of cleaning, unloading materials, and so on. You should report there as soon as you start today. Your day will be over by three."

Sarah had been expecting to be assigned to some boring duties, but this started to sound like someone was intentionally taking a revenge on her. Since she had decided that this time she would not cry, she swallowed the lump in her throat, and quietly said:

"Very well then. I will need to think for a while what to do about this."

Sarah turned around to leave the office. As she opened the door, she heard Margareth saying:

"You should do that."

Sarah started to get the feeling that this was not just a revenge, but that someone had intentionally arranged all of this.

The day working in the school kitchen was surprisingly easy. Sarah had thought about just reporting to be sick but had in the end gone to work. Previously she had not known any of the staff over there except by face, but they had turned out to be very nice towards her and sincerely appreciated the help Sarah was able to give them. They did not seem interested in reasons for her being there and she had decided not to talk to them about it either.

The clock was about to strike half past two and Sarah prepared to finish up for the day. Apparently, she would be needed in the kitchen the coming day as well, for which she in some weird way was even a bit thankful for. This way she would not have to get orientated with yet another new job for one day. Just as she had removed her apron, her phone began to ring. The call came from an unknown number. Sarah answered with her full name.

"Rick Stephenson from Cirencester child protection, good afternoon."

Just as Sarah had managed to get a few less stressful hours, now she again felt her heartbeat growing ever faster.

"I am calling about a report we have received. Do you have a son named Ben?"

"Yes."

"The report is about a concern towards his health and welfare. By law we are required to perform an inquiry into the matter. This is usually done at home with either both parents or the primary custodian present and we typically would recommend taking care of the first visit as soon as possible."

The neutral, distant, authoritarian, and cold tone of Rick felt chilling. He did not strike Sarah as someone who legitimately took an interest in the welfare of children. He was simply an official performing a duty as appointed to him.

"Would you and Ben be at home and free tonight at six, Ms. Stevens?"

"Uhm, yes. I think we will be."

"Splendid," Rick said unenthusiastically.

"Social workers shall be paying you a visit then at your home address in Bibury. There is no need to prepare for the meeting in advance. Do you have any questions at this point?"

"Yes, actually, I was wondering what the report is all about?"

"That is something that will be delved into at the meeting. In order to share that information, I would have to be able to ensure your identity. That is something which I cannot do over the phone unfortunately."

"Fine. But I want to know what this is all about."

"I am certain you will be given all the information needed in the meeting. Have a good day."

Sarah said nothing and just ended the call.

Ben was supposed to be at football practice tonight. Instead, they were both at home, waiting for the visit Sarah had been dreading for and Ben was mostly mystified of. She did not know how to break it to him and much less how to explain the visit from child protective services to an eight-year-old. She had vaguely told him that this was a routine check-up from the local clinic but was most uncertain if she had been convincing enough for Ben to believe her.

Precisely at six, the doorbell rang. Ben stayed in the living room while Sarah went to the door. As she opened, outside stood two women – one of them significantly older than Sarah, and the other one closer to her age, although she was not sure, for her remarkable overweight could most likely fool many into thinking she would be older than she actually was. At a first glance, the older woman seemed stern and unhappy, but as soon as she began to talk, her face adapted a much warmer, even empathetic look.

"Good evening. Cirencester protective services. Are you Sarah?"

Sarah nodded.

"Nice to meet you. My name is Eleanor Mitchell."

"Emily Turner, hi," the younger woman introduced herself. The name got Sarah immediately thinking of her namesake friend Emily.

Eleanor went on:

"We are social workers and here to discuss your situation. May we come in?"

"Yeah, sure," Sarah said.

Sarah turned around and headed back inside with Eleanor and Emily right behind her.

"We can go and sit down in the living room," Sarah told them over her shoulder while leading the way. The women closed the door behind them and followed her. Upon entering the living room, Eleanor and Emily took notice of Ben sitting there, and told him:

"Hi, you must be Ben. I am Eleanor and this is my friend Emily. We work for the county and are here to take just a little peek at how you are doing. We won't be here for long."

Sarah felt that she would also need such a pep talk as well right now, even though she very well knew they were talking to Ben. After the brief introductions, they all sat down, Eleanor looked at Sarah, and began:

"Our visit is based on a report we've received. We have a standardized procedure we're required to follow according to regulations. This means evaluating the conditions you are living in, your status in the society, stage of life, financial status, and so on. We will be filling out a form based upon our visit which you will be able to view and sign to testify that we are writing no falsehoods. All in all, primarily we are here to help and to counsel you, Sarah. Shall we begin?"

Roughly one hour later, Sarah saw Eleanor and Emily out of the house. The time they had spent had gone as Eleanor had implied; with lots of questions to Sarah about her parenting habits and abilities to be able to financially take care of the household and Ben. They had talked to Ben as well, mainly about his attendance at school and his daily habits concerning his welfare. Sarah was relieved to see that they were sincerely polite and kind. They seemed to appreciate the sensitivity of the situation.

Just as Eleanor and Emily had stepped outside and it would have been a natural timing to wish them goodbye, Sarah instead asked:

"The report you mentioned that had been made about me neglecting or even abusing Ben. You never mentioned what it said and where you got it from. I would like to know that."

"In the report someone was concerned about your parenting. They had indeed construed that you were abusing

Ben. You'll probably be glad to know we found nothing to support that theory. Many of the reports we receive in the end turn out to be nothing, but we still are required to investigate them."

"As for the one who made the report, we are bound by confidentiality, so I'm sorry, that's something we cannot tell you."

"So, is this it then? I won't be hearing from you again?"

"I would assume so," Eleanor smiled.

"Of course, we will need to get in touch with you again if there are more reports that have any credit to them. But let's assume there won't be any."

Emily, who had been silent for most of the time, said:

"Have a good evening, Ms. Stevens."

"Bye then."

Sarah closed the door.

It was a beautiful day. The sun was shining, and despite the season, it was warm. Autumn leaves were slowly falling off the trees according to the pulse of a temperate wind that blew. Even though Bibury really shows all the beauty it has during the summertime, these kinds of days in September were not easily outshone by the warm summer days. Some might say this ambience is one of the best things about living in such an idyllic English village.

Except for Sarah, it was not a beautiful day. Right now, she felt that no amount of sunshine and rainbows would be able to cheer her mood. She had barely managed to recover from the visit of the social workers to their home last night, and now, in the morning, just as she had been preparing to send Ben off to school before heading off to work herself, her phone had rung. It was Ben's class teacher from the local school in Bibury. She wanted to meet with Sarah, as she was concerned about Ben.

Instead of going to work, Sarah was now walking towards the village school of Bibury. The teacher had not said much during the phone call, but Sarah could already guess that it would be about the same reasons as with the social workers as well as the problems she had at work. It felt like the last few weeks had been a series of nightmares for Sarah, and they were not even close to seeing their end.

To top it all off, she knew she was most likely going to be late for work because of this. Despite that, she wanted to take care of this as soon as possible, for she knew herself all too well that otherwise she would spend the entire day dwelling in the images of what she was going to be hearing from Ben's class teacher. Before heading towards the school, she had given Ben a lift there and sent him off. She did not want to tell him about this, not for as long as she was uncertain of the agenda of the meeting.

All the emotional turmoil Sarah had been experiencing had clearly rubbed off on her. As she walked inside the school building, all she could think of was how much smaller the school in Bibury was compared to the elementary school in Fairford. She was also slightly worried about running late for work. But at that time, the thoughts of worry about the meeting did not cross her mind. Apparently, she had grown far more robust from these agonizing and stressful experiences.

Her plan to not tell Ben about the meeting got immediately crushed as she entered the hallway leading to the classrooms. The whole school building basically consisted of that single hallway, and there was very little room for anything but the classrooms. Apparently, judging from the loud voices echoing from behind the closed doors, most of the children were already in class. The one exception being the class that Ben's teacher was supposed to have. Instead of meeting in an office, she was standing in front of the classroom belonging to the class Ben was in.

Sarah saw Ben's teacher, whose name she could not even remember anymore, waving at her, with all of her pupils standing right behind her in the hallway – including Ben. They all fell silent as Sarah followed the teacher inside the classroom and closed the door behind her. Sarah did not even dare to look Ben in the eye.

"Please, do sit down."

As she sat down, Sarah noted that Ben's teacher was much younger than the teachers in Fairford, probably still in her twenties.

"I'm so glad you could come at such a short notice. Since they are waiting for the class to begin, is it ok we cut right to the chase?"

"Preferably yes, I need to get to work soon," Sarah said.

"Of course. The reason I called is that there is a disturbing rumor circulating in the school about Ben, which involves you as well. I don't know if Ben has heard of it yet, but some of the pupils and my colleagues notified me about it."

There was a disturbing silence which felt like eternity to Sarah, who finally asked:

"Well, what is it?"

"They told me Ben is not being given a chance to eat proper food at home, that he is suffering from malnutrition. According to the story, you have financial trouble and can't afford it. The wildest part of the story is that you have been feeding him dog food."

Instead of being shocked, Sarah felt her eyes opening. She could not tell who was behind all this, but it was apparent that this had also caused her problems at work as well as yesterday's visit. In all her years of living in Bibury, she had obviously heard many wild stories and rumors circulating but had never experienced what it was like being the object of those stories. Now she knew.

"What else can I say but that it is not true?"

"I figured as much," the teacher whose name Sarah still could not recall said and smiled. Sarah saw that she did not believe her entirely.

"Killing these rumors can be very difficult. Do you have any idea what might have been the cause of all of this?"

Of course, she knew now what the back story in all of this was about. The discounted meat in the butcher's shop. She was uncertain what to do about it, though. In that moment, she decided not to tell Ben's teacher and to solve it by herself.

"I really don't. And it boggles me if it is appropriate for the representatives of the local school to go and spread these rumors any further."

"I assure you; we will not be doing that. The only reason I was told is that it involves Ben, and otherwise we are bound by confidentiality," she said with a smile so exaggerated it seemed anything but sincere to Sarah.

"It goes without saying I will not have Ben being picked on because of this and I assume you will help to do your part if you saw something like that happening here at school?"

"Most certainly. We do not tolerate any kind of bullying here, rest assured of that."

"I need to get to work now. I need to think about what you said, but in the meantime, it is vital that we do not spend the rumor any further, ok? It is false and can cause trouble especially for Ben."

"Absolutely. But it is good that you know now."

With that, Sarah left the classroom. As she left, the pupils began swarming inside. In the hallway, she quickly told Ben that they would talk after school. She needed to clear her head and think.

Thanks to her new position at work, Sarah arrived home before Ben. She had run late, as she had imagined she would, and that would need to be compensated some other day or else the time would be subtracted from her salary. But she did not care about that right now. All day, she had been wondering what she would do about the situation so that it would cause the least trouble for them.

As Ben's teacher had told her, the rumor concerned food. Sarah could immediately connect the dots to her visits to the butcher's shop and her buying discounted meat in bulk. It felt so silly and absurd at the same time that if she was not experiencing this herself, she would not believe the story. For the first time ever, she seriously considered them moving to a big city. She felt deep hatred for the people who had been spreading these lies about her. For the first time ever, she saw the dark side of living in a small community.

Naturally, there was also the question of who the original rumormonger might be that bugged her. Agnes was the first one to see her visiting the butcher's shop, but on the other hand, it might also have been someone at work. Her natural instinct was to try to get back at people for causing all this trouble to her. For now, she would have to push those feelings aside, and consider what would be best for Ben and for her in the end.

When Ben arrived home from school, Sarah explained to him as best as she could what happened and what she had heard. She left out some parts of the reasons for the visit of child protection so he would not get too scared. Ben told her he had not heard of the rumor and had not been bullied because of it, for which Sarah was very thankful for. Sarah felt relieved to see that Ben had gone surprisingly unaffected by all this thus far and she was intent on having things remain that way.

Now, she knew just what to do.

It was the week of the harvest festival, which marked the end of summer season in Bibury. It was not the only annual festival and get-together the villagers had, but one of many. If you asked a local about the significance of these gatherings, they would most likely hold them to a high regard. Many found them important not only because of tradition, but also because of the boost these events gave to community spirit. During the week, there had been small events and markets arranged in the village. The main attraction, however, was the weekend full of celebrations that lasted from each morning until late evening, and every night culminated in joint dinners where everyone who lived in Bibury had been invited.

Community spirit was not something that was being celebrated in the Stevens' household. Sarah knew that the horrible stories being spread about her would inevitably come to an end, but it would not happen within a week or two. She was determined to attend the festival that weekend since she had given a promise to participate and bring along some home-made pastries as well. The unwritten rule stated that everyone attending the dinner would have to bring something, and Sarah intended to honor it.

What dimmed her mood even further was that ever since meeting with Ben's teacher at his school, Ben had also been getting strange looks both at school as well as at his football practice. The word had been spreading, and it seemed unfair that her little boy would have to suffer because of the behavior of a few in-bred, petty, and gossipy locals Sarah had previously considered neighbors or even friends.

Even for the most devoted local festivalgoer it was rare to attend the harvest festivities all the way throughout the weekend. Most of the people attended one of the communal dinners, while coming and going as they pleased throughout the weekend. At the same time, it was also highly irregular for one not to attend any of the festivities. Especially under the current circumstances, Sarah wanted to stay out of the spotlight and do just as she normally would have done. In the Friday evening right after work, she had prepared three apple pies to bring along to the festival, which already was far more than most would contribute.

Now, it was Saturday afternoon, and she and Ben were soon to head to the fields of the local cricket club, where the main festivities would take place. She surprised even herself by how calm she was about the gossips. After all, why would anyone spread rumors and gossip out in the open, when that was the exact opposite of talking about someone behind their back?

She was worried about Ben, however. Ben had always been a calm and prudent boy. Even as a baby, Sarah was constantly amazed by how little crying and defiance she had got from him. Yet as a mother, her instinct said that Ben cared about stress factors in his life far more than he let it show to others. These past few days he had been visually calm as always, but Sarah could tell that he had been shocked by the recent events just as she had.

Now, the time to head off to the festival with him had arrived. Despite Ben attempting to convince her that he wanted to go, Sarah prayed to herself she would not have to come to regret bringing him with her.

Anyone that has visited England, especially during the autumn, knows that rainy weather is not an exception, but a common rule. This is something the whole town had been preparing for in the arrangements of their common gatherings. Upon glancing at the harvest festival area, one who was not from around there might have thought the circus had come to town. The high-rise tents with loud music and surprisingly large crowds all signaled that there was something big going on, and all the major activities happened inside the warm and dry tents.

Sarah could not help feeling a slight breeze of joy upon seeing the area, even if the totality of the situation was otherwise uncomfortable. She had never been to Central Europe or their folk festivals but was certain that the Bibury harvest festival would not pale in comparison to theirs. Pure and cheerful festival bustle filled the air.

She and Ben were dragging the pies she had made in a large cooler bag. The first thing she wanted to do was to whisk them off to the largest tent where they would be having dinner later on.

"Mom, can I go play over there?" Ben pointed at a site designed for children with multiple swings, slides and some small amusement park devices installed.

"Just help me carry this inside first, then you can go," she told him.

As they entered the tent, there was a crowd of perhaps 30 people already inside, most of them familiar faces to Sarah. People were sitting by long, wooden tables, enjoying locally produced tea, ale, or cider. Sarah was unsure if it was all just in her head, but for a while it seemed like the chatter lowered down and eyes turned towards her and Ben as they came inside. They walked towards the counter where warm food was already being prepared to drop off the pies. Some of the local volunteers were typically there to receive whatever was being left there, but since everyone seemed busy, Sarah and Ben simply unloaded the pies covered in foil at the counter. As they were about to leave, a man from the other end of a long wooden table shouted:

"Hey, hey, hey! Don't you dare to leave those there!"

Sarah turned to see where the voice came from and saw a man with a pint of ale in his hand. Sarah knew his face; he was a local, alas she did not know him. He was drunk.

"Yes, I'm talking to you. I'll not have you bringing no maggot food or whatever it is there."

At this point, the whole tent had fallen silent, and everyone stared at Sarah and Ben. Why, oh, why had Sarah not just let Ben go play and carry the pies inside herself?

"Excuse me," a voice from behind Sarah called. It was Agnes. She was standing behind the counter.

"Can you believe this drunkard?" Sarah asked.

"Yes, very inappropriate," Agnes said.

"But still, could we not make a fuss out of this, and just go without your foods? You are still welcome to stay here for warm drinks," Agnes went on.

Many in the crowd began to whisper to each other. At that point it dawned on Sarah: no matter how much she had been preparing for this, facing down with the people spreading lies about her was too much for her to take. Now, she was being publicly banished from the village gathering by someone she considered to be her friend. A tear rolled down her face and she did not dare to look at anyone.

At first, there was a long silence which seemed to last forever. Gradually, people at the tables began to chatter as before. Agnes tried to make eye contact with Sarah who was just staring at the ground. She seemed uncomfortable and uncertain herself, too. Then, she called her name:

"Sarah? Are you ok?"

The drunk man from the other end of the tent raised his voice again:

"Begone for all I care, who cares!"

"Let's not make a scene out of this, Sarah, ok?" Agnes said, almost in a pleading tone.

At that point Sarah felt some primal force awakening in her. The single teardrop on her cheek fell to the ground. She slowly raised her head and looked at Agnes. Right there and right then, if she could have, she would have burned this tent to the ground right along with everyone else in it with the power of her mind. She could not contain her anger anymore as she raised her voice, almost shouting:

"Fine, I would love to! Why would anyone want to spend more time here with any of you?"

The tent fell silent once more. Sarah did not care, but went on:

"The truth is you are a bunch of losers. People who never dared to venture outside of their own comfort zone and who now take pleasure in life making fun of others!"

"You blame me for not taking care of my son? Me, who has risked and put everything on the line for him? You have no proof, of course, but you don't care!"

Sarah pointed at the drunk man.

"The greatest risk my son is facing right here and right now is the rambling village idiot who has been drinking and driving intoxicated for years. For some reason, you as a community wish to protect him."

Sarah turned towards Agnes.

"Or you, Agnes. From you, my son might learn how to steal flowers and plants from the local fields, just as you do."

Then, she raised her voice again:

"Oh and no, I will not name which fields she has been stealing from, you can go ahead and gossip about that amongst yourselves!"

She took two deep breaths, and said:

"But worst of all, my son might gain influence from this hideous group of people, from all of you, who love to make others suffer. Tonight, as a pure atheist, before going to sleep I shall kneel, cross my hands, and pray to God I will never have to set my eyes on any of you ever again!"

Sarah looked at Ben who seemed terrified by what had just happened. With the empty cooler bag in her left hand, she took Ben by his hand with her right hand, and told him:

"Come. We're leaving."

As Sarah and Ben left the tent, not a word was spoken. There lay only deathlike silence.

Sarah woke up to a new day. The first thing she noticed was the small humming of traffic that could be heard inside their new home. Ever since moving, the amount of noise and various voices had been the first difference both Ben and Sarah had noticed. After Bibury, where the sole voice to be heard was the birds singing, who could blame them?

She walked from her bedroom to the small kitchen right next to it. Ben was already up and getting ready for school. The Oxford city schools for some reason seemed to have their first classes of the day earlier than the ones in the countryside. Sarah did not know why. Since her own workday would start soon, too, she did not have the time to wonder about it right now.

Right after seeing Ben off to school not far from the apartment flat in which they lived now, she went to the bathroom to brush her teeth. Everything in their new home was smaller than before, since housing costs in Bibury were much more affordable than in a city center. That was the price both of them had been willing to pay, though.

They had been living in Oxford for two months now, and both Sarah and Ben had gotten well used to their new life. Ben had quickly adapted to his new surroundings and gotten friends at school, and Sarah – with the help of her friend Emily – had landed a job as a general secretary in the same office Emily worked. Her salary was not much, but still more than she made in the short term she worked in Fairford as a part-time general assistant. Additionally, she had plans for the future to apply to university to study law, just as Emily had. Right now, she was preparing for a day of working remotely from home and enjoyed her new job.

After the episode they had gone through at the harvest festival, Sarah and Ben had unilaterally made the decision to leave Bibury. That had not been part of Sarah's initial plans, but seeing the worst of the community manifest itself in such an explosive way made her see that it is worthless to fight against windmills. She also had to consider Ben, who mattered to her the most. He would not have a bright future in such a close-minded rural village. That was something she had always known, yet somehow pushed from her thoughts.

During the last days they still lived in their old house in Bibury, Sarah had heard that the focus of the villagers had now shifted. They still talked of Sarah and Ben, but it was now Agnes and that other man that were receiving most of the heat. Despite her feeling gleeful about it, she knew that this only strengthened the idea in her head that leaving Bibury was the correct decision for them. Those people would never change.

As Sarah fired up her laptop and checked her calendar for the day, she remembered she had arranged for a meeting with a lawyer working in the same office who specialized in labor law. They had briefly discussed Sarah's former situation in Fairford, and the lawyer felt confident Sarah had a potential case to be entitled to a compensation for her rights as an employee being violated.

Relaxed and confident about her and Ben's future, Sarah took a sip of her cup of tea and began to prepare for her first tasks of the day.

A SHOPPER'S SAGA

Emma was hurrying along the crowded streets of Manhattan. Being Friday afternoon, the traffic was particularly bad. At one point she had thought about driving to her destination but soon discovered the whole idea doomed from the get-go. Just attempting to move on foot proved to be challenging enough during the rush hour, let alone getting stuck in one place with a vehicle.

It was almost weekend, and what better way to start that than by heading to Bloomingdale's major discount campaign, she thought. Not only because of the prices, but she was also in dire need of new summer shoes and dresses. Just last week she invested in new trousers in anticipation of warmer weather, so why not?

With vast experience in clothes shopping she had gathered throughout the years she browsed through the racks in the women's clothes section. For an occasional bystander her actions might have seemed strange, to say the least. Emma had developed the habit of picking up many, at times even more than a dozen pieces of clothes in one go. After trying them all on she made up her mind whether she would buy them or not. She did not tend to buy all of them... most of the time.

Today's visit had been a slight disappointment to her. She had managed to find a lovely pair of new sneakers, but no dresses that pleased her. This meant that she would have to pay a visit to Goodman's on her way home as well.

"I'll just order the rest of these from the Internet," she muttered to herself as she headed towards the checkout.

Emma lived in a flat in Jersey City, within a reasonable commute from Manhattan. Upon arriving home, it was evening. It may have taken her some time, but shopping at several different stores had nevertheless been a success. She exhaled deeply as she dropped the large bags in her hands onto the apartment floor. Even though she was satisfied by the thought of not having to think about work for two days, she was also excited by all the great discoveries she had made in the form of new clothes.

She knew she could not really afford all of this but had concluded that passing up on all the great discounted prices would have been dumber than simply using credit card to take advantage of such bargains as these. At least that was how she justified the shopping to herself tonight. The total cost of a few dresses and the pair of shoes had set her credit back roughly 600 dollars.

Her home was not as luxurious as her daily spending habits. The small apartment of two rooms, a shower, and a kitchen was far more affordable than the similarly sized ones she had been able to find in New York. She had taken her time to furnish her home neatly, though. All the furniture and decorations inside were either brand new or in mint condition, and no doubt a professional in that field would immediately have noticed the harmony of the colors and shapes the tables, the couch, a few paintings, and many other items formed. Unsurprisingly, Emma had consulted an interior designer on the matter.

At a quick glance, the only thing that disrupted what some might call feng shui were two huge piles of cardboard boxes piled up in the corner of her small kitchen. Many of them were labelled with brands known in the fields of fashion or décor, or simply with logos of department stores. She had opened a few of them, yet the items were not unboxed, whereas some of them seemed to be tightly sealed and in the same conditions they would be in at the hands of the postal office or a parcel service.

Emma stepped into the kitchen and placed the new shopping bags on top of the other pile of boxes. They could wait there until she had time to wear them. Then, she opened the door of the reasonably large fridge she had. A glass jar dropped down from the top shelf, and with lightning-like reflexes she caught the falling jar in her left hand. The jar falling was hardly a one-time incident. Considering her crammed fridge, it was in fact quite surprising that nothing had fallen out and broken on the kitchen floor, at least not yet.

After about ten minutes of warming up whatever leftovers she had from that week sat down in her kitchen, enjoying a mixture of bread with butter, salad, and some chicken. While chewing on the incredibly dry meal, she browsed through the receipts of today's purchases. A bit expensive, but nothing that was not to be expected, she thought, and threw the receipts inside the shopping bags. She knew herself well enough to tell that after eating she would be exhausted and ready for bed.

The next day, Emma was strolling around the shelves of Whole Foods Market in Manhattan. There were plenty of grocery stores closer to home, obviously, but she loved the vibe of Manhattan too much to skip an opportunity to go there even during the weekend. Besides, she wanted to do her shopping in a place she considered worth her while and penny.

As usual, she could not resist the temptation of splurging on food, even if for just a little bit. Some organic strawberries, artisanal cheese and pasta, and gourmet chocolates found their way into her shopping cart. It was all a mix of both healthy albeit very expensive options as well. At the checkout, Emma got a weird feeling as the cashier scanned her items. The total amount seemed a little higher than she had expected. It all added up to almost one hundred dollars.

As she walked along the bustling streets, the city bathed in radiant sunlight. Emma saw people entering and exiting some of the stores she tended to frequent herself, and felt the urge to go in. Resisting the temptation, she decided to head straight home so that she could get her groceries in the fridge. She felt a growing sensation of nervousness inside her at the thought of some of the expensive items she had bought spoiling.

After getting back home, she took a look at the receipt from the Whole Foods. It was 121 dollars. The looming anxiety she had recently experienced grew a little bigger. There were still almost two weeks to go until her next payday and she had been using credit card to take care of today's groceries. For many years, she had not cared or been worried about her spending, but having to use credit card was something new to her.

She felt nervous. At that moment, she decided to go through her bank statement and bills. To begin with, there was her bank account, as it was the easiest one to take a look at. It held several hundred dollars, just as she had expected. Nothing spectacular, but it meant that she would have to forego a lot of shopping before being credited with the next salary. Next up was her credit card bill. She knew it would be something a lot harder to digest. Her eyes grew wide as she saw the total sum.

Her credit stood at 20 dollars from being maxed out. On her next due date, she would be paying close to one thousand dollars in interest only. She heard a wheezing sound in her ears, took a look at the ceiling, then turned her eyes back to the iPad screen to check if she had seen the numbers correctly. The numbers were still the same. Up until then, she did not have a clue her situation had gotten this bad.

After paying her rent and necessary bills, there still remained the loan payment of consumer credit she had taken one year back to take care of for that month. It had been to buy a new television set. By instinct, she took a quick look at the television she did not even watch that much and cursed to herself.

She did the math in her head and came to realize that after taking care of all of those payments, she could not afford any more food until her next salary. The anxiety she had been experiencing had now transformed into a full blown-out panic in her mind. In the physical world, she was just intensely staring at the screen, her heart racing. In her thoughts, she heard a voice in her mind screaming incoherently.

As her credit score was still enough for the application, she quickly surfed to the website of another bank and applied for another loan for five hundred dollars to get her through those few weeks. She did not bother to look at all the details included, just that it promised a quick application processing service.

Before long, her bank account balance showed 500 dollars more than it had before. It was as if a load of stones had been lifted off her chest. Simply the feeling of being able to survive with what she had without having to sell anything off felt incredible to Emma.

At least she knew she could sleep peacefully now knowing that she had it made for a while now.

On Monday, the week at GothamStrat Solutions headquarters in Manhattan, New York City, had begun as usual. Even though many would expect companies working at the heart of one of the major commercial centers of the world to be swarming with people and energy during daytime, they were the exception that proved the rule. Located at the southern end of Madison Avenue, the office was relatively quiet and calm at 10 o'clock in the morning.

The big open office area had been left mostly abandoned because of many choosing to work remotely from home. From one side of the office, one could barely hear someone lightly tapping their keyboard and sipping on their morning tea at the other end of the space.

GothamStrat Solutions focused mainly on marketing services for their clients. Despite the impressive annual revenue in sales, the business seemed all but harsh and competitive judging from the serenity that reigned over the office.

It was not all just deathly silent there, however. Even in such a calm office space, there was one place where you could hear lively chatter coming from. That was the break room. Without a doubt, this area attracted many of the employees several times in a single day all thanks to the easy-going and careless atmosphere the place had.

Solely because of the nature of the office, switching jobs had not crossed Emma's mind for years. She dreaded the thought of having to look for some other place and getting used to constant stress and sense of urgency. As a marketing coordinator, among many others, she had very few dreams or aspirations of achieving higher positions. In fact, the very median salary she made had always been enough for her. That is, at least for now. She loved the life she had with no constant interruptions to her time off work because of her job.

This time, however, the loud discussions and chatting had gone unnoticed by Emma, even though she was sitting right there in the break room along with her co-workers. Despite the amount of money she now held in her bank account, she was still feeling restless because of her financial situation. Suddenly, she was awakened by a comment:

"Seriously, I could never imagine ending up in debt myself."

The one speaking was her colleague, Jim. Even though she had not been following the discussion, it was obvious to Emma that what Jim had just said contradicted everyone else in the room. Not only because of the choice of words themselves, but because of the sudden silence that had fallen after Jim had spoken. In such a female-dominated industry, it was not surprising that the only aberrant statement came from a guy.

"I know that there are people who are drowning in credit card debt and other crazy stuff. It's a huge problem in America. For a while now, I've tried to live as free from spending money as possible. It's incredible. I even have this cousin who has…"

Lauren, another colleague of Emma, cut Jim short: "I could never live like that! You know what happened just last weekend, I can't believe it I…"

At that point Emma faded out again. She looked at Jim, then sank into her thoughts. Perhaps Jim had a point. Perhaps Emma needed to revise her life. She had tried executing lifestyle changes before, such as eating only organic foods. The results had been lackluster. Considering her situation now, after all, how could it hurt? For a while she thought about asking Jim for advice, but decided to opt out, since in such an environment it might be construed as something entirely else. Besides, Emma was not interested in Jim the tiniest bit in any other way.

After some miserable days at work, Emma was now back at home browsing the Internet., She had found out that trying to reinvent one's life was surprisingly hard. Besides Jim at work, she had thought about asking other people for advice. She did have a few cousins who – at least to her recollection – were in financially good positions. But then again, she was strong and had been able to survive all her adult life by herself, so she would not need anyone else to advise her, at least not directly.

Surfing the web for answers was complicated as well, though. Unsurprisingly, there were plenty of websites, blogs, and influencers to be found that all dealt with the topic of household economy and saving. Knowing where to start proved to be hard. Some of the sites were clearly just a façade in an attempt to sell some product or a service. Since Emma figured that to be the exact opposite of what she was aiming for, she skipped those immediately.

After a few hours, it was late evening already, and even though exhausted, she felt excited as well. She had compiled a list of steps to take to achieve a more balanced life when it came to spending money. She had found hundreds of pieces of advice, and had now filtered and compiled a list of six actions she would have to take:

1) Start at home. Look around and see if there is anything you can save on in the place you are living in.
2) Plan your budget and shopping in advance.

3) Wherever possible, pinch pennies.
4) Pay off loans and prepare by saving extra money.
5) Avoid eating out.
6) Commute as little as possible.

"That's fairly simple," she thought.

She could just do one thing at a time, and then be able to cross an item off her list. At the end of the month, she would have a new life.

On top of those measures, she had stumbled across various healthcare services she had access to as a benefit from her work, and seeing a trained therapist might be an option. If everything else failed, she could try that out. But first, she wanted to see if she was able to succeed on her own.

So, it would start. Emma turned 360 degrees slowly around counterclockwise in her home. At first, she was staring out the biggest single window in her apartment, in what some might call the living room. To her left, there was the entrance to the kitchen. Right next to the doorway, a big pile of boxes rose up towards the ceiling, containing some of the stuff she had been ordering online and had not had the time to open yet. Just inside the kitchen, on the other side of the wall, she knew there were two more piles just like that waiting for her.

That's where she would start! She was exhilarated by how quickly she had managed to find and identify something she could try to change. Some of those might be returnable, and even if not, then perhaps she could see what mistakes not to repeat.

The first box on top of the pile was a big one, although not too heavy. Unsurprisingly, inside were the results of last month's clothes shopping. She was pretty sure she had tried some of them on, but certainly not all of them. Also unluckily, they had all exceeded the 30-day return window by now. Now she would have to figure out what to do with all of them. Most of them were dresses, with the occasional exception of a skirt here and there. Overall, there must have been more than ten pieces of different clothes in there.

"That's right!"

The memories came back to her slowly. These were the results of shopping from a single store for several months now. She laughed a little at the idea of ordering that many products online at once. Then, as she realized how she now literally laughed at her own irresponsible behavior, she stopped and put on a more serious face.

The second box had nothing in it but packaging material. She remembered it used to contain cosmetics, all of which she had tried already so they were no longer returnable.

The third box still included some gift wrapping. She remembered it contained decorative items she had ordered to be used as Christmas gifts. She had ended up keeping them to herself and giving out gift cards, instead. Needless to say, she would not even want to get rid of them. How great would they look in her apartment in a few months?

After two hours, Emma was exhausted. She had gone through the entire pile of things and found nothing returnable. Her eyes widened with surprise and shock as she noticed it was almost midnight, and she would have to get up at six o'clock in the morning to get to work. The feelings of anguish and anxiety clutched her insides again as she prepared to go to bed.

Right before falling asleep Emma still kept thinking about the list of measures she had made and about promising to renew her lifestyle. With already almost in sleep, she reminded herself that she could not let go of the objectives she had set for herself. She had become instantly obsessed by them. She felt her whole life depended on it.

Emma was sitting in an armchair coated with leather. To her, the leather seemed cheap and fake. Yet, it was comfortable. She had sat there for but a few minutes without having barely said a word. Most of the time there, both of them were silent. But now, the woman in front of her, an occupational health therapist called Claire Ross, began to speak. Having introduced herself already as Emma had entered her office, she now jumped straight to the point. She told Emma she was there for the treatment of her shopping addiction.

Emma had never thought of her situation as an addiction, and thus it all sounded strange to her, even a bit demeaning.

"According to the contract we have with your employer, you will be entitled to ten therapy sessions annually. After that, I will be able to still keep working with you or alternatively refer you to another expert, but the costs will have to be covered by the patient or some other party."

Emma felt disgruntled by how Claire referred to her as "the patient" instead of talking directly to her. The wound-up look the woman who was old enough to be her mother had did not help her to stomach the situation. She began to think that she might not be attending the therapy for more than this one session.

"Typically, you will be the one doing most of the talking here while we are in session. After all, it is your life we are trying to observe here. This first time is an exception since I am legally and also professionally required to explain the basic structure of therapy sessions and the contents of your employer's occupational health care contract to you."

For the first time, Claire smirked a little and said:

"I will shut up now. It's your turn. Tell me what ails you."

The change in her tone caught Emma off guard. She froze for a couple of seconds, after which she told Claire about her monetary situation and how she had identified habits and patterns she had developed over the years of her adult life. Emma had been preparing for the question beforehand and had rehearsed how to share her story, so it came out smoothly and naturally.

Her new therapist barely blinked an eye while listening to Emma. There was something eerie yet soothing about the calm, almost cold professionalism around Claire.

"Have you done something about your problems yet?"

"I tried making a list of things to change. It didn't go so well. I have some items at home which I ordered online, but I wasn't able to return them any longer... all I found was this endless stream of boxes full of stuff which I can't get rid of now."

"After that, I got really depressed about the whole plan I had and forgot about it for a few days. Then, once I remembered I can soon no longer afford to buy food, I booked this appointment."

For most of the time she had been talking, Emma had been gazing at the floor. Now, looking Claire directly in the eyes, she said:

"I really did not want to come here today, either. If I could have put this off some more, I would have."

Claire slapped her hands together, smiling, and said:

"Honesty! I love it. Go on."

"There is nothing more. Now, I am here."

"Nonsense. There is plenty more we can go on from. Now, tell me about your earlier life."

Half an hour later, Emma was exiting Claire's office back to the streets of Manhattan. Despite having had a good session, she felt ashamed for going to therapy in the middle of day on a Friday. It was not even noon yet, and she was supposed to be working. In her situation, she most certainly could not risk losing even an hour's pay. Still, she knew that something had to be done about her addiction and habits.

For the rest of the session, Emma had told Claire about her childhood and adolescent years. Instead of being able to give her some insight right there and then, Claire took notes in a huge notepad like which everyone had accustomed to seeing therapists use even in the movies. At the end of the session, she gave Emma tasks to complete before their second session in the next week. But most of all, she had gained the confidence to even book the next appointment and summoned the willpower to decide to show up.

That Saturday, Emma was feeling low again. At first because of the overall situation – she was even a little embarrassed about having to attend therapy – but also because there was nothing for her to do. Everything she liked cost money! She was wary of opening up the envelope in which Claire had given her a list of tasks to complete. In fact, she even felt somewhat terrified. She had, however, made up her mind to book the next session, which meant it would be mandatory for her to attend – unless she wanted to end up paying for the missed timeslot herself. And since she was going to go, she hated the idea of going there empty-handed.

The large A4-sized envelope had not been sealed and contained just the one piece of paper on which stood her list of tasks to do. The first thing that made Emma gasp as she read the list was the number of things to do: all in all, there were ten different tasks to complete in less than as many weeks. Most of them would require her to make big changes in her life, too.

As she felt emotional burden starting to weigh on her chest thinking of all those things, she decided to proceed one step at a time. With that in mind, she calmed down and read the first bullet point:

"Sell off, give away, or throw away five items you own."

Despite sounding quite easy and simple, the idea sent shivers down her spine – and not in a good way. The simplicity of it made Emma also feel stupid, as if she was the one special needs student in a class full of normal people. Nevertheless, she began to instantly think about the belongings she had and right away thought about getting rid of any excess clothes she might have. Somehow, her mind guided her towards her wardrobe.

Since Emma had always been very strict about wearing only fashionable clothing that was in pristine condition, choosing something to give up on would be hard. On the other hand, there was plenty of which to choose from. For the last five years, she had been buying clothes almost weekly. That is also why she made up her mind not to just give the clothes away, but to sell them.

Apart from her outdoors clothes and shoes, she had four large cabinets and a cupboard which were all full of clothing.

An hour passed as she combed through everything those stashes held inside.

Alas, she found no garments which she was ready to give up on. At that point, out of sheer frustration, she picked up a dress she had gotten tired of and decided to sell it. She would later on find a new one to replace it, after she had managed to steer clear of the bane of her loans and credit card bill. No one said the five items would have to be clothes. Despite clothes being her first instinct turned out to be harder than expected to choose from. She would find the rest of the items somewhere else.

A week had passed, and Emma found herself yet again sitting in the hallway right outside Claire's office. Even though she knew the office itself was just what everyone would expect from a therapist's reception, the hallway was not. She did not know what all the other office spaces were used for, but judging by the looks of the people passing by her there were other healthcare functions of some clinic based there, perhaps even a private hospital. In any case, with people constantly buzzing around, it made the waiting seem longer and less relaxed than it should have been.

Finally, after maybe five minutes, which at that moment had felt like an hour, Claire opened the door and invited Emma in. As soon as Emma had taken a seat in the same leather armchair Claire wasted no time and jumped right to the list of tasks she had given her.

"We're done with the first week now, how are you doing?"

"Well, I managed to complete the first task on the list. It's a start, I guess."

Claire contemplated for a while.

"It was the one where you are supposed to eradicate some of your belongings. Five things, right? What did you decide to rid yourself of?"

Emma had been half expecting Claire to ask her to report some of her actions to her, so the question did not come as a surprise.

"My initial idea was to sell off some of my clothes, but it turns out that most of them were mandatory for me to have, actually. But there was this one dress I decided I will sell; I can always get a new one to replace it. Apart from that, I have been holding on to a toaster which has been broken for almost one year now. Instead of having it fixed, I figured I'll just throw it away. Also, a bag of black pepper in my kitchen had expired, so I just threw it away."

Emma took a short break to take a look at the paper of tasks listed in her hand, and went on:

"After that I could not think of anything else! Everything I have and own is useful."

Claire intensively looked at Emma in her eyes with Emma returning the look. After a few uncomfortable seconds, Emma said:

"That's what I figured, at least."

"The schedule you are on here is tight. You know that, right?"

Emma imagined the question was rhetorical, so she did not answer.

"We have ten appointments together, one of which is gone already. In between the sessions, you have ten tasks to complete. There will be no more, nor will there be less, but that will be expected of you, should you want to gain something from all of this. The last session we have together will not be spent dealing with the list I've given you, but it needs to be finished before that."

"You have ten things to do, and two months to do them. Have you taken a look at the rest of the list?"

Emma then took a look at the list, only to notice just the second item say:

"Sell off, give away, or throw away five items of importance to you."

Claire interrupted her reading by saying:

"That's right. They will get harder and harder. Now, even the first one you've barely half-assed. It's not done yet, and you know it yourself as well."

All this time Claire had retained her professional calmness, even though her words cut hard and deep. Of course, Emma knew she had not managed to succeed in the first task. She needed more time for it.

"Another thing you need to understand," – Claire went on – "is that this therapy is not about me somehow healing you. It is about me helping you heal yourself. But that will not happen unless you are up to it."

"So, the question is, are you? If not, we should just call it quits right now, since wasting the time paid for by your employer will not only not help you, but also place you in unnecessary risk of having to pay for any extra appointments by yourself."

How could Emma say no? It felt like Claire was blackmailing her by giving her no good options.

"Yes, I am."

After a long, thoughtful look at Emma, Claire said:

"Very well. I seem to recall the last time we talked about your early life. Let's now pick up where we left off."

Emma had never imagined she would be working as a salesclerk at Costco. But there she was, in the warehouse in Eastern Harlem, working an evening shift. It was not just the third task in her list, which said "Find a new source of income," but Emma also found it to be a sincerely good idea. This way, she could kill two birds with one stone, since the fourth task would have her find a new way of saving money on everyday expenses.

Now, she had the advantage of earning an extra penny, plus she would be able to do shopping with some employee discounts after her shifts. The obvious disadvantage to all this was that she now had to spend time on two jobs instead of just one. In spite of that, she now discovered that she had actually found some excitement in her new challenges. She got to earn, save money, and find new people to mingle with all at the same time. She had always enjoyed meeting new people, after all.

After her shift, just as she was approaching the checkout with her groceries, she noted that her shift manager, Mrs. Johnson was working there. Since Emma was feeling particularly thrifty today, she decided to try out her new skills at haggling for even lower prices.

"Well, hello there Emma, ready to head home?" Mrs. Johnson, whose first name Emma could not remember greeted her as she began to beep up the groceries.

"Did you know that besides this side job, I've also been studying the art of negotiation. How about a deal on these groceries?"

Emma approached Mrs. Johnson quite boldly, especially since she had only been working there for two days and did not know her basically at all. Luckily, instead of being angry she seemed just amused.

"That's not something you get to hear every day around here. A deal on groceries? Very well, try me."

"Very well!" Emma cleared her throat and took a look at the items she had placed on the conveyer belt.

"See this carton of eggs here? I've studied the general price levels, and even with the employee discount, three dollars would be a more reasonable cost instead of three-fifty."

"I'm sorry dear, but that's a discounted price as set by the company. I cannot affect that." Mrs. Johnson chuckled as she kept on scanning the items.

"Ok. Let's say that's the price, then. How about you throw in this pack of napkins as well, for the same cost?"

Mrs. Johnson looked like she was holding in laughter.

"That's creative. But their price is set as well. Sorry, I cannot do anything about it either."

"You're a tough one to haggle with, I'll give you that." Emma smiled. Luckily for her, she had managed to break the ice and open up a conversation with one of her new bosses, and thus the conversation had not been for nothing. Mrs. Johnson just smiled, shaking her head slowly from one side to another.

Back at home, the results of Emma's attempts on her tasks number four and five could be seen. The piles of cardboard boxes were gone, but the place looked no emptier than before. Instead, the trinkets, clothes and other items were scattered all around the living area. The objectives given to her in therapy included tasks of saving money, obviously. In fact, in the tasks numbered four and five Claire had told her to find a way to spend less money on everyday things as well as to find a way to save a bigger sum of money in one go.

So, Emma had gotten hard at work. In the case of routine everyday savings, she had started to gather coupons with which to pay less for any purchases. For now, that had resulted in her buying small stuff more often than before, even though she paid less for them. As for the one bigger go at saving money, she had decided that she would arrange a garage sale later on to get rid of things she did not need while getting some of her money back.

The current state of affairs had her nervous, though. Not only because of her financial situation, but also since she was having a hard time relaxing in her home, which had now become far too chaotic to her taste, even though she knew it would not be permanent.

All in all, she had not yet managed to save a penny, and even her first paycheck from her new job was yet to come. She felt too busy to be concerned about it, however, for she had convinced herself that she was on the right path.

The next day at work Emma felt fatigued. Not only because of having two jobs, but also because the various projects she had set up for herself to save money took quite a lot of time out of her day and even nighttime sleep. Her position made it possible for her to work from home most of the time, however, there were days when it was mandatory for her to come to the office of GothamStrat Solutions. This was one of those days, with two face-to-face meetings to attend to with the entire marketing team she was a part of.

Now, in the break room, sipping coffee, she was dreading the thought of having to sit through those honest-to-God boring meetings. She had not gotten enough sleep, which made it worse, on top of which she felt a tingling sensation all around her ankles which made her want to scratch her feet all the time.

The sensation was not just of a mental source, but the socks she had knit for herself and was wearing today no doubt played their part in agonizing Emma. In fact, one of her more ambitious projects to save money had been an attempt at producing clothes for herself, either by knitting or simply by putting parts of old and partially worn-out apparel together. Unfortunately, these home-made socks were right now driving her crazy.

Not even being able to concentrate properly on what the others in the break room were discussing, she decided she needed to get another cup of coffee and went to pour one for herself. As she came back to the round table full of her coworkers and began to sit down, she quickly realized that the itchy socks were soon going to be the least of her problems.

As she sat down, a loud ripping voice sounded in her ears, and it clearly came from her. She blushed and kept her cool as well as she could as she observed the reactions of others. Amazingly, either the others genuinely could not hear the sound or pretended that they had not heard it.

Emma knew there were two possible options: either her shirt which she had sewn together had torn apart at her back or the same had happened to her old pantyhose she had fixed at home. As she discreetly took a look down at her feet while simultaneously feeling a cold breeze in her back, she understood both of those scenarios had occurred at the same time.

By now she remained convinced no one else had an idea of what had happened; they were far too absorbed in whatever discussions and chitchat were brewing in the break room at the moment. Emma had no idea what those were for she was far too shocked by her clothing literally falling apart on her.

Since she had been silent for a while now and no one was talking to her anyway, she bent down to pull up the sleeve of her pantyhose which had fallen apart and down her leg, attempting to somehow string it to the other end right above her kneecap in as much as secrecy as possible. After that, she casually stood up, walked over to the counter next to the dishwasher without exposing her back to the small crowd gathered at the table, placed down her cup of coffee, and walked slowly out of the room in sideways motion, all the while hoping her hosiery would not fall down her right leg again.

It all would have looked ridiculous had someone paid attention to Emma, but thankfully, no one seemed to notice a thing. As she rushed over to the office cubicle where she worked, the pantyhose sleeve fell down again. Since the office was as empty as always, she decided not to mind and simply took the broken pantyhose off in the cover of the open-space office cubicle and threw it in the trash. Then, she just put on her jacket to wear for the rest of the day.

In spite of the feeling of being an emotional wreck for having to wear clothes which literally tore down on her, she appeared calm on the outside. She would be able to make it through the rest of the day like that. She just needed to revise her strategy of saving money yet again as soon as she was done with the work for the day.

A few days later, after some time had flown by, it was already Thursday. That meant tomorrow would mark the third meeting with Claire. Emma felt completely disappointed. Every attempt she had made at changing her habits had somehow failed. Working a second job would only be a temporary solution and nothing that she could keep up doing indefinitely. It depressed her even further to think that instead of enjoying the weekend off, tomorrow she would have to head to Costco right after her day job.

She had not found a way to cut down on her daily expenses, either. Sure, she would pay closer attention to price tags, but it was not like she had managed to rid herself of the need to buy groceries. The garage sale was yet to come, and she did not even want to think back to her attempts at repairing old clothes.

Almost a month had gone by, and she had barely managed to scratch the surface of doing something with her financial skills. She felt utterly pathetic.

Then, just as she thought about simply spending the rest of her evening in front of social media and what television would have to offer, her phone rang. It was Lily, another employee of Costco whom she had exchanged numbers with.

"Hi Lily," Emma picked up.

"Hi! You on the evening shift tomorrow, too?"

"Yep, I am… not the whole eight hours, though. I'll be there as soon as I'm finished with my other work."

"Oh, that's right. Anyway, great news you'll be there. We're gonna have a great team there tomorrow. Friday evenings tend to stress me out, you know. Because it's not as smooth working with everyone as it is with some, as you may have noticed."

"Yes, I have," Emma laughed.

For the next ten minutes, Emma and Lily talked about their work and life in general. Even though she had not gotten to know everyone at her second job very well, Emma had noticed that working at retail the team she was with had an immense effect on how enjoyable the shifts ended up being. Working with Lily had been fun, and she generally liked her as a person.

After hanging up the phone, Emma felt better. Even if the totality of her situation had not faded completely from her mind, she came to conclusion that not all her efforts that week had been in vain. She had gained a new friend.

"The last two times we've talked a lot about your childhood. You see the pattern there, don't you?"

Claire's question confused Emma. Her expectations of the session had been that she would have to report on her progress to Claire, but as soon as she sat down, Claire had opened up with discussions about Emma's life back when she still lived with her parents.

"I… guess so?" Emma replied.

"You guess so?"

"Yes?" Emma said hesitantly, unsure whether she was making a statement or throwing the question back at Claire.

"The time we have spent here talking about your former life has all revolved around how poor and stingy your family was and how it affected your life."

"I agree. That is why I'm terrified my life will now become like that once again."

"Emma, I'm not a financial advisor, so I cannot help you directly with financial issues you're struggling with. I can, however, tell you that by changing your habits you will most likely avoid having to return to such conditions," Claire explained with a much warmer tone than before.

"I can also tell you that the main reason you are struggling now is overcompensation. You have gone from one extreme to another. In your fear of having to re-enter your childhood poverty, you've been continuously over-consuming. It really is that simple. I wouldn't be much of a therapist if I wasn't able to see it even though we've only sat down together three times now."

Emma remained quiet, letting Claire's words sink in. Before long, Claire went on:

"Now, that was the easy realization. The real challenge is in you being able to take a step back towards a more moderate level of spending."

"I always figured it was just the times we lived in. In my childhood, I mean," Emma said.

"In any case, I had never thought about it like that."

"Now that you do, does it make sense to you?"

"Yes. I mean, no, there is no sense in spending too much money, but the theory does make sense."

"Do you think that you are now a victim of the current times?"

"Well, the purchasing power has gone down incredibly fast in the recent years, and more and more people are struggling financially. So yes, of course those play a part in everything."

"And what might be the part that you can play? What sort of things around you can you try to enhance? I'm sorry to spoil the excitement, but that will be a task for you later on in the list as well."

"Everything else?"

"Don't ask me. It's something you need to find the answer to by yourself. Oh, and do remember – you should have completed the first half of the list by the next time we meet in one week."

Claire's rigid way of giving therapy made Emma feel as if she was in a boot camp.

Two days later, Emma had finally set up the garage sale she had been planning for. To be precise, it was technically not a garage sale, but she had simply set up a table outside her apartment. A small green patch right outside her building made the entire setting seem rather inviting, even if she said so herself.

There was plenty of stuff to sell, too. Most of it were clothes, but there were also plenty of home appliances and décor for sale as well. The small table she had in her kitchen was the only thing there that she did not plan on giving up. It was there only to help arrange rest of the stuff and could barely even hold everything she had brought for sale. Some of the stuff Emma had to simply keep inside the carton boxes. It was perhaps not the solution most pleasing to the eye, but it would have to do.

No one had yet stopped by to browse through her items, but it had been only 15 minutes, and she had prepared herself to stay there for the entire day, if need be. It was an urban and crowded area of New Jersey, which meant that there was continuous light traffic there. Therefore, Emma had not yet become discouraged.

Not before long, an old, bearded man stopped by to take a look at the wares Emma had set on the table. With a thoughtful look on his face he gazed at the items, turning his head slowly from left to right, and finally upwards so his eyes met Emma's.

"What's the story behind this, are you recently divorced?" the man inquired.

"Not at all," Emma replied with a smile on her face that made her feel phony.

"I have just been wanting to get rid of some of this stuff for a while now. I need to free up some room in my apartment."

"Is this some political climate change thing?"

"No! I just sincerely need to get rid of this stuff."

The man stood quiet for a while, after which he offered up to buy one of her artisan glass birds:

"Ten dollars for this?"

"Sold! Thank you."

The old man left with the glass bird which had been one of Emma's favorite ornaments at home. She had originally paid fifty dollars for it. But now, it just had to go, and Emma was glad she had managed to land at least one sale.

As an experience, each sale she would make turned out to be more valuable than she had thought. One hour passed, with a few people curiously slowing down next to the table to take a look at her wares, yet no one actually bought anything. Sales seemed to be slowing down. Soon, a young woman maybe a few years younger than Emma arrived at her table.

"This is so amazing. And look at that, so many clothes. Are these yours? I'm asking because we are even almost the same size."

Emma was surprised and even a little bit bothered by the woman's reaction, since it reminded her of her own reactions from time to time when she had been shopping for good deals. The young woman even looked a bit like her.

"Um, yes. They are all mine. All are for sale, have at it. And if you're interested in all of them, I am certain we may be able to negotiate a fair price for the bulk."

Around five minutes passed as she went through the items Emma had brought out for sale. Emma obviously had no room available for her to try the clothes on, but she had figured she would overcome this obstacle by simply offering prices that are low enough so the customers interested in them will risk buying them anyway. As this strange young woman measured the clothes with her eyes, she looked a bit disappointed not having a chance to fit them on her. Despite this, she kept going through the clothes one at a time.

"These are all in such a lovely shape. Even if they don't fit perfectly, I'll always find some use for them. In any case, I can always sell them out on the street like you do," she laughed and kept piling on clothes that she had taken an interest in.

Emma kept counting what went in the pile just so she would be able to give her a price just good enough so she would be able to rid herself of those clothes.

Finally, as the woman reached the end of Emma's table, she quickly glanced at all the other items Emma had brought out but showed no interest in them. Emma was excited, since the pile she was interested in was well more than half of what she had for sale. She figured she might be able to net 100 dollars, which would be a ridiculously low price for everything in there, yet low enough so the lady would end up buying everything.

"I'll take these," the woman announced. "And I have a proposal for you. 300 dollars for the entire stack of dresses and pants I have here."

Emma could not believe her ears. That was around the same cost she had initially paid for them back at the shop. Now, she had been offered the chance to erase the mistake she had made in buying all the excess apparel.

"Sold!" Emma stated.

"Well, that was hardly a tough negotiation," the young woman smiled.

"There you go."

"You need any help with those? I wasn't prepared with bags or anything."

"It's ok, I have a car just around the corner. Thanks!"

With surprisingly agile moves the woman grabbed the pile of clothing, walked away, and disappeared around the corner of the block.

Emma stood there with mixed feelings. First and foremost, she was happy. She had exceeded all the expectations she had for her garage sale and all she had left to sell now were some miscellaneous wares and trinkets she could now all unload on the table. On the other hand, she felt bad. She saw herself in the young woman whose name she did not even know. She had bought secondhand clothes from her without any fitting, meaning that it was not possible she would be completely pleased with everything she had bought. On top of that, she had paid the same price she would have had to at a retail store. Had Emma taken advantage of her?

The rest of the day went by slowly with only two customers who bought Christmas decorations from Emma. She had set the table up at ten o'clock and was now finishing up for the day at six. The vast majority of profit she had made had been from the young woman shopping for clothes, with the rest of the stuff not selling too well.

"Perhaps I could try setting up a table at a flea market, unless that's too expensive," Emma thought to herself.

As Emma arrived back at home and unloaded the items she had not managed to sell, she took a critical look around her. Apart from knowing that the wardrobe was now emptier, the place looked hardly tidier or cleaner than two weeks ago. Upon arranging her wares, she noticed she had hardly any room on the tabletops left for them. Most of the surfaces were filled with newer ornaments she had gotten at discounted prices from coupon clipping she had started a few weeks back as soon as Claire had urged her to find new ways to save money. The more she bought stuff at a discount, the more she would save, she figured.

Emma stuffed the various items inside the wardrobe which used to hold the clothes she had sold off today. The feelings of guilt for selling the clothes were gone, and she was starting to question whether she was seriously mentally ill herself.

It had been one month since Emma had started going to therapy because of her financial situation and spending habits, yet it felt like she had been going there forever now. The worst part of it was that despite all the hard work and efforts she had made, she had only gained very little from all of it. But as of right now, Emma had the feeling that she had thoroughly succeeded in changing one of her habits.

As she closed the lid on a plastic Tupperware box she had acquired she felt certain of it. She had begun food prepping as a way to save money and hopefully simultaneously eat healthier as well. She had done the math, and quickly realized that paying well more than ten dollars and a tip for a single meal in a restaurant was splurging, considering that a single home-made meal cost her only a few bucks.

She placed the box in her refrigerator next to many others she had prepared for herself. Finally, something with which to cut down on daily expenses! Emma was no cook, and the meals consisted mainly of vegetables, chicken, pasta, rice, and some occasional minced meat. Still, she rested assured she would get better at it over time.

She took a look at the first five items on the list of tasks she was supposed to complete. The first two ones – giving up on ten items she owned – were easily taken care of in the amazingly successful garage sale a few days back. With that, she could also cross the task of big one-time saving off her list. The food prepping she had just started gave her a way to save on daily expenses, and her side gig at Costco provided her with an additional way of increasing her income as well as with employee benefits when shopping there.

Things were starting to look better. She now stood ready to face Claire for the fourth time.

It took Emma by no surprise that Claire began their session by yet another different approach. This time they did no recap of their past meetings nor talking about the early life of Emma, but they delved straight into the tasks Emma had been given.

"In therapy, I always want to highlight the importance of the work done by the patient. Thinking from the perspective of the first five tasks, could you describe me what kind of ways have you found to change your life?"

So, Emma went on to tell Claire about her new job, describing the discounts she had access to because of it, while also telling her about the big success of the garage sale where she had sold even more than ten items that she owned. She did not neglect mentioning her failed attempts either, such as haggling for better prices at Costco checkout or coupon clipping which only resulted in her acquiring more worthless belongings than before.

"Which one of those do you think has been the greatest success so far?" Claire asked her.

Without much thinking Emma replied: "The garage sale was a huge success."

"Why so? Do you think you could repeat it as successfully as before?"

"I could do it again. How successful would I be? I don't know. The first time could have just been blind luck."

From the look Claire had on her face, Emma knew she disagreed. Even so, she replied simply: "Ok. And your second job? Do you think you will have the energy to keep doing it even after we will have finished with our sessions?"

"I haven't really thought about it that far. Maybe."

"I can see that you have identified some points which will help you to advance further in your life, yet I am still uncertain whether you have actually changed your daily habits. Have you in fact managed to steer clear from buying new things and how has that made you feel?"

"I've been so focused on doing these new things I don't think I have even had the time to consider it. In any case, buying new expensive things is not really an option for me anymore, either, since I have already maxed out my loans everywhere I know."

Claire sat there, pondering about Emma's situation. Then, she said:

"In that case, your daily habits are what we will be focusing on for the remainder of these sessions. You can forget about the original list of tasks; I will be giving you new ones instead."

"All in all, from now on I want you to make sure that your everyday life revolves around more frugal habits. Whether you will accomplish that by keeping yourself somehow busy or some other way is up to you. The ultimate goal for you, however, is to adapt to a completely new lifestyle."

"Sure thing," Emma replied. It all sincerely made sense to her.

"The first thing I need you to do is pretty technical. Take notes, now, you don't want to miss anything. Each payday, I want you to start by budgeting your income. Take care of the mandatory costs such as your rent, food, and utility bills first. Then, pay off your loans with as much as you can. Finally, set aside some money for savings. Then, and only then, budget whatever you have left for anything you might consider a leisure."

"The second task is, find a way to do everything you are doing right now by spending less money than before. Cut the costs on food, get a more affordable mobile phone service, commute less, and so on."

"Finally, give up on shopping. Don't consider it a hobby, but something you have been filling your days with, and as something you have tried to compensate with for the days of scarcity in your childhood and adolescence."

As Claire was speaking, Emma wrote what she said down on a piece of paper right after her five original tasks. While writing, she did not have the time to digest what she had heard just yet, so she just replied:

"Consider it done."

When Emma had been enlightened of her dire situation and started to seek help from her occupational health care services, the spring was about to end. Now, as the second half of her therapy rushed by, it was already summer, and the weather outside was warm and lovely. Once Emma had begun her therapy, she had become excited about it and the challenges offered by Claire and even her very detailed list of tasks.

Alas, her experience now got very different. The changes she had made no longer seemed to be as interesting as they used to, and even the tasks were no longer specific challenges to complete, but broad and rough. The current season did not help the situation, either. The warm evenings and nights were just inviting Emma to go outside and have fun with her friends, enjoying activities which by no means were suitable for her new, frugal way of life. Just after a little more than one month, her initial excitement of the therapy had blurred away.

Gradually, she stopped trying. At first, she could not find any new changes to do in her life. Then, she came to understand she had more important things to do than working a second job on the side. Finally, she started to slip towards buying new clothes for summer and heading out to bars for drinks. She could afford this by postponing payments on her loans wherever she was able to, just taking care of the interest payments instead.

The return back to her old normal was easy for her. After all, this was how she had lived for years now, and the last few weeks seemed simply just like an experiment that had passed now. Meetings with Claire became a necessity because she did not want to seem like a quitter. She simply stated that everything was like before, and that she was trying to adapt to her new lifestyle without revealing too many details. Most of the time in sessions with Claire they spent sparring about new ideas for her to execute to save some money in everyday life. The last few therapy sessions had become a theatre play to act out, nothing more. It all lasted for a good number of weeks until something happened.

Emma was certain she could remember it as clear as day for the rest of her life. It was Thursday. She had taken an hour off her marketing work at GothamStrat Solutions on the account of her therapy session. In the evening, she would still have to do a short shift at her second job at Costco. The time they had spent with Claire that day had gone like any other session before that – most of the first 45 minutes they had spent talking about different ideas on how to save money.

Even though Claire was not there to give her any kind of financial advice, at this point it would have been hard not to mistake some of the things she had been saying into anything else. The thing that struck Emma the most was when Claire started to talk about the effect of interest rates and high-interest debts overall had on Emma's life. Naturally, up until that point Emma had told nothing of her relapse back into her old ways. At that moment, however, Emma thought of the 1000-dollar credit card debt she had taken just the day before that. That was the number she had managed to save up and pay back at the start of the therapy, which she now had squandered in the blink of an eye.

As Emma was about to answer, her voice cracked. She produced a high-pitched tone which pictured the perfect mixture of sorrow and despair. Since she was about to begin by saying: "I…" from outside of the room it might have even sounded like a sudden shrieking sound. Then, she burst into tears. Claire – as stone-faced as ever – handed her a tissue, which was hardly enough for Emma to properly wipe her face.

After a while, even though she was still sobbing uncontrollably, Emma confessed to Claire her slipping back into her former ways of life. Looking back to it, it was hardly anything but a tangled mess of a story, yet the main idea could be understood from a few key words here and there. But for Emma, the most shameful part of the session was yet to come.

Before Claire had time to respond, and even as Emma had hardly gone quiet herself, she bounced up from the chair she had been sitting in, grabbed her purse, and ran out of the room and into the busy streets of Manhattan, still sobbing, with her face now bright red from all the shame and crying.

Emma's attempt to cure herself from relentless and constant shopping that she could not afford had failed. Now, a couple of weeks after her last meeting with Claire, she had sunken into depression – or what felt like one, at least. If feelings and actions could have been described with colors, her days were now gray. She woke up, went to work, came back home, and simply existed, wallowing in her pitiful state. She had not managed to gather enough strength to go do any extra work at Costco anymore, and sometimes on weekends even getting out of bed seemed like an impossible thing to accomplish.

All this had a bright side to it. Despite the initial shock and wave of emotions which followed right after, she had managed to do some introspection. She discovered that the worst feelings of depression had lately been subsiding, and she had planned out activities to do. The last time she met with Claire was her ninth therapy session, so there would still be one left that she was entitled to on behalf of her employer. Encouraged by that thought, she booked the final meeting with Claire one week from now. She knew she needed the closure.

The second thing she realized was that all these weeks she had been depressed her financial state had actually taken a turn for the better. She had only been doing the absolute minimum required of her. So, she had been working, paying off her bills and loans, and most importantly not been out shopping for more clothes and trinkets. She gloomily chuckled at the idea that perhaps living entirely passively like a zombie would be the answer to her situation.

Now it was weekend and Emma was visiting her sister Zoe who lived near her in Brooklyn. Her life seemed far more consistent than Emma's – as far as Emma knew, she had no debt besides mortgage, and had a well-paying job and a career in the financial district of Manhattan. Zoe was almost ten years older than Emma and lived with her daughter who was fifteen now. They had never been particularly close, so Emma did not have in-depth knowledge of the life of her sister, but judging from the looks of her life, she was still envious.

They had just finished a lovely dinner Zoe had prepared. Emma was slightly shocked and depressed as she caught herself thinking how lucky she was someone else was kind enough to offer her a warm meal which she did not have to pay for. After the usual dinner conversations and chatter about how everyone's life had been, Zoe left the table for a while to prepare dessert for them. It was a slightly uncomfortable moment for Emma, as Zoe's daughter Olivia was a typical teenager with whom it could be very awkward to talk with. As soon as Zoe left the room, Olivia went for her smartphone.

Despite not being good with children and teens, Emma decided to go for it, and asked Olivia what she planned on doing after finishing up high school.

"Not sure yet. College, maybe," she replied, not even lifting her eyes from her phone.

"Good, that's wise," Emma said, after which there was an uncomfortable silence.

After a while, she decided to try again:

"Got any plans for the rest of the weekend?"

Olivia took a quick look at Emma, smirked, and said:

"Off to do some shopping with my friends."

"Really? Where are you heading?"

"Bloomingdale's, probably. We'll see how much allowance Mom grants me this time. Gonna head out in any case."

This sounded just like the plans Emma used to have for years now, which sparked her interest even more:

"Wow. You do this often?"

"Pretty much every week."

At that moment, something in Emma's mind clicked. She knew what Olivia was talking about. It was the exact thing Emma struggled with.

"You know, you could try saving up some of that money instead."

Olivia looked at her as if she was insane, then went back to her phone. Emma decided not to give up so easily, but to try another approach.

"I used to do a lot of clothes shopping as well. Do you mind if I come and join you sometime? I promise you it won't be weird, and I'll be gone in a second if you want me to."

Olivia seemed to think about it for a while, then shrugged her shoulders, and said:

"Sure, fine."

Emma was genuinely thinking that perhaps that way she would be able to affect Olivia's behavior to make sure it would not get out of hand the way that it did with her. She had gotten all the practical tips from Claire, and even though they did not work out well with Emma, Olivia was a lot younger than she was, and thus easier to influence. Obviously, she should let Zoe know as well, although explaining the matter might turn out to be challenging.

The next week Emma arrived at Claire's reception well in advance. The patient before her was still inside, so she would have the time to think about how she would face Claire after the show she had put on the last time. Truth be told, her being ashamed had been the first and foremost reason she had avoided coming back here. On the other hand, she knew she was being ridiculous. In reality, it was not as if she would be required to answer and report back to her therapist in case she did not want to. Still, that was how she felt.

She thought about the last few months and what a rollercoaster they had been. She was 33 years old, and never before had she had that many upheavals in such a short amount of time. The last time she had been so depressed must have been when she was still going out with her ex-boyfriend, but that was whole another matter and story.

She had started with anxiety and hopelessness, then got quickly excited and put herself hard at work to produce a change in her life, only to fall back right where she started, with a slight aftertaste of depression as well. Right now, she felt stale and tired. She did not know if she had the strength to keep leading the change in her life. She struggled there, too. She did now know whether to tell Claire of her thoughts or not.

She was certain she did not want to go through all that negativity again. She was too afraid of the possible consequences of either drastically falling back into her old ways as a method of overcompensation, or alternatively sinking back deep into depression. She knew she had managed to get several things correct the first time as well, though.

Even though working at Costco was not something she would be doing for years to come, the idea of getting a side hustle had proven to be something well worth sticking with. Especially since it was a great way to make new friends and connections. Food prepping had also been a success. While she did it, she had been able to save a significant amount of money from her restaurant and grocery costs. Finally, managing to identify the possibly risky behavior of her niece was something she was even a little proud of, even if she would not be able to influence a change in Olivia.

Just as she had finished that thought, the door to Claire's office opened, and an elderly man stepped out. He closed the door behind him and left. Emma wondered what he must have been seeing Claire for. Obviously, she was not the only one with issues in controlling her spending, and at the root of it all could very well have been a psychological issue for someone else as well. Then again, in the case of that old man, him visiting Claire could have been about any other thing as well.

She knew these thoughts were all about simply evading the inevitable of having to face Claire soon while still not sure of what to tell her. She also knew that in theory one should feel free to let their therapist know everything without any doubts, and that would have only positive outcomes. In practice, it was not as simple and Emma certainly knew that there would be wisdom in not letting her know everything she was thinking, especially since this would be the last time they were going to meet, anyway.

Perhaps she would only tell her what was absolutely required of her: about the spectacle she caused by storming out the last time they were in session, and then a few vague truths about her life right now. Of course, she could also add in something about the feelings she had been going through. And the successes she had scored.

The door opened, and Emma saw Claire was standing there in the doorway.

"Emma! Welcome back. Come on in."

Emma stepped inside Claire's office.

DIARY OF A MILLIONAIRE

SEPTEMBER 7ʰ, 2023

I'm exhausted. Not unlike any other days, though this time it's worse. It used to be you could just work the best you could, and the word would spread, and bingo, thus you have customers. But no, nowadays you need to take care of marketing – especially social media – by yourself to be able to attract anyone. It's either that or hiring someone else to do the marketing for you, and that will eliminate all the margin from your business.

The day at the shop wasn't that bad. The same handiwork as always. But having to keep going with this after getting home and barely saying hi to the family is too much. It is now one in the middle of the night, and I have to get up in five hours. I just sent the last email for today. I can't keep going like this. If I hadn't gotten the authority over myself by quitting my day job at the factory, I would go rushing back there in a second.

At least the kids are doing great. As far as I know, that is. Now their hobbies have become at least slightly more affordable for us. That makes this all worth it, right?

If the government didn't rob the fruits of my labor, I would be a millionaire. Seriously, I am now doing the math in my head, and I would be earning a million in a few years being an entrepreneur if it wasn't for the ridiculously overpriced taxation and other governmental costs. It is insane.

But hey, this has only been going for a few months now, and the bigger prizes are still on their way, should I succeed. Maybe writing my thoughts down starting from now will help me clear my head to remember why and for who I am doing all this. Just a few years, then we'll be done with the mortgage. Or I'll be done with the mortgage, it's not like Gladys has one. She'll look after the kids during the days.

Just a few years, then we'll get back to more normal life as a family.

SEPTEMBER 8th, 2023

Friday! Party! Yeah, right! Actually, maybe it's party time in a way, even for an entrepreneur. Tonight, I got home at eight and managed to wind down for a while. Tomorrow I'll work only six hours, call it quits a little earlier, then head home for an evening with the family. If all goes well, Sunday will be completely off duty for me. That is, if the old Ford of that one client doesn't give me any trouble tomorrow after I've popped the hood.

I originally designed these writings to be a way to unburden myself from the stress that work gave me. But tonight, coming home just to receive a huge load of nagging from the wife and screaming from the kids was even more stressful. Since it all ended up being because of trivial reasons, at least everything calmed down. For now.

Of course, I would not trade my family for anything. I love them all. They are also the biggest reason for me to do this hard work and the long days that come with it. I can't dream of a much bigger glory than that right now.

Tomorrow will probably include playing board games with the kids or watching TV with them. A better-than-average dinner, too. A beer or two. Perhaps something just for me and Gladys after the kids have gone to bed… that is, once I get off work. We should be heading to Mark's theatre play on Sunday, and after that, there are no plans for the rest of the day – thank God.

As I am writing this, I am thinking of trying to take a weekend off, maybe a few weeks from now. With the family, perhaps, but with my old friends from the previous job, even better. We'll see. The problem is that every weekend (or any other day as well) I take off also drives me away from my goals by that one day, and I wouldn't want to hinder those plans. But everyone needs a day off from both work and family from time to time, right?

SEPTEMBER 11th, 2023

I'VE WON! I'VE WON!!! TEN MILLION, BABY!!!

SEPTEMBER 12th, 2023

I CANNOT BELIEVE I WENT TO WORK YESTERDAY! I did a WHOLE DAY before finding out I won!!

OK now, I know I need to calm down. And I have – in fact – considering that it's only been one day since I found out I won BIG on the Saturday drawing. Even after taxes, I will be able to keep well over seven million from the winnings. Actually, I stand corrected: we will be able to keep them. This money will ensure a good and well-balanced life for my whole family and allow me to never have to work again. Gladys wasn't working in the first place, so we're all good in that front, too.

This does NOT mean we can go crazy with money, now, though. Today went by real fast, I think we both needed the time to digest this piece of news. The kids don't even know yet, and they won't need to know, either. They're not that old yet.

Today I stayed at home and just basically thought about the situation. I was too ecstatic to go to work to finish anything up. But since I want to do this cleverly, tomorrow I will head to the workshop the first thing in the morning, finish up with the rest of the jobs I have there, and then close the place for good. Assuming I get the cars in shape by tomorrow, I will be able to start closing down the day after. I want to do it in a classy way, not stupid. It's not like we can go insane with this amount of money, either.

Gladys was speaking of us taking a vacation and a trip with the money. I guess that's fine, but not the first thing we need to be doing right now. That will be the first trip we take as a family of four, after all. I do need to get her to understand the plan of not wasting too much money. We need to invest a hefty amount to secure a wealthy future for us. Use what's needed to pay off the mortgage and other loans, too.

But that's enough of writing for now. I anticipate tomorrow and the next few days are going to be quite busy.

SEPTEMBER 13th, 2023

It all went even better than I anticipated. I managed to take care of the unfinished jobs – well, almost all of them. But I will not be going back to work tomorrow. I don't need to! I'm a millionaire! I'll just pay for someone to go there instead and terminate the rental contract for the place. I'm not the least bit worried about closing down – not a bit!

What annoyed me today, however, was my beloved wife. I arrived home just to notice that she had been ordering stuff online with our joint credit card. I mean A LOT of stuff, worth of a couple of thousand dollars. I got mad at first, but then agreed with her that we could afford it, since things like a new television are nice to have now that we can. The thing is, she should have consulted me before doing any decisions. It was me who won the money for us, after all.

I just also finished sending a message to my bank about wanting to take care of the rest of my mortgage. It felt good, but it will feel even better once I see the debt cleared off my name in the statement on the screen whenever I log in to the banking services. Speaking of which – we need to figure out if we need a personal banking expert or a financial advisor now. After all, investing wisely with this much money is of utmost importance. I wouldn't trust a commoner such as myself to take care of it all by ourselves.

I have yet to decide if I want to tell the news to my friends or the rest of my family, such as my parents. I've heard stories of people completely changing or even turning against their former friends or relatives because of them becoming rich. Well, I guess I should let my parents know eventually. As for the friends… maybe I'll just enjoy a glass of whiskey now instead of going to meet them at the local pub just yet and let this all sink in properly at first.

Taxation is truly evil. I know we are still rich, but having to pay millions to the government just for winning Powerball is just disgusting, considering the way that money gets spent and that I have been paying a ridiculous amount of taxes all my life already. That is probably the only thing right now that feels unjust about all of this.

SEPTEMBER 14th, 2023

I'm feeling terrible. The glass of whiskey turned into another, and a third, until the whole bottle was gone. The wife was mad too, having to take the children to daycare all by herself. What does she have to complain about? I'm the winner, not her. She isn't even working! To be honest, I don't even know why we are paying for the daycare at all. I guess she has that same headache every day, which forces her to just lay down and not do a goddamn thing around here. She really should pull herself together.

She is not the only one, though. I need to get my shit together as well. I know it's been only five days, but it's about time I got something constructive done. I still need to empty the garage I rented to use as a workshop. Also need to check to see if my mortgage got taken care of by the bank. Then there's the investing plan to devise, too. But that's for tomorrow, since right now I feel like I am going to puke.

I really am worried about Gladys, though. She is acting as if it was her who won, not me. She has been reckless before, like that one time she used up all the allowance on her credit card to buy shoes or some other stupid stuff I can't even remember anymore. She could turn reckless again, but I won't have it, not with this much at stake. I need to set up a plan and we both need to follow it, including her.

I know just what I need: a celebration, just the way I thought of having it even before all of this. Just with friends, no family. Maybe even a little trip, if those poor bastards can afford one, hah! Hell yes, that's what I'll do.

Still feeling terrible, though. Hopefully it'll be better tomorrow, so I'll get around to planning all that there is to take care of. I remember taking a drink used to help me overcome hangovers in my youth, as long as it's done with great care, and not overblown. Perhaps I'll try that now, just so that I'll be in better shape and be able to perform tomorrow.

SEPTEMBER 17*th*, 2023

Took me but three days, but now I'm feeling better. Still drunk, though. I am dreading what tomorrow is going to be like. I no longer am the young man I used to be, drinking for several days in a row. But hey, I am a lottery winner now! I am entitled to celebrate and to have fun.

The wife's been getting on my nerves. She is nagging me about closing the business down and wanting to buy more crap. This day and the day before were filled with us fighting, and she better learn to respect me and the fact that this is MY money, not hers. I will of course handsomely take care of her, and that should be enough, but no. Up until this day the thought had not even crossed my mind, but today it dawned on me that I may just be able to get a better, younger wife now, too. She'd better realize that as well.

But enough about her. The truth is, I am pissed off at myself, too for not taking care of the shop. I just sort of forgot about it all once I began drinking, and especially once I headed out with all my friends. They were flabbergasted by how I wanted to keep buying all of them one round after another, but that's all the hints I am going to give them about my life now! I most definitely don't want no beggars behind my front door nor pestering me on phone either.

In any case, I really need to get to work now in proceeding with closing down the business. It is a ridiculous thought, really… having to get to work as a millionaire. But a man's gotta do what a man's gotta do. Plus, just keeping paying the bills for the rent and not selling all the equipment would be a stupid way to squander money. The plan is not to go broke despite winning the lottery, but to save my life with the money.

Speaking of the plan, which is something I have been trying to figure out recently, as well. The first stage is getting rid of the old life: the work, the duties outside of family life, and all the other annoyances. The second stage is saving a part of the money and investing it cleverly. The third stage is defining a budget with which to live by. In these I might need some outside help from an expert.

I don't know if it's still the liquor talking, but I have also been wondering if I should see a psychologist. I have no idea how to feel about all of this. At first, I was ecstatic, and now, it's been fun, but still very much like everyday life. If this turns into constant fighting it's going to become annoying as hell. I should feel glad, happy, optimistic, and positive right? Then why am I not feeling like that?

The night out with my friends turned out to be depressing in the end. Miserable old shits whining about their lives, and meanwhile I am unable to tell them about the happiness that's been given me. Even alcohol didn't make it better, it was as if I just skipped right past the phase of getting drunk and ended up with a hangover straight away. In that condition, who cares about Mark whining about his motorcycle being toast? I mean really, who cares? I know I don't.

As I am writing this, I am feeling the hangover starting to creep up on me. Again. Once that happens, I know I will be unable to do any proper soul searching – let alone the duties required to exit my old life to enter the glorious stages two and three in my plan.

The last note I will make this time is that I haven't seen my kids the entire weekend and that makes me sad. I did not want them to see their dad wasted, of which I am truly ashamed of. Even if Gladys didn't start to act in a way she should in order to deserve a life with me, the kids most certainly will still have me in their life, and I swear I will make life better for them. I will not let them down. In fact, I'll begin right now by transferring 10k to their savings account. That's 5k for each of them. That's a start.

Once that is done, I will head to bed to sleep and wake up sober tomorrow. Should everything fall perfectly in place, I will make up with Gladys, say hi to my son and my daughter, and then head to work to finish up with everything. It is just for a day or two, and then it will all be better. Besides, what a great day that would be.

I felt awful once I began writing this, but I am feeling better now. Tomorrow is also going to be a better day for sure. I'll make it a great and productive day.

SEPTEMBER 19th, 2023

The last day at the office was alright. I'm now done with the lease and don't own the equipment anymore. I know this one guy who was supposed to come and pick it all up and buy it for himself, but surprise, surprise, he offered me peanuts. Since I can now afford to say "fuck you" whenever there is someone deserving of it, I will, and now, I did. It felt good to tell the workshop to go fuck itself. I was of course pissed off because of this and the family did not take it well. Told them to go fuck themselves too – in my head, that is – and headed straight to the bar.

At least I'm not hungover now, but feeling pretty good actually, considering that the wife and the kids will need some appeasing. I think I will go and find that financial guru for me after that, it is about time I invested a part of the money to start earning some of them dividends. After that, I'll just need to figure out what to do with the rest of my time. The kids will be hard to spend time with, since they'll be at school. But I certainly need to come up with something, or alternatively send Gladys off to work instead of me, haha!

If my friends were not so up to their ears with their jobs, perhaps I might do something with them. Unless they are my former friends now, that is. In which case I would have to find some new ones. Maybe I'll take up golfing and try to find some new buddies there, who knows?

Alright then, I just went out to the kitchen and had to come back to write this one last thing down. Gladys just told me she thinks I owe half of my winnings to her. At first, I laughed at her, but now I'm furious. Who does she think she is? The cow thinks she's entitled to something? She's entitled to shit. This time I told her to fuck off to her face and stormed out. Seems I am heading back to the bar again. Cheers!

SEPTEMBER 20th, 2023

This is it. I need to and I am going to stop drinking. My life is going to hell if winning a single lottery is enough to throw me so completely off track. I think it did the same for Gladys as well, since she hasn't been the same as before either. The difference between us is that she is acting stark raving mad for someone who didn't even win but is just simply close to someone who did. I, on the other hand, have every reason to have difficulties getting adjusted to this new life. Especially with her dragging me down now with these outbursts of emotion.

I am going to help myself and the both of us by setting some distance in between us. We need to cool ourselves down before having any big talks about our future. I just booked a two-week long vacation for myself to Hawaii. I simply have to get out of here for a while, and it will do good for her too, and help her to clear her head. Too bad I cannot have a buddy there with me, but they all have to work. I guess it's a good thing I'm not too bad at making new friends.

Two weeks of sunshine, warmth, relaxation, and sobriety sounds great to me. For now, it's aloha!

OCTOBER 5th, 2023

Charlie's back! And guess what? No, nothing is better now. Upon entering the door, Gladys started screaming at me, and that's all she does now. Apparently, she didn't get the note I left and thought something had happened to me. Too bad, her behavior is still completely unjustified. Whenever she sees me, she now begins to scream and actually broke some of my things when I came back. Lovely. I had to take the kids to my parent's place. They should not see their mother acting like that, it simply cannot be healthy for them.

Apart from that, the trip was absolutely fantastic and just what I needed! No alcohol, just sunny beaches, warmth, and rest. Got to know some locals too and partied A LOT, hell yeah! Apparently, the clichés of Hawaiians being relaxed turned out to be true, even though they're a democrat state, can you believe that?

Not to turn this into a holiday diary, but my typical days consisted of sleeping in, enjoying a huge buffet breakfast, sipping down drinks at the beach or at the pool, eating some more, and just chatting with people. Oh, and partying every night. Met some great people, too, but I'd better skip the nasty details here.

The most fantastic part about all this was not having to stand all the fighting and stress of everyday life – obviously. But besides that, I've never been on a holiday during which I did not have to worry about money at all. Can you imagine the things you can do when there is no budget to follow? Before this, neither could I. I spent a crap-load of dollars there, but it was all so worth it I would do it all again in the blink of an eye.

Oh, and need I say anything about the weather? I don't think so. Just that here it is cloudy and raining. Just like what my mood is slowly but surely becoming like, too. I'm still happy, but afraid that the everyday life will take that away from me soon. In fact, even though I love my family, I don't know how to go on from here. I would not want to spend a second in the house with my wife right now.

For now, she is shouting and screaming and threatening to destroy my belongings and kick me out. Yeah right, she'll calm down. This is all her fault in any case, and I won't let her drag me down with her.

OCTOBER 19th, 2023

Things have been calmer now. There is no fighting when neither side is talking to the other one, you know? But it's all good, and I prefer this to that constant fighting and screaming. I have enough on my plate already as is without exterior interruptions and harassment like that.

Even though the weather here is horrible when compared to Hawaii, what I picked up from there is that we humans are made to party. I have been doing that here at home as well ever since coming back, because why not? I've met some cool new people in the local nightclubs I have been frequenting. The drunk, miserable old men I used to hang out with have thankfully disappeared from my life, and I don't miss them at all.

The guys I met last weekend, for instance, are just awesome. Jean and Jacques. It's rare that an older guy like me makes new friends with younger people, but it's really a pleasure to hang out with people who have great business ideas, similar values, and overall love to party hard. Truth be told, I am quite certain that they may be a gay couple – something I am totally not into. But hey, who am I to judge? They have a positive vibe in their overall life and that is what counts.

That is one of the things I have totally been looking into the last few weeks: finding new, better people to hang out with. I came to realize that I must have been lacking success simply because there has been no success around me. With better new contacts, I will have a whole new world of potential, options, and opportunities opening up to me.

Speaking of which, I wonder whether my family, or my wife at least falls into that category of low-quality people. Not talking to her has been great, but it could also be one of the first signs of an impending break-up and divorce. Which reminds me of the importance of trying to protect my assets now that I am rich. I for sure will not want her to have half of MY winnings.

Who knows, maybe I should try talking to Jean and Jacques about my family situation to exchange some ideas. They may have some insight into situations like these that I don't have. I am also afraid that she might turn violent. Her throwing things must have been a warning sign that something like that might happen in the future.

OCTOBER 21ˢᵗ, 2023

Went out to the club the other night. I forgot to mention I now have "the club" of my own. The owner of one of the fancier nightclubs here heard about me and my friends having wealth, and since we have generally been spending quite handsomely while at his place, he generously offered a prestigious private lounge area of his nightclub for us to enjoy. Think about that. It seems so silly how I have been bothered by little troubles at home, seeing how great my life is in every other way.

Met Jean, Jacques, and a couple of other guys there, too. I could not help opening up to them about my situation back at home, and they had plenty of advice to give me. We actually talked about the whole mess for quite a while. To cut long story short, they told me to be very careful and to try to avoid getting a divorce for as long as I did not have a proper prenup – and preferably even then not get a divorce. I should probably get some legal advice, considering that Gladys may already have something going on behind my back. Thankfully, the guys know a great lawyer I am planning to get in touch with. So, oh my dear diary, should I get divorced or not? That's the problem.

Considering that the whole divorce scenario revolves around monetary risks, we talked about finances as well. Jacques is actually quite a miracle maker in many ways, and he had a guy to recommend for investing advice. I will get around to that shortly as well, at latest as soon as I am done with consulting the lawyer.

That is what I basically am nowadays – a rich guy discussing important matters with some other significant people. I used to just go out and get drunk, but we hardly even drink alcohol anymore. Sure, we may enjoy some euphoria of intoxication every now and then just as any other man, but that's a story for another day.

Right now, I have three things to do:

1) Get in touch with the lawyer.
2) Get in touch with the investment advisor.
3) Hell, I might even give up alcohol. Why would I need it anymore? There is no need for me to escape the reality any more…

OCTOBER 23rd, 2023

I can see I wrote up my list of three tasks a few lines up! It's been two days now and I got around to doing those. Let's recap how they went.

I called the lawyer the guys recommended. At first it seemed to be all good, he was a pro with 20+ years of experience. His name was Michael, and I discussed our situation first on the phone two days ago and met with him at his office just yesterday. He wanted to clarify that the whole situation was as I had described, and he did not misunderstand anything. Turned out to be a real slimy guy. We spent three hours revolving around the subject, and most of the questions he asked me were simply stupid. Like for example, what have the details of Gladys' hobbies got to do with anything? I get that her habits of spending money may be important in a divorce battle, but as we neared the end of our meeting, Michael did not forget to remind me that this first consultation was not free of charge.

In the end, we agreed not to do anything, but he is still insisting on billing me! Over my dead body, I told him, and left. What a crook. Let him try; I'll make sure the guys won't be hearing the end of my feedback about their recommendations any time soon, either. Right after leaving his office, I went almost straight to the financial advisor recommended by Jacques.

Thankfully, that turned out to be a better deal. I will be handing a great deal of my new-found wealth to him to invest in various assets in my to-be portfolio. Not blindly, of course, for there will be contractual disclosures in case of him or his company trying to rob me of my money. He will take a small fee for the service – naturally – but it's not like I can't afford it. What I can't afford are guys like that Michael character was, a pure cheater. Still, I do need to find some legal counsel. I cannot just let Gladys drag me down with her as she decides to trip over and land belly-up on the ground.

As for the drinking part, I've been alcohol-free for two days now. Woohoo! I would rather just opt for stimulants and nothing that is even associated with alcohol, which is truly some vile stuff. Speaking of which, I think I should be heading back out to the club soon to get some more of the good stuff the boys have in store over there.

OCTOBER 26th, 2023

It's been one hell of a week, I must say. Even though I've hung out at the club every single night up until tonight, it's been like putting money in the bank. My investments made by Mike – yes, that was his name I had forgotten already – are rolling and growing in value. I wish I had taken care of that even earlier.

Like this, I am safe and secure to live as I please. No matter what I do, I will just keep earning more money!

And damn what a time it is I've been having. I cannot remember even the days of my youth being this wild. To imagine that this all happened in my forties instead of my teen years or twenties. I get to play a dad in the daytime and party like madman in the nighttime. There has not been much time to sleep in between, but hey, I am feeling great. It's like I don't even need sleep anymore. It is almost the other way around: I have been having a hard time getting any sleep after a night at the club.

Well, that's not just because of chemicals. The other thing that has been keeping me up has been Gladys. It has been the worst week of our marriage by far. Every day I have seen her has been full of constant screaming, and she is again threatening to throw stuff at me, and speaking of taking the kids away, too. I'll show her.

But she is right, of course. We cannot keep living like this. She either has to calm down or one of us has to go. I will suggest she choose the first option. Maybe then I can talk some sense into her. It's not like I've started these arguments so I obviously cannot end them by myself. Nevertheless, I shall remain stoic and do my part to tame her. Otherwise, there is the looming risk of a divorce in the air as well.

I'll take tonight off from my new life and stay home. Take care of the kids first because that is what a good father does, and then have that talk with Gladys. One of us has to act like a grown up, so let it be me in this case.

OCTOBER 27th, 2023

Had an AWESOME party at the club last night. It was absolutely insane. Have you ever taken a drink of alcohol by first pouring it in between and straight through the buttocks of a striptease artist? Well, neither have I – since I don't drink alcohol anymore! Something else, perhaps… but now I've seen the trick done, too. Like I said: absolutely insane. Took me until eight in the morning until I made it back home. Thankfully it was silent as everyone else had gone to school or somewhere else. Who knows where Gladys had gone.

Last night was actually so awesome I am heading back there in a while. It is now almost nine o'clock in the evening, got some sleep in between and now I am ready to roll again. I am expecting nothing less than what last night was like. After winning the Powerball, I may have become a millionaire, but now I am finally feeling and living like one. All that we are lacking is a limousine. Which makes me think why on earth have we not thought about that one yet. I really have to let Jean and Jacques know that from now on I will be arranging a limo for us.

The talk with Gladys did not go well. The thing I am glad about is that I managed to remain at home for the rest of the evening that night. Other than that, it all went badly. She just would not stop screaming and shouting at me, you know. She is claiming that I am irresponsible, wasteful, selfish, and a horrible father and a husband. Of course, the message gets a bit blurry as she is constantly just shrieking out loud for as long as I am there.

Well, like everything, I managed to solve it too. After more than one week of listening to her high volumes, I gave her a fair, open-palm slap in the face. Not too hard to seriously hurt her, but hard enough to make her cheeks turn red. That shut her up well enough to allow for us to have a talk. Or to allow us to try it, at least, since she after that would not say anything anymore. Whatever, her loss.

I don't know if it is because I am such a great storyteller or a problem solver since the guys completely cracked up as I told them about it. All the troubles and fear mongering about a potential divorce were long gone as well. Them being high as a kite might have had something to do with it, too.

OCTOBER 28*th*, 2023

The awesomeness just won't stop. I had the craziest dream last night. Or actually, it was this morning as I was getting back home. In fact, it felt more like a hallucination rather than a dream. As I stepped inside, I dreamt of Gladys bitching at me once again, but this time instead of being pissed off I felt GREAT. The mirth just wouldn't stop, and everything was hilarious, even her reaction. I can remember continuously slapping her to make her go quiet again, while laughing all the time. It was as if I was using a clenched fist, too.

What a weird vision. I just woke up, and I am convinced that I heard some noise coming from downstairs. But there was nobody there. Made me feel anxious, which I dislike. Like right now, my phone just rang, and I didn't want to answer it just yet, so it just kept ringing for ages, for one hour, at least. Or perhaps it was just ringing in my ears. For years I've heard the sayings and teachings of how drugs are bad. Could this be it?

Shit's ridiculous. I could hardly even find anything to eat in this place. Just had a bowl of cereal with milk because I could find nothing else in the kitchen. I am not feeling particularly hungry anyway, though. Perhaps a little pick-me-up is all I need right now, or maybe just a cup of coffee. I realized I had not even planned what to do later today. Heading to the club seems like an automation now, not even like a spontaneous idea. Hell, as soon as I am not feeling so nauseated anymore, why not?

You know, this is also the first in a long time when I don't have too many recollections of what happened last night. That is strange, especially considering that I have erased alcohol from my life. Unless I had some last night and just can't remember any of it. Which would be terrible; I am not a hobo, am I?

Tonight, I will stay 100 % sober from start to finish, even if I decided to head out. I swear. Life like this will kill you, you know? But for now, I need to grab something to eat. If not at home, then at a restaurant.

I just can't shake the nagging feeling that I am forgetting something important. Must've been nothing too special, since I've forgotten about it already, right?

OCTOBER 30*th*, 2023

Today I understood why the place was empty the other day and why I have got to enjoy life all by myself. After two days, Gladys showed back up. She came early in the morning, and I was somewhat asleep when she woke me up by trying to sneak up to get to some of her stuff in the bedroom.

It was confusing at first, really. Having just woken up, I was feeling groggy, and she just kept whispering as if she did not want me to wake up at all, not realizing I had awoken already. After that, she just told me to stay away. Still halfway out of this world, all I could think of to say was: "Pardon?". How stupid and absurd is that?

To nobody's surprise, it didn't take her that long to start screaming at me again. Unlike the last time, however, this time she was absolutely hysterical. After a while, I just lost it and let her have it. She tried to strike but was not quick enough, so I hit her back hard enough so she would not try that again. If I am that lousy wife-beater now, then why am I not feeling the slightest bit ashamed? Maybe because she had it coming?

This does solve the mystery of her disappearance, though. Apparently, the last time I came home was not a dream, I think, and she kidnapped the children and left. Seems like she forgot some of her stuff back here. That's in how much of a rush they were to get away from their husband and dad. Sounds ridiculous, doesn't it? I thought so, too. From now on, she can do as she please, I don't care. But the kids I want back. I will fight for them, even in the court if need be.

Nope, not feeling remorseful, even though I try to. The fact is that she is the one who has been dragging me down ever since my winning of the Powerball. She is the one who wanted to stand in the way of our dreams, not me. Now let her weep in the streets for all I care. I will rescue my children back from her clutches, even if that's the last thing I'll do.

But the first thing I'll do is try to get some sleep before tonight. Gonna be a big night at the club, and oh yes, I most definitely will report back to Jean and Jacques about this mad stuff at home. We'll set up a plan for the divorce lawyer as well then, together. What a crazy world it is that we live in, right?

OCTOBER 31ˢᵗ, 2023

My mouth and my throat are hurting from all the laughing. Jacques told a ridiculous story of his other friend who is sheepishly working a nine to five job and struggling with his interest rates and inflation. Of course, as soon as Jacques gave him any advice about how to make his life better, he would just crawl back up in his shell and continue with his regular life and job. No balls, no gains. Oh well, I guess it was funnier the way Jacques told it last night while making these imitations of the dude.

What made the guys as well as myself crack up was also how I described my situation back at home to them. Gladys' whimpering was just what ridiculous. Joking aside, though. The situation is quite serious, and they could not take it seriously enough. I will not be falling for another scammer like the one Jacques recommended to me earlier, but I do in any case need a lawyer. I shall dedicate today to browsing for a new one. It shouldn't be too hard since it's not like I have a shortage of cash.

Another thing I will have to do today is that I need to find out how my investments are doing. I haven't been in touch with my consultant for a while and need a status update. It is weird they have no internet service to see the state of my investments and funds in real time. I'll just give the man a call. Now that I think of it, that is probably the thing I have thought I might have forgotten about. It's a good thing I figured that out now.

I have also been thinking about how to explain my situation to the lawyer. Maybe I'll just briefly tell him that I will be ending up in a situation where a divorce will be imminent, and that there will most likely be problems with custody issues as well. Thinking about any further specifics got me thinking about if I could actually be the bad guy here? But no, not really. Thinking about how Gladys acted up before all of this, yes, it's definitely her fault.

Whoever that will be – I'll just tell the lawyer the brief version of everything.

NOVEMBER 1st, 2023

It just hit me that I might actually be a lousy father and I might never see my kids again. I miss my family. Even though she can be difficult, me and Gladys, we did have some good times. Most of all, I had a family here at home with me. Now, I am alone, and the isolation is starting to gnaw at me. I may have had a reason to get mad, but this is not what I wanted.

Today I just remembered what I had forgotten about. Just last week I was supposed to take the kids to the school theatre. Patrick was performing there, and Alice was supposed to go to the audience just to watch. I forgot about it all, must have slept through it entirely. Maybe that was what Gladys was also screaming about? I am not sure, but I am feeling so terrible words cannot describe it. Maybe it was that day I slapped her in the face?

Is there coming back from any of this? Have I lost them for good? I haven't heard from them ever since I saw Gladys the last time.

It is like a terrible pressure in the back of my head – both squeezing and banging at the same time. I cannot even cry because I'm afraid my head might explode, I just can't…

NOVEMBER 2*nd*, 2023

Nope, still cannot write. I will just lay down and wait for the inevitable. Or perhaps I'll end it all by myself before that.

NOVEMBER 3*rd*, 2023

So today I grabbed myself by the balls and got some things done. For the first time in a while, I woke up reasonably early in the morning, had some breakfast and a cup of coffee, and headed out to meet a prospective divorce attorney. Even though I have not heard of Gladys, by now it is obvious what is coming, so I might as well be prepared. There was no way I would have been able to take care of this sober, but getting things done is something, at least.

After a quick web search, I found this guy called Alexander Stone of Stone & Associates law firm. Despite the peculiar name, he turned out to be quite professional. We talked about my situation, and he straight up told me he is going to be honest and told me the odds are not too good. He did tell me, however, that he might have a few tricks up his sleeve concerning the erratic behavior of my spouse. That could help balance the odds even without a prenup.

He also told me to stay off drugs and alcohol, which annoyed me at first – it's not like I'm visiting a lifestyle coach here. But then again, now that I think about it, noticing such things about a client also speaks volumes about the experience this guy has. I will be assigning him to the case as soon I get the papers served.

Since my life is apparently a total rollercoaster now, no way could I have gotten only good news in a single day. When I got back home, I had received a letter from that scammer Michael. He is demanding me to pay 10 000 $ for his consultation that one day. The guy is obviously a thief. I will not be responding to him and threw the invoice away already. Jacques will not be hearing the end of this for a while once I get started on telling him about his 'wonderful' recommendation for a lawyer…

Nevertheless, I will be making sure that I have some money at my disposal. Even though this Michael character will not be getting a penny from me, my new attorney will be expecting to get paid at some point. Even though I will do all I can to make sure Gladys gets to pay for him as well, you can never be too prepared for anything.

NOVEMBER 4th, 2023

Ok, so today was a weird day. It seems I hardly have any other kinds of days anymore. Alexander asked me to secure a part of his payment up front, which I did – it's a reasonable request. Except that I did not since I could not.

Upon logging in to the personal financial management account, an error came up. I called the lady over at their office – Sarah was her name, I believe – and she promised me that she would do everything she could so they could transfer the money required back to me. It should arrive shortly, within a day at most. I am not particularly worried, ProsperSafe is one of the most well-known corporations around here and I trust them.

I was pissed off yesterday, so I only stayed at the club for a short while. Jacques was there, too. You can already guess what happened. I let him have it and told him all about what I thought of his recommendations concerning this Michael guy. Imagine my reaction when he got aggravated and started making fun of me. The guy who is probably not even worth 10k is mocking me for following his stupidest advice ever. In the end, I couldn't stand looking at him for any longer, so I simply left. Now that I think of it: great, I am out of a friendly club environment, too. He has probably already told everything about it to Jean and the other guys over there.

Oh, I also asked Alexander about Michael's bill. I've got him working on it as well, since he actually seems to know the guy from the past. Over the phone he quickly pondered whether it might be easier to just pay the bill, but I say hell no. Let's investigate other options first.

NOVEMBER 22nd, 2023

A lot has happened since I have bothered to write anything here. Mostly just turns for the worse, even though I am happy that things are finally proceeding the way I have been anticipating for a while now. Where to begin?

Let's start with the divorce papers. They were served to me on Monday. The application included a mention that Gladys will be going after half of my possessions, including the lottery money. The bailiff actually had "the decency" to remind me that these cases are usually judged for the benefit of the women. I was so happy because of him reminding me that the thought of punching him in the stomach instantly came to me. Thankfully, I managed to contain myself and just let it go.

In any case, this is it, then. The end of a marriage that would soon have turned 20 years old. Well, in a couple of years, anyway. My life is not going to change a lot in practice, since I've been feeling alone these last months, anyway. Not having any other voices under the same roof with me will be different, obviously, especially since the children are away, and most likely will stay away, too. I guess it's mostly just the idea of being single again that will be different from before.

Should I manage to deal with the ransom demands she is making, this won't be bad. Without her, I can live, that's for sure. And I am not just talking about the money, but about the rights to see my kids too.

Last week, even before hearing about the divorce, I got a call from the state police. It seems that Gladys has also filed charges for domestic violence and assault. The police will be interrogating me later this week, but I trust that it's nothing that Alexander can't handle. I don't know the details, but we'll see if they even have any evidence against me, or if it's just her word against mine.

Oh, and the best part: she will be suing for monetary compensation as well. You can see the pattern here, right?

Speaking of money, Michael still has not dropped his demands of charging me for the consultation visit. He has sent me another invoice, including extra charges for the delay in payment. Well, he can be expecting many more delays to come if he still wishes to be paid for something he initially told me would be free. Thank God I have Alexander handling it, too.

One thing I will have to prepare for is also the battle for the custody of my son and my daughter. When it comes to that, I will not give up easily. She will be trying to grab them all to herself alongside the divorce application and the criminal charges against me. The social workers have already called me, and they will want to have a hearing with me – to which I will also be bringing my lawyer. This did not come as a surprise, but something I had been expecting for a while now. Fine, if she wants to play dirty, let's play dirty.

The one thing I haven't gotten yet is the money I tried to transfer back to my day-to-day bank account from my investments. The financial advisors at ProsperSafe haven't returned my emails yet, either. I haven't been too active about the whole thing myself, either. That is something I will have to seriously start working on now, since I will be needing that money by the end of the coming week to be able to pay Alexander up front for his services. Without him I would most definitely be screwed.

All in all, things are not too hot, but I have gotten over being panicked about it. I have decided that I will just solve each of these problems one by one – I am a millionaire, after all, even if I have managed to spend a big amount of the winnings as well.

One of the more surprising matters of annoyance is that I got kicked out of the private lounge in our club. Jean and Jacques got furious after I told Jacques what I thought of his advice, and because they know the owner of the place and basically everyone over there, for all intents and purposes, I am basically banned from the place. I guess I could go to the public area of the nightclub, but they are all fiendishly hostile towards me now. This begs the question: why was I even trying to make and stay friends with such losers anyway?

So, I am facing divorce, losing my kids, being charged for services I did not agree to use, have lost my last friends, and am potentially facing hefty fines, and maybe even some jail time. How am I feeling right now? All in all, pretty good, considering the current circumstances. The weekend was bad. I had a hard time getting out of bed back then. But now that I have managed to process things, I am feeling better again, and that is even without benzodiazepines or any other medication, too. I will just have to act rationally one step at a time to solve this equation, and I will be back on my feet in no time.

The next step will be securing enough money to be able to pay Alexander and his firm – and to make sure they get the damn online service fixed for me to be able to access my investment portfolio, too.

DECEMBER 1ˢᵗ, 2023

Alexander just told me he is backing off my cases. Every single one of them. I was unable to come up with the money for him, and it's his policy not to continue working for clients with potential solvency problems. Since he did start working for me already, he too, will of course be sending me demands of payment in the form of invoices, just as that rat bastard Michael has. But that is the least of my problems right now.

I am starting to feel terrified by the fact I have not even after all this time been given a chance to liquidate any of the money invested by my financial managers, nor have I seen any of the money I sent on their platform as I began using their services. On top of that, it seems that it is even hard to get in touch with anyone at their office anymore. I am starting to get a bad feeling about all of this. I have less than ten grand in my bank account, and the millions that have presumably been 'invested', only that I am now not able to manage my so-called investments. Have I been scammed?

I don't have any facts to back that theory up just yet, but it is certainly starting to feel like it. Losing my winnings at this point would mean a start to what is going to be the end game for me, and a very miserable one, too.

But what I don't get is how could it be? I know I got the recommendation for using ProsperSafe from someone who ended up being an untrustworthy guy, but even as I browsed the internet afterwards, I could see lots of praises for them, with only a few disappointing reviews and bad experiences. I just don't... get it.

Even if it was a clever scam, I bet that the police would be able to help me with it, but how long will it take? A year? Two years? Ten years? That will not help me, I need the money NOW to survive. This is the most chaotic time in my life. Even after I have done everything as I was supposed to: I went to school, studied some more, got a profession, a career, a family... sure I got lucky in winning the Powerball, but does that mean I have to be punished like this?

I still do believe I can overcome this situation rationally, step by step. But to succeed I need that money. There is no way I can succeed or survive without any cash to fix the situation with.

DECEMBER 6th, 2023

It is all over now. I can see that ProsperSafe has taken down their entire website, and I cannot reach anyone at their office anymore. The last time I heard from them was maybe one week ago, when a lady on the phone promised me that she would get back to me. I am still waiting for her call. What I don't get is how they managed to pull this off so well – even all the articles and reviews online must have been faked. I just don't understand. Were Jean and Jacques behind it all? Maybe it was all a great conspiracy in which Michael and Alexander were involved as well?

DECEMBER 7th, 2023

Got really drunk last night, and not just that. I basically abused every single substance I could find in the house. Shit happens, I guess.

My family and the kids are gone, and there is no chance in hell I am going to see them ever again. In theory, should I be able to pay for a lawyer, I might hold a small – a very small – fighting chance. But under these conditions, nah. But at least I have managed to keep my DNA alive and going forwards on to the next generation, and that's what matters, right? In any case, my children have been taken from me. Shit happens.

The idea of having to work once again to make a living is hideous enough, but last night I was checking for open positions announced by some local employers, and nowadays it seems to be fashionable to have potential applicants go through various security audits. Seeing as how I will be convicted of violent crimes, there is no point in even applying for those jobs. And yes – without a lawyer, I most definitely will be convicted of all the crimes I am suspected of, too. I guess I could go and work for McDonald's, I hear they don't perform too vast background checks on their applicants. Again, shit happens.

Last night I also felt something I had forgotten about: the feeling of loneliness. The friends from my past life are gone; I drove them away. The new so-called friends I had are gone too, which in the greater scope of things is probably a good thing, since they cheated me. Why am I still missing them, though? Getting wasted and high alone felt like shit. Shit happens.

Shit also happens in the way of me being almost out of what little money I have left. One bright thing is that at least Michael and Alexander will not be getting a dime out of me – unless they were co-conspirators in that whole ProsperSafe scam.

My marriage is also over. The divorce application has not finished processing yet, but we all know where this is heading. Not that it bothers me that much, to be honest. That is probably the least of my problems.

All in all, it is not just the money that is gone but so is my entire life along with it. There is nothing to look forward to, just bad things in the form of convictions, loneliness, poverty, homelessness, and shame. Maybe even addiction since I have lately been super cranky unless I use something to cheer myself up. Everything is just darkness now.

I think I'll grab the rest of whatever refreshments I can find, pay a visit to the medicine cabinet, ingest all of it and just OD tonight.

UNHEALTHY COMPETITION

"Ryan Thompson, nice to meet you."

Ryan cleared his throat, then extended his hand:

"Ryan Thompson… nice to meet you," he stuttered, with a far greater break in between words than what would have sounded natural and confident. He also could not help being bothered by his facial expression he saw from the mirror he stood in front of. In spite of him trying to act happy, his face spoke volumes.

He had a job interview scheduled for tomorrow but was now more than certain that he would not succeed in it. In fact, he was not even convinced he was going to attend it. It was a part-time offer for a junior systems analyst position, which was not what Ryan had ever studied to do nor what he was passionate about. He had not even paid attention to what the company did exactly.

If he had been going through an experience of sudden loss – which he had – he had not yet reached the stage of trying to solve the situation. After losing business of his own, trying to find a new source of income made sense, especially since getting a position like that prior to graduating from a bachelor's degree would have been exceptionally lucky. Especially since he had just been sending applications here and there as a means of trying to solve the equation of getting back up on his feet.

The initial stages of chaos and grief he had gone through after his company ended belly-up two weeks ago were long gone, but Ryan was still far from getting over it. In fact, he did not even intend to, but instead had sworn never to forget about the events. As a 24-year-old student in robotics and artificial intelligence, setting up a company and becoming an entrepreneur in the field was hardly exceptional. Clutching at a business idea that would not only end up making him a millionaire but also something that would be considered a guru in the field of artificial intelligence was something he did not intend to simply pass by and give up on. Therefore, all that getting snatched away from him he would from now on treat as a very expensive lesson in life.

Needless to say, his resolve had not been quite as strong a few weeks ago when the inevitable series of events had occurred. He did hit what he considered the rock bottom of his life, and just quit operating on everything he had going on: his company InnovixAI, which was like a child of his own, his studies, and even his personal life. He had sunk into deep depression and avoided every single human contact he possibly could. And that he could.

Now, as he reclaimed the lost parts of his life the way that it used to be, it was also the first possible moment for him to try to make sense of the events that had occurred and had led to this point. Not but a month ago, alongside his business partner, fellow student, and a friend, they had been the youngest rising stars in artificial intelligence in the United States – and perhaps even in the whole world.

InnovixAI – the company Ryan had started from scratch – was now a thing of the past due to a complete and absolute lack of funding. Not only that, but besides the trust of the investors, the company and Ryan had also lost the trust of the public. Everyone knows that it takes years to build trust, and mere seconds to lose it all.

InnovixAI was not just any start-up corporation operating in the field of various AI solutions. The service portfolio Ryan planned to have the company offer to its clients included many things that were well-known and quite basic to anyone with any knowledge of information technology: search engine optimization, website design, and general IT consulting, to name a few.

The trick Ryan had up his sleeve, however, was the way he had managed to write the leading product of InnovixAI. Albeit an official comparison was yet to be made, he personally believed that he had managed to create the most versatile and intelligent AI program to find intelligent and efficient sales and marketing solutions up to date. The program could detect leads and promote products and services of the one utilizing it to a prospective client. After that, it would be able to take care of the whole process of negotiations and landing a sale all the way up to a successful closing. In theory, if the end user so wished, all that would be required of them was the final signature in a contract – and even that was only for legal reasons, since legislation would not recognize an entity with artificial intelligence as someone with the mandate to represent a person or an entire company.

The public and a large group of venture capitalists agreed with Ryan – this was going to be something close to a revolutionary step forward, especially with a young student at the helm of the innovation. With this, Ryan would take a significant step towards wealth, fame, and status he had never dreamed of at the moment he had decided to enroll into university to pursue a career in robotics and AI. Except that nothing in the life ever goes as originally planned, especially nothing as big as this.

A few weeks ago, on an otherwise ordinary Tuesday morning, Ryan had barely fired up his laptop before he received a call from one of their biggest investors. They were pulling back their intended funding because of business risks associated with suddenly increased competition. After exchanging a few awkward phrases, Ryan came to know that his former partner in InnovixAI, Lucas Anderson had gone behind Ryan's back and formed a company of his own. Lucas was now offering the very same services that InnovixAI was and had all but directly stolen Ryan's innovative ideas.

What made Lucas' turncoat behavior even more heinous – and frankly, stupid – was that he had not even bothered to name his company brand very differently. Now, a new AI company focused on marketing and sales called Novix AI roamed free in the market, whereas InnovixAI had not even properly begun offering their services yet.

If Ryan still had his funding, he would have been able to compete with Lucas, and if sheer will could monetize business, there would have been no problem. Alas, that is not how the world works, and there was no way Ryan could pull it off without taking significant risk in the form of a loan. At that point he was convinced that Lucas had also started his own company the same way. Later on, Ryan came to find out that Lucas had managed to snatch and lure many of InnovixAI's investors behind him, helping him to start up Novix AI. Even though Ryan was the brains of the business, Lucas had always been more talented in pleasing people and acting in a more confident and convincing manner in general. In this case, that had worked to his advantage.

Of course, what had disappointed Ryan greatly, was also the fact that he had considered Lucas a friend. The origins of InnovixAI had formed in the hallways of the university they both attended, when they were both studying the same courses on the subject matter. Even if Ryan had been the mastermind behind the ideas, Lucas had done his share in contributing to every part of setting the business up. Not just that, but they had fun doing it. Up until the latest turn of events.

Now, Ryan had his mind set on getting his life back together. It involved some wild attempts and moves he even considered a bit desperate – such as applying for jobs he found no true interest in. But as he lived from day to day, life also seemed brighter with every day that passed. His mind was becoming clearer, and his focus was coming back to him. He was already almost at the point of getting employed to help balance his financial situation. More than that, he already had some new ideas with which he might set up a new business in the future.

But most of all, he had been regaining his determination. In the back of his mind now constantly dwelled the idea of taking down Novix AI and completely ruining Lucas' life.

"Now, with the groups you've been assigned to, get organized, and start preparing for the first seminar the next week. Remember, the key is to already have a presentable plan ready by Thursday, so you'll know what kind of research to start planning for. When there's time for that, remember to also enjoy your weekend, everyone."

As multiple voices were still responding to wish for a good weekend back over the Zoom call, Ryan exited the lesson without saying anything. He looked over his laptop to the other side of the table in the university library, and asked:

"You know what gets me? That we are planning to do research on how to market an ecommerce business instead of actually doing something like that in real life?"

On the other side of the table, Lucas lifted his head up from his laptop screen, briefly looked at Ryan, then went back to staring at his laptop, and mumbled:

"You know what gets me? The way the teachers and professors are always wishing a good weekend on Friday, even though they know that unlike them, the students will have to keep on working and studying on weekends, too."

Ryan rolled his eyes for a while, but then went on:

"I mean, think about it. What are we getting for doing this? Credits for studying, but that's it. At the same time, we could be doing this for real, in real life."

Lucas looked at Ryan, closed his laptop, leaned backwards, and asked:

"Alright then. How would you do that?"

"Look! Look at this!" Ryan frantically pointed at his laptop screen. There stood the seminar project they had been forming up for the university course of whose remote lecture had just ended.

"We are using a huge amount of time doing a marketing plan for a fake business. Why? Why would we not just form a marketing plan for a real business, and then execute it?"

Lucas looked at Ryan with a sarcastic look on his face.

"You wanna start a dropshipping business?"

"No. The profit margin of that has shrunk too much. Which adds even more weight to my original question. The reason we chose a dropshipping business for this project was because it was easy to utilize, right? In real world we would never do this because we are not stupid. So why are we doing school projects for the sake of stupid ideas instead of executing good ideas in real life?"

Before Lucas had time to respond, Ryan went on:

"In marketing, for example, what is it that businesses are constantly looking for? The right target group, of course. So far, it's been done manually by people. The kicker is, I believe that I can find a way for a computer to do the work from start to finish. Who wouldn't want that? And just imagine where else to expand from there on."

"Where would you expand, then?"

"I don't know yet. But I will know once I get started. I could use some help. Are you in?"

"Okey, now we are talking…" Lucas said quietly, almost whispering, as he entered what in his terms was an illustrious penthouse in downtown Providence, Rhode Island. For him, even visiting such a luxurious and vast apartment as a university student and a start-up entrepreneur had been off his limits and even his wildest dreams for quite some time.

"This is quite something, indeed," the real estate agent who had offered to show him around the property that was now up for sale confirmed, smiling.

Lucas turned around and asked:

"The asking price was one million, right?"

"999,000 $, to be exact," the agent replied.

Lucas turned around once more, took a look around, and said:

"I'll take it."

As Lucas got back to his current home in dormitory, he was relieved that he had not bumped into Ryan. He had no regrets for what he had done but was in any case anxious to get out of the same premises with him. Not that we would be opposed to being able to live like a millionaire, either. He was thankful his new home would be ready for moving into at any time. If he started packing what little possessions he had right now, he might be done by tomorrow evening.

He had successfully launched Novix AI, and everything was online and working, at least in theory. The first accounts he had using the services would need to be supervised rigorously, though, since besides the launch of the business this was also the ultimate trial of whether the code he had put in place worked. The first few days and weeks would determine whether it all could last.

But at the same time, he had identified the risk of Ryan attempting to hinder his plans. So, moving out of the dorm to build distance in between them would be essential, too. Even though the company had existed for a while now, the operations of his AI solutions had begun just today. Lucas cursed at not having moved out earlier, since this would mean having to answer calls from his customers around the clock and having to move at the same time. When would he be able to sleep?

On the other hand, failure was not an option. The mortgage he had taken would be too big to handle without the business, and he had also put his university studies to a halt because of this. He knew the risk was great, but so were the potential rewards. He had been toying with the idea of getting a business partner, but the company was at too critical of a stage to risk having someone come and do espionage and hinder his plans. He did not have anyone he trusted enough to help him even with the customer calls.

Lucas sighed, walked over to the closet, and pulled out cardboard boxes to start packing his belongings into them. He sighed once more as he just remembered that even if he managed to get most of the stuff over to his new home tonight so he could spend the night there, he would still have to stay up to monitor and adjust the performance of Novix AI's sales tools. For the first time, he was having doubts about leaving Ryan's business idea hanging to set up his own company, but there was no turning back now.

"You've done… nothing?" Ryan asked, with more disappointment than anger in his voice.

"Well, I did finish that university project," Lucas shrugged.

"But really, I had no time for this. I mean, for us this is still a side hustle, a hobby, right?"

"No. Get a grip, man. If we want this to work, you need to be in this as well. It cannot be just me coding the programs, setting up meetings to gain partnerships, and luring in customers."

Lucas said nothing. Ryan was now thinking that maybe he would be better off alone. That way, if he actually managed to make a profit, he would not have to split it with anyone, either. Although it would mean a whole lot more work for him alone. But what good would a partner be if they did not contribute to the project?

"Ok, let's chill down for now."

Lucas looked at Ryan like he wanted to say something, but before he could, Ryan went on:

"We have that meeting with the first potential investor coming up. Let's take a break until then and go on from there, ok? Just make sure you know the product and service plans by heart once we get there."

Lucas nodded.

In two hours, Lucas and Ryan entered a small skyscraper that one might expect to see in a show like the shark tank. The setting was not far from that, either. It felt very old-fashioned to them; despite remote meetings being a thing of the day, apparently, many investor institutions nowadays still preferred meeting new acquaintances face to face. This made the situation all the more exciting. TTT Venture Partners was the first venture capital firm to openly show interest in InnovixAI, and this meeting could very well determine the fate of the company.

The feeling was truly what it must have been like when entering the shark tank, or perhaps a lion's den. From a grand reception hall, Ryan and Lucas took the elevator up to the 15th floor, where after checking in with the secretary, they were led into the office of the vice president of TTT Venture Partners, Gary Newman. Despite the illustrious hallways they had gone through, his office was just a regular office room, not much bigger than an average cubicle. Despite having dressed formally – just as could be expected – he greeted the guys casually with a quick glance, without standing up:

"Howdy!"

"Good… hello," Ryan began, distracted by the informal greeting.

Gary Newman then lifted his eyes from his computer screen, stood up, and extended his hand, sharing a strong handshake first with Ryan, and then with Lucas. Then, he sat down behind his desk, and Ryan and Lucas sat down in front of him in the chairs facing him. After the first greetings, no one had said a word, and tension created by the silence was rapidly getting alarmingly uncomfortable.

"So… I guess we should begin," Ryan started, and coughed a little.

"I trust you've had the chance to review some of the material I sent to you prior to this meeting?"

Mr. Newman did not say a word, just shook his head.

"Oh, ok then…" Ryan went on, clearing his throat one more time.

"I'll begin with the basics, then."

"Please do," Mr. Newman said with an impatient tone.

The next fifteen minutes Ryan introduced his vision of the services InnovixAI might have in the future, and potential product plans. Even though he had always been good with computers and information technology, Ryan had never been good at presentations, or showcasing his ideas to other people. This time it did not go any better, and Ryan felt it too. What had probably been not much more than fifteen minutes had felt like an hour to him, and he could tell by Mr. Newman's expressions that either he had not understood what Ryan had said, or he was simply not impressed.

"Thank you, that was very nice," Mr. Newman said, followed quickly by:

"Let's cut to the basics, however. Key factors. What kind of a budget are you planning? What is your expected revenue and profit margin?"

Yet again, there was an uncomfortable silence. Then, Ryan opened his mouth, as if about to say something, but instead just froze there with his mouth open. In any other setting this might have been comical. However, the strange moment was broken by Lucas, who jumped in but half a second later after Ryan had frozen up:

"What we need the budget for is equipment, marketing, and communications. In IT and AI, it is all about the combination of hardware and software. The code for the software we have – no problem. But the hardware we have now is just for testing out the applications, it is not enough to have the software running comfortably and risk-free for real-life customers around the clock."

"Once we have everything set up, there are no boundaries – after that it is all just about finding customers."

Lucas was sitting with his back straight up and he confidently waved his hands in the air while explaining the situation to Mr. Newman.

"I understand you need some numbers. With twenty thousand, we can have a few machines up and running to support up to ten clients. Give us ten times that, and we'll be running operations for one hundred clients simultaneously."

"And here's the best part: after that, it will be all about just doing the work. The costs will be related to electricity, marketing tools, and an occasional hardware update here and there. After the initial investment, we are anticipating a monthly net profit of easily more than 100 %."

Silence fell in the office as Lucas was done with his little speech. Meanwhile, Ryan experienced a shock-like state – they had never talked about precise numbers before and had no idea whether they could succeed in what Lucas had just promised. Mr. Newman's eyes had widened slightly upon hearing Lucas' estimate of their potential profits. Although he hid it well, it was clear to both Ryan and Lucas that he was impressed by the promises. He turned to Ryan and asked:

"Can the applications you have coded actually produce these results?"

Ryan had no idea if they could, but he wanted to believe so. Even less of an idea Ryan had of why he so confidently answered with the words that then came out of his mouth:

"Yes, I believe they can."

For yet another while, everything seemed to stand still, even the time. Then, Lucas came up with an idea he could not resist sharing:

"Actually, Mr. Newman, I just began thinking of what our first mutual campaign slogan might be. How about 'Via AI, re-discover your time to enjoy the land of the free once more', with people firing AR-15's in the background?"

Ryan, who had just raised a bottle of water to take a sip barely managed to gulp down the drink instead of turning into a human fountain. Had Lucas lost his mind?

Mr. Newman's reaction was quite the opposite, however, since he burst out laughing. After regaining his composure, he looked at Lucas, smiling:

"First of all, call me Gary."

"Second, I love the humor, but I don't think that might appeal to just everyone out there in the public. Lastly, I like that you are willing to take risks, as long as they are not needless ones."

Lucas pointed out to a small sticker Gary had on the side of his computer screen, which spelled out 'Freedom firearms':

"I thought it might not be such a risk saying something like that to you."

"I can see you're observant as well," Gary seemed truly impressed. He then leaned forward and said:

"But the thing you must understand, I and the company I represent are taking major risks here, too. This is why I must be rigorous when investing in start-ups. Although I must say your thing here seems promising so far."

Gary leaned back on his chair again, and continued:

"Tell you what. I need to contemplate this for a while. Please email your business idea with your expected key financial indicators to me, and I'll get back to you. Either with an offer or with a rejection."

Barely being able to cover their excitement, Ryan and Lucas then shook hands with him and left the meeting.

"That was incredible! How did you do that?" Ryan asked Lucas in the elevator.

"I figured he seemed like the kind of guy who needed persuasion and confidence, most of all. I mean, there is no way I can improve on your apps any further, so I decided to focus on selling him the ideas."

"But how are we ever going to hit the goals you just promised for our budget?"

"How can you be so sure we won't?" Lucas raised his eyebrows, smiling at Ryan. For the first time that day, Ryan felt relaxed and began laughing, and they made a high five before stepping out of the elevator back into the lobby which they had come from.

Overall, the success of InnovixAI had not lingered in Ryan's great ideas, but it turned out to be the combination of those ideas and Lucas' skills in sales and negotiation which made the business truly soar. That is, until the bitter end was met by the two masterminds splitting up.

Ryan was seething because deep inside he knew that without him, Lucas would have been nothing. How many would form and innovate ideas such as Ryan had? Perhaps one in a million. How many would be able to use cunningness and treachery to trick people into investing in business ideas, and then double-cross their partner?

"Practically everybody," Ryan answered his own question.

He had drifted back into his own thoughts again, even though he had made every attempt to push those thoughts back so they would stop eating at him from the inside.

Lucas would have no way of competing in the industry once he encountered a problem with his current services and had someone who knew more about the technology to partner up with. On the other hand, Ryan could do nothing about the situation by himself, either. He would need some backup.

As Ryan was browsing the web for new open positions to apply for, his eyes suddenly brightened up.

A few days had passed after Novix AI's services had gone online. Lucas had dark circles under his eyes and a dead expression on his face as he was typing a reply to a customer request. He knew that if he did not get the applications he was offering to his customers working by themselves without him constantly maintaining them, he would eventually have to get himself a pair of helping hands. He was hesitant about that, since he knew that in spite of employees being potentially great assets to his business, they would pose a great risk to it as well.

At first, he had laughed at the idea of running automated apps based on artificial intelligence, which still needed constant human supervision to work properly. Now, the thought hardly amused him any longer. He clicked on the 'send' button in Outlook to reply to the ticket.

He felt and heard his joints clicking and snapping as he stood up from the office chair to stretch. He took a little stroll around his luxury apartment which he had just moved into. Taking a look out the window, he remembered how much he loved the magnificent view it offered over the city of

Providence. Then, at the same time he was reminded that for the last three days he had hardly any time to even acknowledge its existence.

"A golden cage…" he muttered to himself.

"Ryan Thompson. It is a pleasure to meet you."

Ryan still felt uncertain whether the line he had been rehearsing for these interviews could have been the best one, but it was now out there and would have to do.

"Likewise. My name is Carlos," the man in blue suit introduced himself while shaking hands with Ryan. Then, he pointed towards two seemingly expensive armchairs:

"Please, let us sit down."

As Ryan took a seat in what inarguably was a very comfortable chair, he felt his anxiousness subside. Nevertheless, the sharp determination of him being able to score this vacant position still remained. Carlos Rodriguez sat down too, facing him, and with a heavy Latino accent, dived directly into the reason for why they were there today:

"So, you applied for a sales coordinator position at Capitán. Are you at all familiar with what we do here?"

Ryan instinctively braced himself up in his chair. He had not been waiting for this topic to pop up among the first questions in the interview. In his thoughts he thanked himself he had done his homework about the company.

"I have formed an idea, yes. In fact, Capitán has been mentioned as an exemplary company when it comes to prosperous growth businesses in my studies of robotics and artificial intelligence back at the university. In short, IT consulting. Everything from coding websites to solving more complex issues when it comes to handling information."

As Ryan talked, Carlos kept continuously nodding his head as a sign of both agreeing but with a hint of impatience as well. Before Ryan could go on to satisfy that impatience, Carlos interjected:

"Yes, that is all true, but you left out a very important detail. You explained our line of business, but what we actually do is also a family business. Capitán is my child, and therefore, I only want the best for it as if it was my actual offspring. Here, we take care of each other, and work all for the good of the company. You may find this strange, but it is of utmost importance to me. I expect everyone here to be dedicated to that goal."

On the inside, Ryan rolled his eyes. But on the outside, he just happily stated:

"I understand you completely. It is like with my studies, except that there is much more hard work to put in and more risk to carry. I even had an idea of becoming an entrepreneur myself a short time ago but decided to give up on that idea."

"What I would expect from you in this position besides dedication is strong will to help grow the business. To close sales, and to even form partnerships should there be a chance for that."

Ryan realized that Carlos seemed to be the type who would be content in letting himself talk a lot more than ask questions from the interviewee. Even though he did not master social interactions the way that his former partner could, he had picked something up from constant negotiations he had to go through when setting InnovixAI up. As Carlos went on, Ryan came to understand how to play the rest of the interview to his advantage.

"I understand that I am asking for a lot and since this is an entry-level position, I cannot pay you very much. But in exchange for your efforts, besides pay, you will receive the full support of what I like to think of as Capitán family. You will indeed become a member of a family."

"Don't worry, Mr. Rodriguez, I have not even graduated yet, so all I am looking for is the right opportunity for me to prove myself and to set my career on the right path right from the start. The pay you are offering will do fine for me. The most important things for me are that I can get to a position where I can learn new things and actually influence the growth of your IT business."

Clearly, Ryan had hit home, since the face of Carlos Rodriguez turned seemingly content and happy upon hearing those words come out of Ryan's mouth.

"Let's discuss the potential contract, then. When would you be able to start? And please, call me Carlos."

Lucas had a hard time focusing on browsing through websites and offers of different service providers. One week had passed since Novix AI went fully operational, and severe sleep deprivation and general irritability had been building up in him ever since. The applications Novix AI offered to his clients ran by themselves – in theory. Nevertheless, Lucas had identified several fields in which he desperately needed a helping hand.

First, there was the dealing with crashes, errors, and malfunctions. Although the instructions he had originally received from Ryan worked well, the reparative measures took hours which he could very well have used for something else. Help in this field would require him to hand over some rather critical rights to the third party, so they would have to be completely trustworthy.

Second, he still had no idea how to deal with invoicing. This would be the lifeline that kept the business together, yet he had no time to take a look at it at all. This was something he would have to outsource sooner rather than later.

Lastly, finding new customer relationships and taking care of the existing ones was a major hurdle which could swallow his focus around the clock – if it were possible. Even though Lucas' talents really outshone many of his opponents in this field, he could not go on like this forever. He would initially have to take a day off some time in the future and find someone to cover for him during that time.

But that time for the days off would not be now. He would have to find a partner to take care of invoicing and errors for him. A couple of potential options existed already, but he would have to look a little deeper into them. It took him but a few minutes to draft up requests for quotations and send them to a couple of potential service providers.

In a few weeks' time, Lucas sat down at a dinner table on the night of the Christmas Eve. Visiting his family for the holidays, he was glad he could finally take some time off work. As a new entrepreneur he obviously always had his laptop with him should a problem arise. Right now, however, he felt confident that he would be able to relax for tonight and take an entire day off work on Christmas day.

As a single young man living by himself, he had a fairly traditional way of spending the holidays with his family. Coming from what most would call nuclear family, present at the table sat his little sister Sophia, and his parents Sheila and Terrence. Taking part in carving the turkey and exchanging gifts very much opened an entire new universe for Lucas, who had spent his weeks in front of a computer screen, working on his business and living constantly in that reality. On the bright side, the business was blooming, and the constantly growing revenue guaranteed a very comfortable position for him in the coming years, as long as everything would work as well in the future as they had for now.

Yet, on the darker side of things, besides work, he had been missing out on life. Unlike his former partner Ryan, Lucas enjoyed social interaction so much that it made it easy for him to keep honing his customer relations and striking new deals. But, on the other hand, the work required many other things to be taken care of as well, and he was left unsatisfied for not having enough free time to socialize with his friends anymore. He, after all, took care of all the duties of Novix AI by himself.

As could be expected, his inarguable success with the company became one of the topics of discussion at the Christmas dinner.

"When will you be returning to school to finish your degree, then?" his father Terrence asked.

Baffled by the question, Lucas answered:

"Once I get this thing going properly, I don't see why I should return there at all. I mean, I have everything I need right here. In theory, I could make this business an ultimate success, and sell it in a few years, and I'd be set for life."

A short silence fell over the table. Terrence and Sheila looked at each other, and Terrence, with a very serious and dark tone, said:

"We feel it would be better for you in the long run if you would. This – the way you are doing it – is far too risky and you are placing all of your eggs in one basket by doing this."

Before Lucas had an opportunity to say anything, his phone rang. It was one of his biggest clients, a pharmaceutical company.

Without raising his eyes from the phone he had reached for to pick it up, Lucas muttered:

"Yes, right. Excuse me."

As he noticed the caller being the marketing manager of his client company, he stood up and walked out of the dining room while answering the phone:

"Lindsay! How can I help you?"

"Hi, Lucas. I am sorry to bother you at this hour, but I've just received a disturbing call from our headquarters. It seems that some of the focused ads you have been creating for us are guiding consumers towards our competitors' websites. I am celebrating Christmas with my kids at the moment, and understand that you are probably doing something similar, too, but with the pricing for the ad products you have given us this absolutely cannot wait."

With each word he heard her speak, Lucas' hands shook a little more. He just could not catch a break. Instead of revealing his disappointment, he just masked his tender voice as well as possible:

"I am so sorry, that sounds terrible. I absolutely understand your situation and will get right on to fixing the problem, whatever the cause may be."

"Lovely. I need to go now, but please take care of this as soon as possible. Merry Christmas!"

"Thanks, and the same to you," Lucas ended, uncertain whether he was able to maintain his composure during those last words over the phone.

Upon resting down his phone he began pondering about his options. By firing up his laptop he would have to step away from what was going to be his last chance for relaxation for a while. He could also take his chances and just ignore the call for now and get back to the problem in the morning. He had only been doing this for a such a short while now that he did not know if the company or Lindsay would actually keep a close track of how fast he reacted to their complaints. On the other hand, could he afford the risk of losing the client?

Lucas stepped back inside the dining room and announced his family:

"I'm sorry, but there has been an urgent matter at work, and I need to take care of it right now. I'll get on it right away on my computer and get back to you as soon as possible."

He then turned around and intentionally stepped away before giving his parents the time to react verbally. The shocked expression on Sheila's face and a light smirk Terrence gave him, however, revealed their thoughts more openly than words ever could.

Lucas headed upstairs in the house he had lived in for most of his life. He knew the room he used to occupy as a child was still somewhat unattended, since his parents had not figured out any practical use for it – besides the occasional storing of their less-than-important belongings. Unsurprised by the fact that his old desk he had used for taking care of his school homework still stood there, Lucas closed the door behind him, sat behind the desk, raised the lid on his laptop and started working.

The sound of loud clanging and doors banging echoed throughout the old house. Lucas slowly opened his eyes to notice that the smell of cinnamon had floated all the way to his old room. The second thing he immediately felt was the hangover-like state he was in, even without consuming any alcohol. Having spent many a Christmas with his relatives, he knew that it was traditional for them to get up early on Christmas day to start preparing for the breakfast and opening of the presents.

Lucas held back the reflex to throw up. His nausea was not because of the scent of cooking but sleep deprivation he suffered from. He had stayed up until five o'clock in the morning until he had managed to fix the bug in the code and report back to his client that everything worked properly now. In the middle of the night, he had started wondering if there was a chance he could charge them for the work he had done.

Turned out that he could not, but to Lucas' horror upon examining the bills sent he found out that in the last two months he had been missing out on several invoices he could have sent out. In other words, he had been working without pay. This had also kept him up for a few hours later than the sole handling of the bug alone would have.

With the sickening sensation in the morning of that Christmas day, he made the decision to finally hire a partner or a subcontractor to take care of some of his administrative work. Up until this point, he had been reviewing various quotations and offers he had received but had not summoned up the courage to sign up for anything. This, however, was the defining moment in which he decided to act quickly to make his business more manageable.

But right now, in front of him loomed the long day of holiday festivities and pleasantries to participate in, despite him feeling like a wreckage. Lucas sighed.

On the 27th of December, Lucas electronically finalized and signed agreements with two different companies to take care of Novix AI's invoicing, accounting, and a part of the customer support duties. This would cut into Lucas' monthly earnings quite significantly, but he still made a fair amount of profit even with these services. Yet this way he could focus on keeping in touch with his clients, and at the same time learn more about coding various AI solutions by himself. Maybe one day he would be as good as his former partner Ryan, allowing him to develop his company's solutions even further.

As Lucas thought of Ryan, he started reflecting on the past, and wondered how he must have been doing. He had intentionally tried to keep Ryan out of his mind, since on some level his own actions had bothered him. Up to a certain point, he had considered Ryan a friend and still did so even now, although the feeling would certainly not be mutual.

Then again, at the moment Lucas had made up his mind to set Novix AI up, he could not understand why he should not do so. With the knowledge of how Ryan's applications worked, he possessed all the skills needed to make the business prosper. The way he saw it, Ryan alone could not do it without him, but Lucas alone could, so why would he split profits with someone else? He just wished he could have done it without less attention in the media and among the investors, whose backing out of the investments in InnovixAI had caused the company to crash and burn.

The events had left Lucas doubtful about having any partners of his own, and getting used to the current situation would require an attitude adjustment from him, too. Luckily, the functions he had now outsourced were not critical, and would not result in revealing any of his business secrets to outsiders.

The coming weeks would show Lucas that he had made the right choice. Money would consistently roll in because of the impecunious execution of invoicing service, and he almost every night managed to consistently get eight hours of sleep. His sleep was not hindered by work, at least. What caused him to roll restlessly in his bed in his new luxury home at night-time, however, was the constantly nagging thought in his mind that something was wrong.

Ryan's face had turned red, and his heart was beating fast. In his new position at Capitán, seeing announcements of various businesses searching for advisors, consultation calls, or straight up outsourcing of services had proven to be an everyday thing.

The demand for companies such as Capitán had shown him how the IT field was truly a world of opportunities. He had yet to get used to it, especially since he knew that right now, he was but an underpaid cog in the wheel, whereas he could have been a mogul in the field.

Upon seeing a very particular service request get delivered to a shared mailbox he belonged to at work to had now caused his body and mind to react so forcefully. The thing that separated this one from the most was the name of the principal: Novix AI. Ryan knew his opportunity had come. Lucas had always been hesitant to bring any outsiders to his business, and he for sure would not be doing so continuously in the future, either.

Ryan's mind was racing. He knew he had to do anything it took to get Capitán to sign a deal with Novix AI, yet he was not in charge of making these decisions. He knew that with the abundance of job offers, most of them would simply be ignored on the account of not being profitable enough or simply because of the lack of manpower the small company still had. To make the matters even more challenging, Lucas was looking for someone to take care of Novix AI's invoicing and customer support. Capitán was not in the business of financial services, so the customer support and account management duties were the only option Ryan could attempt to take a strike at. Even then it would not be a profitable contract nor at the core of Capitán's business concept.

To get the deal, he would need the blessing of a sales negotiator in the company. Ryan thought hard for a few seconds, then grabbed his phone, and called Manuel.

"Hey, what's up, Ryan?"

"Hi. Listen, I think I just found an opportunity for us. Check out the mailbox for requests."

Ryan could hear Manuel clicking his mouse on the other end of the call. Like most of the employees of Capitán, they were both working remotely.

"Novix AI," Ryan added.

"Yes, I see it. But I don't know… I'm supposed to be focusing on expanding our sales in the programming sector. Besides, I don't have to the time to continuously babysit a customer. This sounds like an intensive gig."

"Don't worry – I'll take care of the actual work involved. I am starting to get the hang of my current accounts in any case, so it's no trouble, really. Besides, I can't imagine anyone getting upset over you scoring a sale for us," Ryan rushed in to prevent Manuel from backing out.

"Really? I thought you had your hands full, considering the junior position you're still in," Manuel laughed, half-joking. It was true Ryan had been upset about the workload, since he got paid what might be considered the minimum salary in the industry.

"Yeah, but making sacrifices is the only way to advance, you know? Well, of course you do, since you're even newer here than I am. Come on, if I was you, I wouldn't say no to this, either. It's a win-win scenario."

It pissed Ryan off to no end, knowing that Manuel was as young as him, but since he was an actual blood relative of Carlos, the managing director, he was better paid and in a far more secure position than Ryan, too. But right now, Ryan had to swallow his pride and suck up to him to ensure that his only purpose for getting this job would become reality.

"Well… the service request is so simple it's doable, as long as you are willing to take care of it. I'll draft up a quotation soon, run it by you, and then send it over to Novix AI. Is that ok?"

"More than ok. Talk to you soon, and thank you," Ryan ended the call.

Ryan smiled widely as he put the phone down. His heart still raced as his over-anxious self could not stop worrying if Manuel would actually do as he promised. After the deal it would all be in his own hands, but right now, he trusted no one else. This all felt so personal it surprised even himself. Right now, he had a few clients under his belt to take care of, but the tasks involved were menial. He hated his current job.

Ryan did not have to wait for long, for quite soon Novix AI's request got answered by Manuel, with Ryan in the list of blind carbon copy recipients. A grim smile appeared on Ryan's face.

"I'm still sorry about the Christmas, Mom. I know it wasn't what you and Dad were expecting."

"Never mind about the Christmas, but we worry about you, Lucas. The way you had to rush out back then, and the way you have distanced yourself from us. You hardly ever come to visit anymore, either," Sheila frantically explained to Lucas over the phone.

"Things have been quite intense, I know, I know. But it has gotten better already; I don't have to worry about so many things right now as I used to."

"We told you should never attempt to become an entrepreneur all by yourself, but just finish university first. Have you made any progress in your studies at all? We never even got to ask you that before. You know we wouldn't want to put pressure on you in front of your sister who is doing so magnificently in Harvard."

There was a short break in the conversation. Lucas had to swallow his frustration prior to answering.

"You know I am focusing on this right now, not on my studies."

Lucas heard an overly dramatic sigh made by his mother over the phone. He went on:

"But you know what, things are getting better now. Right now, I am living what might be considered a normal schedule. I hardly ever do more than nine to ten hours of work per day, thanks to some partners I hired to take care of some of the simpler tasks involved. Everything is going exactly as I've planned."

"Promise me that you'll finish your studies as soon as possible."

Sheila now had the stubborn tone in her voice, and Lucas knew very well what it meant. There would be no point in trying to talk sense to her, but to just rather end the call quickly. He had learned this about his mother as early as in his childhood."

"Sure thing, but I gotta go now. Please tell Dad my love and I'll talk to you soon."

"Bye."

Lucas was amazed by how convinced his parents were that the path to success would come from getting a degree, working a regular job at a company, and then applying for a mortgage. Then again, who could blame them, Lucas thought. The generational gap between the baby boomers and millennials was far too wide to expect them to get that what used to work for them does not work the same way anymore. Especially now as Lucas had his business set up and running, it was only a matter of time until he could expand his service portfolio even further, allowing him to basically retire early either by selling the company or outsourcing its functions widely enough so he would hardly have to do any work himself.

And he was more than happy with the deal he had made with his new partners, too. Things were not quite at the point where he would be able to sit back and watch money come in just yet, but that day would come. Right now, he maybe still had to work, but the days of worrying about trivial and time-consuming tasks were over. The invoice handling was basically an automated service, and Capitán Consulting had made his life much easier by taking care of the most basic customer service processes his line of business needed. In fact, some of the things they had done to develop the basic ticketing system Lucas had in place had been quite simple yet big enough to impress him.

As he put his phone down and glanced at the email box he had open on his laptop, there was even now an unread email from the consultants. It phrased out yet another development idea by which Capitán suggested Lucas to expand his business further. This would involve fine-tuning the AI included in Novix AI's applications to identify the customers' key demands without the need for them to manually insert keywords by which to market for new clients.

Lucas felt intrigued and impressed, yet uncertain at the same time. The background work done by whoever at Capitán had drawn up the idea astonished him, because it made perfect sense. He also saw a direct opportunity to grow his revenue greatly, even if the idea did not directly nudge him so much towards growth, but of efficiency. He quickly made the math in his head and understood that this could potentially allow him to double his monthly income. Best of all, Capitán would still take care of the customer service and handling of tickets in this segment.

On the other hand, he was uncertain if his code in the AI – originally created by Ryan – could handle the tasks involved. He would have to make sure of that before going any further. Despite the excitement which made his fingers shake a little, he drafted a simple response, politely promising to look into the idea before proceeding with it.

As Lucas hit the send button, he knew there was no way he could contain himself enough to allow an evening off to start with fresh eyes in the morning. He would look into this right now, even if it took him the whole evening.

Looking into whether the applications would work with the new functionalities did not take Lucas just the whole evening, but the whole night as well. It had been a while since he had stayed up working around the clock now, but to him, this one was definitely worth the effort. Especially since he had found out there was no reason he would not be able to implement the protocols. In exchange for that, he knew that Novix AI's profitability would skyrocket almost instantly.

Even with no sleep and having had way too little to eat and to drink, he still felt extremely excited and could razor-sharply focus his attention to double-checking that everything worked as planned. It did. Lucas sat back and thought about different ways he could handle this. He could implement everything right now and start by mentioning about the new, enhanced AI to his current clients. Then again, something this big might call for a big marketing campaign for him to be able to squeeze every last drop of profit out of it. Or maybe he would just sleep on it and think about his plan before launching anything.

He immediately scrapped the last option. The whole concept simply excited him too much. But he also knew that no way could he market something like this starting from scratch all by himself with no sleep. There also existed the option of consulting Capitán further about the idea – but why should he? After all, Novix AI was his business, and he would make the decision if he wanted to go through with the idea or not.

Lucas made up his mind and decided to add the new string of code to the AI applications immediately. Then, he shot a quick email to his current clients, encouraging them to take advantage of a short trial period of these new functionalities which later on would cost a hefty price to subscribe to. He decided not to reply to the email of Capitán at all – after all, in the best-case scenario he might be able to proclaim this as his own invention, and it would serve no purpose for him to acknowledge in writing that the idea was given to him by an outsider.

It was now eight o'clock in the morning, and as many had just begun their work, Lucas ended his and headed to bed, wondering if he, due to his excitement, could sleep at all. The worry turned out to be for nothing, for in less than a minute after hitting the sack, his lights were out.

Lucas was standing in front of a doorway to the lecture room, wondering if this was the right place for him to be. It was the first day of the course titled 'The basics of artificial intelligence in programming' back at the university, and he felt uncertain about what to expect, starting from the physical location of where today's class would be held.

"You look like you're lost. Need help?"

Lucas raised his head to see Ryan standing there right in front of him.

"Yes, actually, do you have any idea where today's class of basics of AI will be? Is this the place," Lucas pointed at the lecture room next to them.

"I do, actually – nice to meet you, by the way. My name is Ryan."

As Lucas extended his hand to shake hands with Ryan, Ryan quickly withdrew his hand and grabbed his phone, which had begun ringing. Without saying a word, Ryan walked off with the phone still ringing, leaving Lucas there, confused. He had no idea where to go, had not even introduced himself to Ryan, and just heard the phone constantly ringing. It just would not stop but kept getting louder.

Suddenly, Lucas was startled awake by the sound of his own mobile phone actually ringing right next to his bed. It was almost noon, and he had barely slept but a few hours. Even though his eyes had hardly opened, his hand extended sharply right over to his phone and answered it.

"Hi, Lucas," a female voice greeted him before he had the chance to say anything. Lucas immediately recognized the voice to belong to Lindsay, to whom he had last spoken on the Christmas Eve.

"Oh, hi, Lindsay. What's up?" Lucas tried to cover the sound of his tiredness, but instantly knew that he had failed at it.

"I assume you have already noticed that your services are down. We cannot connect to any of your platforms right now."

Lucas felt his heart skip a beat but put on his best face to mask his shock. This time he knew he did rather well at it.

"Yes, I am terribly sorry for the abnormality. We're doing everything in our power to make sure that it'll all be up and running in no time. Be ensured that you'll be compensated for this."

"Thank you so much. I knew I could rely on you. Have a great day!"

"You too," Lucas finished the call.

As he had just woken up, he obviously had no idea what could have caused a potential malfunction in the service. But, since this was a critical interruption, he would have to get on it right now. He stood up on the side of his bed, rubbed his eyes for a while, and then got up to put some clothes on.

Ryan sat in the very same armchair he had been sitting in the day he met his current boss, Carlos Rodriguez, for the first time. That day he had been interviewed for his current position. Now, as an employee of Mr. Rodriguez's company Capitán, it would be about something entirely else – all he had been told was that it had something to do with his current performance. Ryan sensed it would concern the customer relations with Novix AI as well, or what was left of it.

Roughly one week ago, papers in the field of robotics and artificial intelligence all swarmed around Novix AI, with their interest in the rumors of the company not being able to keep on performing any longer. But a few days later, Novix AI announced it would be shutting down all of its operations due to issues encountered in their hardware with which they maintained the production of their services.

Ryan did not have to keep following the news because of an interest in the chain of events. He chose to read them simply because of the hateful glee which filled him every time he saw someone bashing Lucas Anderson or his company. He loved it. What had happened was obvious to him already.

By adding in the strings of code that Ryan with the help of Capitán had fed Lucas, Ryan had gotten him to dig the grave for his own company. The idea of identifying customers' key demands by the AI provided by Novix AI was a step towards development which Ryan was planning to execute with his own firm, had InnovixAI not foundered because of Lucas' doings. He knew very well, however, that by no means the hardware maintained by either him or Lucas would be able to process through multiplied commands created by the new functionalities. The only possible outcomes were either the machinery overheating or shutting down – both of which would result in permanent damage to Novix AI's operations. Hence it was but an idea in development, even to Ryan.

Lucas' processors were toast and there was no way Lucas could continue business with his company without any equipment. This would inevitably lead to him being put into a shameful spotlight and losing every last bit of fame he had gained over this venture. This had already begun happening, Ryan had noticed. Lucas had so far declined requests for interviews by the media, which Ryan found unfortunate. He wanted to see Lucas suffer. To see Novix AI go under, to watch Lucas fall into both professional and personal bankruptcy, and to top it all off with Lucas losing his reputation and credibility.

He had heard the saying of how revenge could taste bittersweet. Oh, how did he disagree right now. To watch the rise and fall of someone who had betrayed him in the most important project he had ever had and trusted someone with in his short life felt even better than the success of InnovixAI's breakthrough. Sure, he would probably have to endure a talking-to by his supervisor because of the loss of the client and go through questions of why he had originally even meddled in the sales process with Novix AI – assuming Manuel had squealed. Being a blood relative of Carlos, he probably had. But afterwards, life would go on and Ryan could continue forming new ideas for the future.

In anticipation of Carlos arriving soon, Ryan grabbed his phone to check out the new headlines with a smirk on his face – and he found just what he had been looking for. Lucas had finally been caught by a reasonably well-known tabloid, and he had given an interview to the paper. What surprised him was how open Lucas seemed to be when giving answers. It even annoyed Ryan a little, since he could not see Lucas squirming in his answers the way that he would have liked to. He ended up scrolling through the interview, until he took notice of a single name which caught his attention: Capitán.

Lucas had named Capitán as the originator of the idea and as a key partner of Novix AI. Ryan's eyes widened as he noticed the related news linked next to the story being directly about Capitán's involvement in the events. The name of Ryan's current employer was now getting dragged through the mud as well – could he be personally named as well, or even sued by Capitán?

The seemingly endless stream of questions swirled through Ryan's mind as the door to the office opened and Carlos stood in the doorway with eyes set on Ryan and a serious look on his face.

RISKY STUFF

"And a receipt for your deposit, thank you, and have a good day, ma'am."

"Likewise, thank you," the gray-haired old lady in her fur coat answered, smiling.

The clock was about to strike quarter to five in the afternoon, and there were no more customers in sight. Being Friday, according to my relatively brief experience here at Aktie Bank, this meant that the last fifteen minutes would simply be preparing to close up and then head home for the weekend. Not that this job saw many rush hours in the middle of the week either, though. I mean, barring the elderly, who in their right mind still visited the bank office for their daily banking services anymore?

As always, everyone else had headed home at least one hour ago already, so I decided to lock the doors one minute to five and do the same. I liked the job. Even though my MBA studies had not exactly prepared me for a position as a clerk and an assistant at a bank, one would have to start somewhere, right? Besides, the people were nice, and my employer did have new positions open regularly up, so there would be potential for career advancements as soon as I had some more experience in the banking industry.

As I closed the back door of my workplace behind me, I felt the familiar feeling of content. With another week of work over, there was the weekend to look forward to. Being single and quite set in the same ways I had since teen years, I simply enjoyed sleeping late, watching TV series on streaming services, and playing an occasional game or two.

The staff door to the regional office of Aktie Bank led me straight to the hallway of the local, 7-11 styled small mall. Why I called it a 7-11 mall was that besides the store there was hardly anything else there. Just the office of the bank I worked at, and a pharmacy. The official name of the mall was Westsider mall, I think, although none of the locals used the name, but simply referred to the place as 7-11.

As usual, I stopped in the store before heading home from work. There were the groceries to take care of for the weekend, after all. I had never cared much for cooking, so as usual, I picked up some fast food which I could simply heat up in the microwave. Some bread for breakfast, chocolate as a snack, and a bottle of coke. That would do it for me.

In my hometown of Lawrence, I loved being able to manage without a car, which would cut way too much into my expenses. For everyday regular needs, I just had to walk the distance between my apartment and the mall. For anything else, even the public transportation was kind of decent. A few miles of walking five days a week also gave me some exercise. My chosen strategy of survival for managing my life with immense student loans included paying them back as soon as possible, with as frugal lifestyle as possible. As for me, I considered myself a mind-numbingly typical guy. 22 years old, medium build, with about as average height of 5 feet and 9 inches and as average weight of 170 pounds as possible.

My home reflected my lifestyle and goals quite well, to be frank. It was a studio apartment with a desk for my computer, a very basic bed in an alcove, and a small corner of a kitchen. My possessions consisted mostly of whatever clothes I had plus kitchenware. My computer was the one thing that had any proper monetary value left. During my student days with no access to a lot of money it had been easy to get used to such a simple life.

The rest of the Friday night passed quickly by with a microwave pizza, coke, and League of Legends. A friend from university surprised me with a WhatsApp message, too. It had been a month since we talked the last time, so catching up with him offered a nice change of pace to what otherwise reminded me of a very typical weekend I used to spend. With friends from my student days all having moved to different states, socializing had grown harder for me than it used to be. I suppose this is what the grown-up life is like for most.

With the rest of the weekend wheezing by in a very similar manner as my Friday night, I soon found myself at work again. It was the start of a new week, which meant starting the week with usual team meeting before opening the doors to the bank for customers. Naturally, customers that physically visited the bank anymore were a dying breed, and we spent most of the time in the meeting simply dividing up various internal tasks to the staff members, plus going through objectives for the week.

Besides the ease of travel, one other thing I liked about my job was the team. Having just graduated, I was obviously the youngest and newest addition. The other five who worked in the office were Regional Manager Tim, Secretary Jane, two Account Managers Philip and Anne, and Charlotte, who worked as the accountant. All of them were in their fifties, except for Philip who was in his early thirties. Unlike one might expect, they were, however, very laid-back people. I for one did not anticipate for them to easily accept in a newcomer to their group, but thankfully they had proved me wrong.

The morning at work began in a very regular fashion. Working here, and in Lawrence in general, they mostly did. Unsurprisingly, I got to sit behind the customer service desk, doing some routine statistics reporting to the bank headquarters while waiting for anyone to step in. I would have preferred to step in and help with back-office tasks – but again – everyone had to start somewhere, right?

The morning passed by quickly, despite only seeing three customers in as many hours. The afternoon half of the day at that point worried me, since I knew those hours would pass by very slowly, should there be no more customers to take care of. I was done with my other tasks and knew from past experience that if I asked Tim to give me more things to do, he would just tell me to take it easy, and that I would have plenty of time to work in the coming years. The general feeling in the town and in the office had been extremely unhurried from the get-go ever since I started here.

But the afternoon had not arrived yet. At twelve o'clock, I headed to the break room to grab a Thai cube for lunch. Inside already sat Jane and Philip. Jane seemed to have just finished with her lunch and getting ready to head back to work, while Philip seemed as if he focused very sharply on something on his phone. As Jane cleaned up the place at the table she had sat at, I sat there with my meal, right across the table from Philip.

To quite a lot of people, the situation might have been uncomfortable. We sat there for a while, at least ten minutes, during which time we simply minded our own meals. Philip kept staring at the screen on his phone, barely lifting his eyes from the thing in the time I had been in the room with him. Even though I had grown accustomed to having no small talk during lunch break, I finally gave up and grabbed my own smart phone. I think I was browsing the news headlines or something as menial when Philip decided to strike up a conversation.

"It's incredible how quickly and sharply the value of AI stocks has risen in the last two years."

I looked at Philip but could not figure out anything to say. He interpreted my reaction as me not understanding what he was talking about:

"Artificial intelligence companies," he clarified.

"Yeah, yeah, I get that," I quickly said, swallowing the last of the noodles I had in my mouth.

"It's just that I've never really taken a look at stock market too carefully so I'm not particularly well up to date on the subject."

Philip eyed me quickly and suspiciously before continuing to browse what apparently were stock charts on his phone.

"Well, you should at least consider doing some investing. Perhaps not directly in stocks, but you're a young guy, and have a lot to gain if you simply spend some time in the market. That is one of the almost fireproof ways to gain wealth, you know?"

I was obviously quite aware of different opportunities that existed, since presenting various products and investment vehicles to customers was a part of my job. Somehow, while showcasing this world to other people in a professional setting had made me disengage from those topics myself. I had honestly never even considered doing anything of sorts myself. Back in school these topics hardly ever even got mentioned.

"Nah, so far, I have been focusing on paying back my student loans. Investing carries risks with it and I'd rather gain surefire financial stability by taking care of my debts first."

"It's of course a good idea to do that, too, but still, I'd advise you to start investing as well. Most don't, and there will be no retirement for many of them ever, either. It may seem distant to you now, but trust me, you won't want to work for the rest of your life."

Philip spoke with a completely different tone than he usually did. He did not shout, yet he sounded fiercer. His facial expression showed he took the subject very seriously.

"Yeah, but one could lose it all, right?"

"Not likely if you're wise. Just diversify by not investing in a single company, for instance, and take care not to pay too much fees when buying. There are a couple of websites that I could recommend to you if you'd like to do some studying on it."

Philip collected his dishes from the table and started placing them in the washer.

"This is also something I could talk about for hours, you know, but I gotta run back to work right now. But let's pick this conversation up at a later time, ok? It'd be nice to exchange ideas with someone. I've found that I'm not able to do it with the rest of the people here. Catch you later!"

At that moment, it did not sound like something I could take seriously. For a second there Philip had sounded like a religious preacher, but after a chat that had lasted for but two minutes, how could anyone be convinced? I was intrigued, anyhow, since he sounded sincere when telling me that I was someone he could talk to instead of the others, even though they were obviously older and more experienced in the banking sector than I was.

The afternoon passed by slowly. In fact, to say it felt slow would be a major understatement. For a reason still unbeknownst to me, Monday afternoons had always been very quiet. Nobody entered the front doors, and the scenario of having no work to do but just sit still had become very real now. The older generation who worked here were conservative enough to frown upon the use of a mobile phone at work, so even the options of coming up with casual entertainment were far too few.

The first hour simply went by with me not doing much anything at all but stare forwards. It may sound unbelievable to some, but it was something I had grown accustomed to while working these quiet hours here. Somewhere around two o'clock in the afternoon the time began to pass by even slower than before. I knew I had to figure out something to make it until the end of the day.

Just then, with a loud beep, Teams informed me that someone had sent me a chat message. Taking a look at it, I noticed it was Philip. There was no actual text, just a link to a website. Before I had a chance to react, he sent me another message. Again, there was just a link without any text. Judging from the URL addresses only, they seemed to revolve around the topics of saving money and investing, just as we had discussed during our lunch break but two hours ago.

Since I had nothing to do anyhow, I began to read. Luckily, the office computer allowed me to open the links with the browser. I knew the computer at the customer service desk had all kinds of restrictions set up. They were both blog posts, one of them from a financial advisor at a competing bank, and the other one from someone who had managed to amass wealth by investing and then retire early in his thirties. The blog posts did nothing to lessen my suspicions, especially since I knew people in the financial sector well enough to know the difference between honesty and a marketing speech. The first blog post appeared to me as a marketing speech. The other one simply seemed way too hype-y to me to appear trustworthy. But at least I got to spend 20 minutes of my workday reading those, even if I left the websites far from being convinced.

Philip's enthusiasm towards the subject of being never able to retire, however, persisted in my mind. Working a job at bank on a day like this also highlighted the idea greatly – was it really worth it to spend your time sitting behind a desk for hours on end, just waiting for someone to enter? Voluntarily, I would never do this if not for a paycheck. But everyone would be able to retire at the age of 65, would they not? Even if I at that time pushed Philip's ideas aside, they did not completely escape me.

Being a young bachelor, I had plenty of time to squander on what many would deem to be useless, and games were no exception. The next weekend, after a week which had felt unnaturally long, on Saturday, there was a notable moment which then defined how the rest of my weekend would go: the internet connection of my apartment went down. Of all the possible days, why did it have to happen on a Saturday evening, the prime time for gaming?

After checking the possible sources for malfunction, I turned to my mobile phone to check the availability of my internet service provider. Turns out the service was down for everyone in Lawrence and the surrounding areas, with no estimations as for how quickly it might get fixed. It had been one week since talking to any of my friends and even if I had been more in contact with them, they lived in different states, after all. My options for spending a quality Saturday evening quickly dwindled down.

By instinct, I opened the web browser on my mobile phone to start browsing. I had another tab open besides the internet operator website. It was one of the blog posts Philip had sent me earlier that week; I had apparently forgotten to close the tab. Not having anything better to do, I skimmed through the blog posts once more. This time, I did manage to pay somewhat better attention, however, for I spotted a few interesting links in the text written by the guy who had retired early.

The first one just led to another article about heavy-handed investing and retirement, but the second one seemed far more interesting. A calculator designed for one to be able to find out when they have amassed a certain profit goal, with the possibilities of typing in a starting sum, monthly investment rate, time spent in the market, and the expected annual return on investment. It seemed unreal but also reminded me of what Philip and the blog posts had been talking about; the message was basically the same.

Considering I was in the middle of a blackout when it came to internet service, I spent some time playing around with the calculator. Turns out that in theory I would be able to become a millionaire rather quickly even with my current savings rate, had it not been for my ambitious plans of quickly paying back my student loans. On the other hand, who said that I could not try saving and investing at the same time as paying my loan back? According to the calculator, expected returns would be quite impressive even with smaller amounts of investments.

Looking back at that moment, my internet connection being down played a huge part in my making the decision of registering as a customer to a bank which offered relatively low fees and then investing in an index fund which was well-diversified all over the world. I invested all of fifty dollars and thought I might start with this, just to see how it all worked. At some point in the future – once I had dug a bit deeper into all this – I could maybe start to consider doing this on a regular basis.

But hey, look at that: my games were connecting to their servers once again. I would have to get back to this at a later time.

The following two weeks passed by as if everything lay in stasis. I just focused on work, not bothering too much with thoughts on investing. Philip had gone on some kind of a training course at another branch, and I think he also did some vacationing the other week as well. I had not bothered checking what happened to my initial investment of 50 dollars, since I knew that not much would happen in such a short amount of time. It is funny how eight hours at work can seem like an eternity one day and then the next weeks will just fly by.

Ultimately, Philip returned from his holidays and one day we were sitting in that very same break room, sipping on cups of coffee. His colleague Anne sat there with us too. By habit, every afternoon, everyone who could make it gathered there for a small break. Having just the three of us there was exceptional, for usually more people tried to make it at the same time. Nevertheless, as soon as we had sat down, I could not wait to tell Philip about my weekend and an attempt at investing a few weeks ago. My excitement about the subject surprised even myself a little bit since I had started up as a skeptic towards the whole thing. Apparently, the ideas of trying to accumulate wealth had slowly but surely grown up on me on the sly.

So, I told him. I could see both Philip and Anne listening to me very carefully. Truth be told, I was not even sure what I expected from the entire conversation; I simply felt like I could not wait to tell somebody and discuss the entire concept more. To my surprise, Philip did not end up being the one to open his mouth after I finished, but Anne.

"Are you really comfortable doing all this?" she inquired.

Uncertain of what she meant, I stuttered:

"I… suppose so?"

"I just think that you're a young man, you should remember to enjoy your life. Paying off your student loans early is admirable, and I wish I had followed that advice as rigorously when I was your age, but investing is a whole another world, you know."

As Anne went on, Philip still remained silent.

"You need to be able to diversify and be able to accept the fact you might not get your money back. I for one would never want to give up living my life to the fullest just for the sake of saving up some money which in the end could disappear. It takes a lot of studying to succeed in investing, too."

I looked at Philip, waiting for him to react, yet he did not. Anne, on the other hand, placed her coffee mug into the dishwasher while still speaking her mind:

"Don't let me discourage you too much. I just wouldn't take that route, but something safer. Catch you later!"

After Anne left, the break room fell silent for a while.

"You'll notice that most people don't get it. I don't bother talking about these things with many, especially with the older generations," Philip broke the silence.

Instinctively, I already had my portfolio open to see if the funds were still there. They were, and my share had even increased a little bit in value. Seeing green numbers and figures on the screen felt incredibly addictive.

Still looking at the screen, I said:

"Yeah… I think we can ignore the last two minutes of Anne's monologue. But why don't they teach this stuff anywhere?"

Philip shrugged.

"I have a couple of theories, but someone might label me a conspiracy theorist if I spoke those out loud. I've come to accept the fact that it's simply a flaw in the system."

"I think I'll keep investing, make it a regular routine for me once a month. I'm not making much working here, but I think I still can do better than fifty bucks without foregoing my plans of paying back my student loan."

"I remember I started with small amounts as well. Sounds good. You are on the right path." Philip smiled.

After the initial introductory conversation initiated by Philip a couple of weeks ago, he had been rather quiet and hesitant to talk to me about investing. It felt really contradictory, for the more I studied the world of investing and capitalism, the hungrier I became. However, as the youngest addition to the workplace, I did not think it was in my place to start forcing topics to talk about to my coworkers, especially if they did not want to discuss them with me any further. Because my friends were still physically very distant to me, I naturally turned to internet and the seemingly endless source of discussions and forums one could find there.

An abundance of views opened up to me. There were of course the typical discussions about saving and investing, and how to budget life in a cleverer fashion. In the low-quality pool of discussions could be found countless of threads of ranting and raving about how to get rich quickly and how to make more money, typically by investing in a snake oil experiment of sorts. In between those far ends was the FIRE movement, which stood for 'financial independence – retire early'. The idea of early retirement and the whole movement really caught my eye because it was something I had never even heard of until now.

Of course, ideas of retirement would not be something a young graduate in his twenties had in his mind, hence it felt so out of place. I did not exactly crave the chance to gain freedom from ever working again. I even had some ambitions in mind concerning my career. But now, instead of spending a typical weekend of leisure watching series and playing games in front of my computer screen, I did still sit there, only I found myself spending hours reading blogs, stories, and discussions about the FIRE movement and investing. A part of that included calculating various potential scenarios in those online calculators I had found a couple of weeks ago. Now, instead of trying to calculate potential profits, I tried to find ways I could reach financial independence as quickly as possible.

Sadly, I also found out that it would not be as easy as some of the blog texts I had read made it seem. I would have to modify my current plan of saving up fifty dollars a month by a lot for sure. Yet, even if I managed to invest ten times as much, the chances for retirement would be decades away. On the other hand, that would also require me to slow down the rate of paying back my student loan. The other options I had would be to spend less money, earn exponentially more, or to significantly increase the return on my investments.

Spending less than I currently do would be hard, incredibly hard. I already led a life of frugality and what some might consider minimalist. Earning more and advancing in my career is something I am anticipating that will happen, but in due time. It would not be an option that helped me in my current situation. The only remaining chance I have seems to be making wiser choices than simply just investing in index funds.

So, I performed a web search on how to make more money by investing. Turns out most professionals do not recommend anything but simply investing in safe, diversified funds and ETF's.

"Most investors will not be able to beat the index," they said. On the other hand, there were plenty of videos scattered all over the internet telling how to make better net profits by investing in riskier asset classes, whether they be stocks, art, or cryptocurrencies. It turned out to become a battle between the more safety-oriented me and the new side in me who wanted to reach for this new lifestyle and potential for an entirely new life as well.

Now, sitting in the comfort of my bachelor pad, I decided to try something new and daring.

As it turns out, the next time I managed to go to work did not end up being the next week, but the one after that. I caught a cold and a fever so bad I was hardly able to get out of the bed the whole week. This being the first time taking the time off for a sick leave, I felt grateful for my employer offering me the chance to take paid sick leave as a benefit. I guess there is some value in working for a large corporation after all.

Once I got back to the office on Monday one week after that, I had already gotten acquainted enough with Philip to jump right back into the part where we left off about the state of our investments. So, after exchanging the usual pleasantries, I immediately announced that besides seeing the worth of my investments in the index funds rise, the small money I had bought bitcoin with had almost doubled in a little over one week.

As is usual with Philip, he did not say much, but mostly just listened. This time, his facial expressions were different than before, however. As I told him about my venture into another asset class – especially something as daring as cryptocurrencies – he seemed genuinely surprised and taken aback by the information. What I did not notice was that Tim, our boss, also overheard the conversation.

"There's a ruling by Aktie that an employee cannot hold such assets," he hissed.

I had never seen Tim like that. He seemed truly angry and anxious, as if his own job depended on it.

"What, really?" I asked, both startled and scared, as well as truly mystified by what I had just heard.

"Yes! You need to sell off whatever you have right now, or I'll be forced to report it onwards, and that could lead to your termination."

I still both needed and liked the job I had, plus I did not feel nearly confident enough to stand up to him, so I agreed to take care of it. He did not seem entirely satisfied, yet he left without pestering me about it any further. Still a bit stunned by the scene we had just witnessed, I whispered to Philip:

"How could he even know if I have sold or bought anything?"

"I don't think he can, but he's right, you shouldn't touch those things. I know I wouldn't."

"Aren't you intrigued by the chance to score such winnings in as little time as I just made? Can index funds do that?"

Philip smiled a little, and I did not know why. Then, he said:

"Don't worry, you'll realize once you've grown up a little more."

After that, he walked away from me. First having Tim react the way he did and then seeing Philip take on such a passive-aggressive and arrogant tone was jaw-dropping. I could never have guessed I would get such a lousy reception at the start of a new work week at this job, ever. But now I had. I could only think that they were simply jealous or somehow afraid of something which I could not comprehend.

Workwise, the rest of the day passed by ordinarily. As for the people, I could not help feeling self-conscious about the events of that morning. It was as if everyone at the office gave me weird looks for the remainder of the day – even the ones who were not there to witness the conversation. It reminded me of my first months as an intern. For a while now, I had grown accustomed to being treated as a whole member of the group at Aktie. On the other hand, why could it all not simply have been a product of my own imagination? Unfortunately, the saga continued that very same week, which ended up confirming my doubts.

The space which today hosted the office branch of Aktie in the property of that local mall had not always been rented by a bank. Besides the floor space being rather peculiar in many other ways as well, there were no toilets in the office for the employees. It may sound ridiculous, but we had to use the toilets located in the hallways of the mall which had been reserved for the personnel of all the businesses in the mall.

On Thursday of the same week of that fatal conversation with Philip, I sat in the toilet booth, minding my own business, as I heard the door open. I immediately recognized two men had entered, and the one speaking was Tim, our manager. Even though I did not hear the other guy speaking, I could tell he was Philip, since I heard Tim talk to him of work-related matters, and I could hardly imagine Tim inviting one of the women of the office to join him in the men's room. I had not made my presence known and I imagine they thought they were alone. For the most part, I could not follow what Tim was talking about; probably a project of sorts that I had not been involved with. Anyhow, what struck me were Tim's words as he stated:

"Originally, I had thought of giving the responsibility of calculating the monthly costs over to Noah, but now I'm thinking I'll give it to someone more trustworthy and more qualified."

I was now holding my breath to make sure I would go unnoticed by them, even though I was certain my quickened heartbeat could be heard by them any second now.

"I see," the other voice which could only have belonged to Philip responded quietly. Had it been a stranger hearing him, it would have been easy to judge the quiet response as him not really caring about what Tim had just told him. But I knew him better to notice that was simply his style of making conversation. When it came to his career, as an ambitious man, he probably cared quite a lot about what his boss had to tell him. After that, they went on to discuss other matters related to that project I had not been aware of, and shortly exited the men's room.

In that moment, I felt crushed. I had considered myself a part of the team and alas, I was not. The first instinct to pop into my mind would obviously be to simply resign and find some other job. Since my employer did not trust me, why should I trust my employer to allow me to advance in my career in the future? Once the initial emotional shock had passed, I obviously began thinking that this would have to be done in a clever way before rushing into anything. At the very least I would have to get a new job before quitting my old one.

Thankfully, Thursday was almost over. Now I would just have to get through Friday before having a short breather by myself to think things through.

The weekend took a turn for the unexpected, for I found myself hanging over at my friend's house in Kansas City, just over the other side of the state border in Missouri. I had come to know Burton in the university. Geographically speaking, he is the closest friend I have, with only fifty miles or so of distance in between our homes. He chased a very similar kind of a career as I did – the only difference being that he worked for an insurance company, whereas I worked in a bank. As people we were not that much alike, but still found it fun to occasionally see each other instead of just spending a weekend by ourselves.

Burton obviously did not live according to the same philosophy I did. Like mine, his apartment also lay in a high-rise building, but it was much roomier and newer than what I had. He had a brand-new car, plus he headed out a lot more frequently than I did and had a few expensive hobbies. I am uncertain whether he carried the same kind of burden in the form of a student loan as I did, but if he was, then he for sure did not focus all of his energy towards trying to pay it back as quickly as possible.

It was still early Saturday afternoon. I had just arrived, and we had been catching up with each other over a few beers. There is not very much we did not know of each other's lives already, for we both still belonged to the same WhatsApp groups we used to back at school. Since I knew of his interest in career and networking, I rather quickly came up with what I had experienced this week at work. After explaining the situation to him, he seemed to mull over the whole thing for a while.

"Sounds to me like you scared them pretty badly," he said, taking a chug from his beer.

"You mean with my investments?"

"I don't know much about cryptocurrencies, but I do know that you probably should think twice before announcing that you're into them. Especially around people who are twice your age."

He then took another sip, sank into his thoughts for a while, and continued:

"You can't really expect them to get it. There's been plenty of propaganda and scare tactics used by big corporations and governments about Bitcoin and stuff like that. Those are the same kind of elderly people, making up rules and restrictions like the one you heard of."

"But what do you think I should do? What would you do?"

"Dude, what do you think I am? A clairvoyant? If I knew what to invest in to get loaded, I wouldn't be here right now."

"No, I mean about the job," I interjected.

"Why don't you just go on, pretend you heard nothing of that toilet talk and if they ask, just tell them you've sold it all? It's not like they are going to find out anywhere that you lied."

Lying about it all had been on top of my mind as well. I just wanted to hear the confirmation of the plan being smart from someone else before proceeding.

"I suppose. But I also suppose that I can now forget about advancing much further there from now on."

Burton shrugged:

"I suppose. Just stay there for six to twelve more months and you'll be good to go to find another job that's higher up than the one you're doing."

Mostly, what he said made sense. It is true that with an MBA and some experience at a large bank, there would be plenty of options for me in the future. Even despite my confident attitude, there obviously always lay the question of whether finding a new position would be that easy once the time for that search came. But for now, the future seemed rather bright.

As the day and the evening advanced, the questions about money and risky investments popped up once more. Although we both practically stood on the same line when it came to our lives, it is funny how mentor-like his opinions and advice sounded to me. I knew he had no more experience than I did, yet somehow acted towards me like a role model from which to learn and to take advice.

"So, if you're not into crypto then what is it?" I asked.

"Last month, I made fifteen grand by selling an NFT. It's almost the same thing… well, not quite, but still an investment in the blockchain tech."

The casual way of Burton saying how much money he had scored made it sound ridiculous. For me, that was a very big number. Apparently, he noticed the way I looked at him and as if in an attempt to balance the odds, blurted out:

"I also lost ten thousand in ending up buying into a scam, though. That's a risk there, too…"

Besides being somewhat amazed by his stories, I noticed he had begun to stammer a bit. All the memories of us hanging out with others in our days as students rushed to me. I still remember he used to drink way too much considering how bad he had always been at holding his liquor. I knew the rational part of our catching up was over the second he said:

"How 'bout I'll now show you around the clubs we have here in the city, Noah?"

I sat in my apartment home in front of the computer. Yet another regular weekend for me to look forward to. I had stumbled upon yet more conversations, message boards, and forums about investing. Only this time, the topics discussed riskier assets than before. Even in the world of Bitcoin, the movements in price were slower than I expected them to be. All the signs pointed in the direction that smaller cryptocurrencies would be the way to go to make fast and big money.

Taking a look at NFTs did not get me excited. It was as if buying art in the hopes of it going up in price, just in digital format. Making a fake duplicate of one also seemed to be harder than faking a Mona Lisa in real life. But still, the idea of randomly buying a picture of a monkey and hoping for it to go up in price sounded ridiculous even to me, considering my state of mind at that time.

Last weekend went as I expected. After heading out to a couple of bars and less than fancy nightclubs, Burton had way too much to drink, and I had to persuade him back to his house in the middle of the night. The other option would have been me having to carry him back or the police picking him up.

Waking up that Sunday morning on a mattress thrown on the floor of his apartment did not have me yearning to stay for any longer. Waiting for him to wake up and recover from what must have been a nightmarish hangover was too much of a price to endure just to hear some more ideas he might have had about modern investing. The bus ride back home being while exhausted myself as well felt it would be enough to go through at the time.

So, I dug into it all alone, just as everyone online recommended: DYOR, which stands for 'Do Your Own Research'. Turns out that most of the coins that people had gotten wealthy or rich with were typically jokes which then evolved into memes, or the other way around. These meme coins had seen ridiculous increases in price. The flipside of it all was that just as the prices went up really quickly, they crashed down almost instantly, too. Many of these projects apparently seemed to be scams, too.

Nevertheless, simply pumping money into index funds or into the stock market in general would not be the answer to the question I searched for. No way would I be able to make money which allowed me to retire early by simply following these traditional means of investment advice. It might be possible if I waited for a few decades, sure, but why wait when I could act right now?

I saw that the new coins of these projects always followed the same pattern: the birth of the coin, alongside aggressive marketing of the project by the creators. Then, if successful, the word would spread, and the price of the coin would pump hard. This pump up would last for anywhere from a day to a few weeks before correcting back down – that is, if the creators did not simply decide to pull the rug from under the investors and vanish before that. With that in mind, I would simply have to identify a new coin or a token like that and then sell off my portion before the price crash.

After some seemingly countless hours which just flew by, I found two such tokens. The first one, Inno Inu with the simple ticker of IINU had some meme value in the footsteps of the countless dog-styled meme tokens. Launched but a few days ago, the price had already soared by more than 300 % from it's original, and the talks about it in different message boards all over the internet had just begun.

The other one had been launched but a few hours ago. An obvious copy of the infamous Terra Luna coin called Luna 3.0 (LUN3). Not only that, but it was also a glaringly obvious scam. But by getting into these scams and exiting quickly enough one could turn up quite a nice profit, so why not.

I felt adrenaline surging as I used 1000 dollars I had originally saved for investing into stock market to buy into these two projects. With that done, I would have to spend the rest of the weekend following the prices of those two assets closely. Concentrating on anything else that night turned out to be hard, as I constantly went back to my browser tab to see if the prices had moved. Looking at hour candles soon turned to following price movements compulsively almost every minute. The clock stroke 4 am on Saturday when I realized I would have to give up and get some sleep. The market would still be there once I woke up.

Lying in my bed, I found it next to impossible to fall asleep. All I could think of now consisted of the prices of my new investments and all the excited movement around them. Some quite seemingly valid theories discussed the idea of those projects hitting even the price of one cent. Considering that the increase in price would then be thousands and even tens of thousands of percents, that would make me a multimillionaire. Even though I would be glad to simply just double what I had invested, the thoughts of becoming rich quickly flooded into my mind.

How could anyone sitting on top of such capital not get excited? The last time I remember taking a look at the time and the prices it was almost six in the morning. Alas, the problem of having optimistic thoughts in my mind was most definitely a positive one. Soon after that, I must have fallen asleep.

That Saturday began at noon with me opening my eyes to see the sun shining directly at my face. Besides the glaring light, the first thing that popped into my mind were the prices of my new-found assets. I grabbed the phone next to me to see that IINU had increased in price by a few percent. Seeing that, you might think it would make me happy, but strangely, I felt nothing. A few percent more meant nothing, considering that I was looking forward to multiplying my original investment – by a few times, at the very least. LUN3 on the other hand had dropped in price by five percent, which immediately made me disappointed.

But still, with the entire rest of the weekend to spend, I did not want to let that get me down. I would have to keep following the prices closely, though. After breakfast, something else I had planned for this weekend awaited: job search. I had decided to follow Burton's advice and try to keep my eyes open to other positions I might pursue. Even in the case of me being offered something, I could take the time and ponder whether to accept or not, I figured.

So, I began the search and fired up my computer intended mainly for gaming. Soon I found out that the hardware would not help me, since I came to understand that I did not even have a CV let alone a cover letter prepared. The job I had at Aktie was my first one, and even that I had acquired via an internship which did not require me to submit anything of the sorts when applying for the position. Some documentaries from my studies accompanied by a motivational letter had been enough.

In fact, just browsing for job openings made me unsure of how to do this. After looking at the websites of competing banks, I had nothing to apply for – where I would be a match when it came to requirements posted, that is. A simple search engine exercise did help me find this one portal which combined job opportunities from multiple employers. Looking at the simple search field on that site, I searched for:

"financial analyst",
"investment analyst", and just simply
"finance".

I did not want to narrow the search too much based on the location of the job, so I just searched across all of the United States. At first, I thought the search had been too broad, for I was overwhelmed by the results, which were in hundreds. After reconsideration, I had the entire day reserved for this. Besides, not going through any trouble in the process did not sound realistic.

Going through most of the open positions, I had managed to filter them down to three most interesting and suitable ones for me. The first one was a risk analyst job at an insurance company I had never heard of in Kansas City, the second a procurement coordinator job for the city of Lawrence, and the third one an analyst position for another insurance company all the way in Saratoga Springs in Vermont – a place I had never been to. Needless to say, the first two options sounded the most exciting simply for being so close by.

Due to my unordinary schedule for staying up so late last night, by the time it would have been customary for me to grab a bite for lunch, the clock was already six in the evening. Waiting for the microwave oven to finish up warming the panini I had, I quickly checked the prices of my new investments on my phone. IINU had barely moved from where it was before, and LUN3 had gone all the way down to 0.0000051 dollars per token, when it used to be 0.0000061 dollars. As I heard the microwave beeping to signal that my food would be warm, I had an idea.

I opened WhatsApp, chose the chat I had with Burton, and began typing:

"As per our meeting, I'm now trying my luck with these," and I then linked both tokens in that same message. After a while, Burton appeared present, and responded:

"Whoa, looks like a gamble, alright. That's some risky stuff right there."

"I know. I'm an absolute degenerate," I typed back, with an uncomfortable grin on my face. I actually felt a bit depressed by the fact that neither of my initial investments had gone up in price.

"As long as you remember to take profits if you happen to run into any."

Burton hit the nail on the head right there. I would sell my positions as soon as there were profits to be made. No need to wait for them to disappear from the markets and then just lose all my money. This was the reason I felt nervous as well. As I sank my teeth into the panini, I could not stop thinking about how neither of those tokens had gone up in price, even though it could still have been expected a while ago. I guess I would just have to be more patient with them.

While eating, I started to construct cover letters and CV's for the three job openings I had found earlier. Thanks to the professional templates I found online, filling in my own information did not prove to be as complex as I had initially imagined. In fact, many websites stated that recruiters rarely had the time to read through unnecessarily long cover letters. This suited me more than well, so I decided to keep the texts short and simple.

Having finished with the applications, it was already late in the evening. My eyes felt heavy and my vision fizzy as the few hours of sleep I had gotten last night started to creep up to me. Besides, it would soon be Monday and I would have to go to work early in the morning. I took one last look at the prices of IINU and LUN3 before heading to bed. The prices had not significantly changed.

Sleep wise, the Saturday night went better. Come Sunday morning, I woke up feeling refreshed with no thoughts of money and investing revolving around in my mind. The first thoughts to pop into my mind were actually about having that day still off before the coming week and that I yearned for a good breakfast. Yesterday's meals had been severely off-balance compared to how I usually ate.

As I rose from bed and headed to bathroom, the first thoughts of excitement and anxiety concerning my investments arose. I decided to hold off on checking out the prices until I had some food in front of me. It would feel even better unleashing all that pent-up energy at the same time as extinguishing my hunger.

Something I never told anyone was that I had never bought any kitchenware myself. The ones I had I got from my parents who gave some of their old pots, pans, and cutlery to me. Despite their age they worked fantastically, even if I rarely used many of them, but mostly utilized just my microwave oven for warming stuff up. I am not sure if now the actual cooking of my own breakfast, the day off, or the long-awaited checking of the prices made the ham sandwich and freshly boiled eggs in front of me seem even more delicious than usual. I suppose it must have been the prices. Before taking a bite of anything, I opened the browser on my phone to see what had happened overnight. As I glanced at the tokens, my jaw dropped open.

LUN3 had been on a steady downwards trajectory the entire night. Not a straight-out crash, but the descent was still significant: my position had gone down by -30 %. IINU, however, had basically gone down to zero. With next to nothing left, even the website of the project had disappeared. The discussion forums had people screaming:

"Rugpull!"

"It's all over!"

And many more alike comments.

The feeling of loss crept up all over me and my body. While a thought that passed by me still told me this must have been a misunderstanding on my or on someone else's part, I knew that it would not be a valid defense. The money was gone, and my worst fears had thus come true. The hunger and the positive feeling I had before passed by completely until I just sat there, staring at the breakfast I had but a few minutes ago been so eager to enjoy. I had never experienced anything like that before.

I grabbed on the sandwich and began chewing. The first thing I made my mind up on right there was not to make rash decisions. I would have my breakfast, finish with a good cup of coffee, and then consider my options.

It did not work.

The food in my mouth had no taste, and the thoughts of these failed investments possessed my mind. How could I have been so gullible? I could hear my teeth gnarling together as I bit on the remains of my sandwich with way too hard bite on my jaw, all the while not quite realizing the eating physically hurt me. I burnt my mouth on the cup of coffee I had poured for myself that had not had the chance to cool down. I just wanted to get through the breakfast as quickly as possible.

At last, as I finished, I immediately headed to the decentralized exchange I had used to buy the tokens to get rid of whatever I had left. In the end, the 1000 $ I had was now converted to measly 300 $. This meant a loss of roughly 70 % of my investment in but a few days, and I had nothing to show for it. And what would I tell Burton?

With my Sunday ruined, I mulled over my decisions sitting on my bed. At first, I still could not gather my thoughts properly. I am not sure how long I sat there, but it had definitely been a while. Then, my thoughts began to clear. It was as if the rational side of my brains had suddenly begun working. This is not the end of the world. I had not lost everything, but just a relatively small amount of money. The third thought I had revealed to me was that I did exactly what I had intended to avoid in the first place: instead of patiently considering my options, I just quickly rushed through my breakfast, and then sold my assets while in panic.

Oh boy, would it take some time for me to get over this. But gosh darn it, I would learn from these mistakes, simply for the sake of not wanting to make them again. One thought in my mind screamed at me in an attempt to get me to invest again in some get-rich-quick scheme in the hopes of winning my money back. Thankfully, I had calmed down just enough to resist those ideas. The situation required me to focus on other things in life and just suffer through the sense of loss – no matter how overwhelming. I would just simply not text Burton at all at this point.

I made up my mind to spend the rest of my Sunday doing what I could to forget about the entire hassle for a while. I did it by doing what I could do the best in my leisure time: by gaming. It may not have been the surefire solution to blacking out from real life, but some League of Legends would probably help ease the pain I felt.

Needless to say, nine hours passed by relatively quickly by simply shutting everything else out of my mind. With hardly any need to even drink or eat, I just played. Ultimately, I grew too tired to keep going, and took a look at my phone, just to check to see if anyone had tried to reach me – and it must have been out of habit, too. Indeed, a single WhatsApp message had arrived. It was from Burton:

"You sold yet?"

He must have seen what happened. It sounded as if he was trying to make fun of me. Then again, I suppose anything he messaged me at that point would most likely have sounded like scoffing to me.

"Yep, lost almost everything…" I replied.

"No shit dude! I checked the prices out myself just now. Sorry, I didn't know what had happened. Looks like you didn't have much of a chance of winning there."

I marked his message read but did not bother replying to him. I still did not want to remind myself of the recent events. The wounds had not healed yet.

The following week at work on my part turned out to be a compilation of mixed feelings. The disappointment of my failed investments – or rather, experiments, slowly faded away as time passed. However, I had the constant feeling of not wanting to work there anymore. On the exterior, everything went fine, but I also knew that my boss along with some of my co-workers no longer wanted me there. My interests had altered, too – I knew that simply working a job and chasing after a classic career path would not satisfy my appetite any longer. I wanted to be financially free.

I often began to doubt myself as well. Had I told my old self what I would be doing in the future, I would have thought I was insane. Instead of trying to land a successful, stable career with its various perks and benefits, I had put my reputation at risk. Instead of smartly diversifying into various asset classes, I was both literally as well as practically gambling my assets away in some of the most volatile things ever to have existed. At times like these, I always thought that nothing I had done would be irreversible; I could always return to my old ways. But what good would come of jumping from one investment strategy to another in such a short amount of time with hardly any consistency?

In some other setting, I might try talking to people about these thoughts to gain some insight. But at work, I knew that talking about traditional investments would cause jealousy and doubt, and unconventional investments could even get me fired. The older generation in general seemed to be far too close-minded and unwilling to talk about money. Then, there were my friends like Burton. I did not feel comfortable talking to them, either. Truth be told, I felt ashamed of my recently failed experiments in investing.

Staring at the blank wall at work – once again during a quiet afternoon, manning the customer service all by myself – I began to think of my previous objectives and the way I used to try to get rid of my student loans as quickly as possible. That project had obviously slowed down now, although I was still paying the loan back quite handsomely.

Maybe the solution would simply be to hold off on making risky investments for a while and to ponder carefully if taking one was worth it. Thinking about what the money now lost could have gotten me felt terrible, which in this moment led me to believe that perhaps the answer lay in having the right balance in everything. I would still have to invest in safer assets, too. Having done the math, I also knew that this would not allow me to gain substantial wealth quickly, nor to retire early, however. For that, I would need more money.

An approaching customer awakened me from my daydreaming session. Much like the few visiting customers we still had here at the bank office, he too was an elderly man.

"Good day," he smiled at me while I nodded back at him to let him know I had seen him approaching.

"Hi, how can I help?" I asked.

"I just lost my job, and I might be having problems with the down payments of my mortgage."

It took me a while to react to that simply because I somewhat blacked out at the point the old man told me he had just lost his job. Not because the case would be anything extraordinary or difficult to handle; I knew I simply had to hand him over to our account managers, either Philip or Anne. The whole idea just seemed incredible, for he must have been at least 70 years old.

"Um, yes, sure… may I have your ID, please?"

He handed his documentation over to me and I quickly saw that the gentleman called Patrick Henderson was a client of Anne. Before calling her, I quickly took a look to see if everything else in his background checked out. Even though I tried to hide my reaction from him, my eyes must have grown wide open as I noticed he still owed more than 100 000 $ to Aktie bank from his apartment home, and that he indeed still belonged to the customer group that had notified the bank they were full-time employees.

"Thank you. If you'll just sit down and take a seat over there right next to the door. I'll call our account manager and she'll be with you shortly."

"I will. Thank you," the old man said, once more with a smile on his face.

I was flabbergasted. In his information sheet on the computer, I noticed he had just turned 73 and still worked daily

– that is, until the loss of his latest job. Not to mention the way he is still up to his ears in debt. Thankfully, there still was a long way for me to go to ever end up in that situation. This got me into thinking that in the end, maybe my situation did not seem so bad. I had lost just 700 $, after all.

The second thought to enter my mind got me into thinking how on earth it would even be possible for anyone to live like that. Sure, I had heard of people who might never be able to retire and who would have to work until they died. Seeing one in real life just made it that much more real. Despite all this, if the looks did not deceive, the old man looked like he was genuinely happy and approached life with positive attitude overall.

"Patrick, please do come in," Anne called the old man from the door to her office. He immediately stood up and headed over to shake hands with her before they stepped inside to begin resolving his problem.

As it happens, Philip walked right by me, probably on his way to the break room.

"Philip, you won't believe this," I told him with a quiet voice.

"The old man who just stepped inside is 73 and still working to pay back his mortgage. How crazy is that?"

Philip looked at me for a while, as if expecting me to go on. Then, as he probably realized I had already made my point, he said:

"Ah, yes. We get quite a lot of those here, to be honest. It's sad. But don't worry, I have a feeling that you're on the right path to evade such a fate."

I must have sounded incredibly stupid since all I could think of in response to him was:

"Alright."

He then went on his way towards the break room. I did of course have many other things in my mind which I yearned to tell him, but I did not trust him enough anymore to be confident that he would keep the conversation between us.

On Thursday evening, that very same week, I sat at home on my computer, procrastinating going to sleep when suddenly my phone rang. The call came from a number visible on my phone, yet from a number unbeknownst to me. Despite being quite certain about who it might be and not wanting to talk, I still answered.

"Hello?"

"Hi, Noah. We were calling 'cos we miss you," a woman's voice slurred. My guess turned out to be right.

"Hi, Mom."

"We never hear from you anymore."

I could tell that she was under the influence of something. Probably not alcohol but some medication of hers.

"I've been busy. What's up?" I said as laconically as I could.

"That's... that's all you can say after all these years?" she sobbed, almost crying.

"It hasn't been years. We talked just a few weeks ago."

If a voice could grow a spine, her voice did that the second I told her that:

"So we did. Anyway, I thought we could still talk."

I said nothing. No matter how hard it had been at first all those years ago, I had gotten used to her mood swings by now. I found it easier for her to just take care of the talking and then be done with it. Just like she did:

"Your dad lost his job. The only income for our rent is now gone, Noah."

"He's not my dad."

That was the least I could say, and a much more polite statement than that person living in what used to be my childhood home ever deserved. I hardly considered him even a human after ruining the last years I still lived there and making my life a living hell.

"So, you don't care we'll soon be out on the street, son?"

It amazed me how she apparently still thought she could manipulate me like that. But I knew it was something that came with her illness.

"Nope," I told her, right before hanging up on her.

I had stopped mulling over the sad excuses I had gotten for parents a few years ago. To be fair, I don't think I should be calling both of them my parents, since my father passed away almost ten years ago. Shortly after that, once the mental health of my mother completely gave up, she hooked up with the guy who shortly took the place as what should have been my father. At least she was still my biological mother, although in her present condition it did me no good.

I did not intend to fall back to my old ways of feeling sorry for myself about that chain of events now, either, but instead it dawned upon me how fortunate I was in my current situation. At least I had my health, my sanity, and my finances in order. I did hold a master's degree and had a job – even if not the coolest job out there, but even so there was always the chance of an upgrade looming on the horizon.

What a strange feeling – for the first time ever, a disturbing call from my mother had taken a turn towards something that actually left me feeling better and encouraged about what the future might hold.

The next I had a shorter day at work than usual and got to head home at two in the afternoon. Some of the other staff attended a conference in Kansas City while others had a day off. In spite of the office closing up early, surprisingly few customers dropped by that afternoon. Since at that point I simply waited for the weekend to arrive, I spent time on my phone checking out potential things to invest in. I noticed the infamous IINU token which had made me lose money mentioned in one of the headlines. I was about to scroll along, but luckily for me, my curiosity took over and I opened to article. As I read it, my eyes grew wide open.

Right before it had crashed, holders of the token had been rewarded with an airdrop of another token. I had not noticed the reward on my wallet up until now. The whole thing seemed to be another meme coin featuring a unicorn, only that this one had actually soared in price. What I had gained seemed to total a whopping ten thousand dollars, should I sell my portion now.

On the other hand, it could become even more valuable in the near future. Needless to say, there was no chance in hell I would be able to focus on anything work-related anymore. Thankfully, it was now time to close the doors and head home.

My ears burnt as if on fire as I walked home, my eyes staring at my phone. As I had quickly confirmed that I actually held the said tokens and stared at the token price chart, an unknown number called my phone. Even though I knew it would probably be my mother yet again, I accidentally swiped green on the call-in screen as I tried to scroll left on the price chart. I stopped on my path on the sidewalk and thought about just hanging up, but then I heard a man's voice talking on the line:

"Hello?"

I decided to answer.

"Hi, this is Noah."

"Oh, hi, must have been some problem with my connection, sorry. This is Dean calling from Verpoint, how do you do?"

At that point it clicked in my head: Verpoint was the insurance company at which I had applied for the analyst position, all the way in Vermont. Before I had the chance to reply, Dean went on:

"Thank you for your application concerning the opening we have for the junior analyst position. We have now reviewed your application and I'm pleased to inform you that we would like to schedule an interview with you if you are still interested in the position. Would you be able to attend one here in Saratoga Springs in the coming week?"

I had no idea how to make that happen, concerning that I would have to fly to Vermont and somehow get some time off work for that, but I still heard myself saying:

"Yes, absolutely."

"That is great to hear. How does Wednesday at 10 o'clock sound?"

"Sure thing."

"Lovely. Please bring by any documents you have referred to in your application concerning your education and employment history. If you have any further questions, you can reach me on this number I am calling from. Have a great weekend and we are looking forward to meeting you on Wednesday."

"Thank you, likewise! Looking forward to talking to you, too. Bye."

As I lowered the smartphone from my ear and watched the call being hung up from the other end, it felt unreal. I had a job interview which sounded like an awesome opportunity – only that it would be all the way in Vermont, even if I got the job. To top it all off, I had no idea how to arrange for myself to get there. Maybe I would just buy the plane tickets and call out sick that day, because who would care, anyway? On the other hand, I could always cancel the interview if I changed my mind, but right now that alternative sounded like pure insanity.

As the call ended, I also noticed the token price chart I had been looking at. Looks like my position was now worth almost 15 grand. Should I sell now or wait a bit longer for the price to go even higher?

ABOUT THE AUTHOR

With vast experience in risk management all around the world, Teemu Lampovaara harnessed the chaotic situation of the western world and took his first stab at writing a book in 2023. Whereas *The Decline of Western Society – Striving for Survival and Success* described societal issues, *Money, Money, Money: Stories of Human Behavior* is now here to let reader delve into the heart of how humans and money act together – whether it be for good or bad.

Make sure to review the book on Amazon.